and Judge Jury

Dedication

This book is dedicated to all the unarmed young black men and women who have been shot down and murdered for no other reason than being black at a place they had every right to be at any time.

Judge and Jury

by Karen Sloan-Brown

BROWN REFLECTIONS

Judge and Jury

Copyright © 2014 by Karen Sloan-Brown

This book is printed on acid-free paper.

ISBN: 978-0-9915517-3-6
Library of Congress Cataloging-in-Publication Data on file.

Editor: Cornelius Brown

Judge and Jury
KAREN SLOAN-BROWN

Judge and Jury

Prologue

Deshaun Gardner was not unlike most seventeen year olds, restless, energetic, and anxious to live his life and make his own decisions. There was no debating the fact that he was a handsome teenager, medium brown skinned, tall and slim with a muscular build. He wore his hair in a high-top fade that got him the steady attention he loved from the girls and he always rewarded them with a smile that slid across his face reminiscent of a young Denzel Washington. Raised way uptown in North Philly, he was definitely street smart with an edge but as far as the books were concerned he handled his business and his grades hovered above a "B" average without him even trying. He loved to draw and the art teacher at his school thought he had real talent. For fun, he liked kicking it with his homeboys in the hood, shooting some hoops at the playground, smoking a little weed on the corner, listening to gangsta rap, and chasing the young hotties on the Avenue.

Deshaun's parents, Mona, a clerk at Philadelphia Electric Company, and Darren Gardner, a loan officer at PSFS (Philadelphia Savings Fund Society), had been attentive and diligent in their efforts to keep their only son out of trouble. Darren was determined that Deshaun would attend his alma mater, Tennessee State University, in the fall and follow in his footsteps as a third generation member of the Phi Beta Sigma Fraternity. Mona was more basic in her desires and realistic about the influences that plagued young black males in the city. Unlike her husband, she never had the opportunity to go to college. She grew up in Chicago where both her older and younger brothers were lost to the streets, one in the penitentiary and the other in the grave from an overdose. Her main objective was to keep Deshaun out of jail and above the ground until his twenty-first birthday, praying that by then he would probably have enough sense to make something out of himself.

A little more than a year ago, after Deshaun's running partner, Jamaal Taylor, dropped out of school and got his first visit to juvenile detention, Darren and Mona reluctantly sold their house of fourteen years. They made the move to South Philly, far away from Germantown Avenue, the temptations, and the pitfalls they felt lay in wait to ensnare the bright future of their only child. As happy and relieved as they were with their new surroundings in South Philly, Deshaun took every opportunity to take the subway back north to his comfort zone, the hustle and bustle on Cheltenham Ave with Jamaal.

Mona monitored his schedule as closely as she could and her constant questions were the cause of much friction between her and Deshaun. He protested as respectfully as he could but he wasn't a baby whose mama needed to know where he was every minute of the day. He wasn't stupid. He kept his hands out of the dirt that Jamaal was drawn to, but that didn't mean he wasn't going to enjoy himself. He wasn't about to stop checking for the young ladies. He solved the problem when he got a part-time job working at the McDonalds in the Gallery. It not only put some more money in his pocket, it got him his freedom back. On many occasions after school he caught the subway up Broad Street to Germantown Avenue to hang with his boy, Jamaal, or catch a movie with a girl he was checking for while his folks relaxed in the comfort that he was off the streets working extra hours making fries and flipping Big Macs.

***

Edward could feel the awesome power of the gun as he held it in one palm and then the other although the weight was lighter than he thought it would be. Turning it over in his hands he eyed every detail, admiring the intimidating piece of black metal and the workmanship. He had planned and looked forward to this day, virtual shopping on the internet for weeks to find the perfect weapon to fit his needs, a Kel-Tec PF-9 9mm semi-automatic pistol. He absorbed the feeling of fearlessness that came over him as he stood there. He already had his gun license in his pocket if anyone asked him for it. They hadn't given him a second look or asked him any questions when he put in his application at the permit office on Spring Garden Street. They were more concerned about him paying the fee than anything else.

He raised his arm and pointed the gun at the mirror behind the long table of weapons at the Gun Show and grinned at his reflection. He thought he looked like his favorite action hero, Russell Crowe. Nobody would dare to disrespect him in any way when he carried this piece. He'd specifically chosen this firearm because it was the same one that the Philadelphia Police Department carried, and they had denied his application to join the academy. He didn't need their permission to protect himself or his neighborhood.

"I'll take it and give me two boxes of ammo," he told the vendor.

"Good choice, do you want to add the waist holster too?" the gun seller asked.

"Yeah, I do?" Edward said, pleased with himself.

With one swipe of his credit card he made his purchase and was now armed and ready to confront the dangerous element that threatened his peaceful community.

"I just need to check your ID and get your signature," the vendor said.

"No problem," Ed answered, pulling his wallet back out from his rear pants pocket.

"Edward Landauer," the clerk said, pronouncing each syllable as he read his driver's license.

Ed waited in silence while the seller wrote down his pertinent information. As the pen moved slowly across the paper he stared at the man's hand and forearm thinking his weathered skin looked like tan leather. He kept watching him as he placed the gun back in its case and then put the case in a bag with the holster and the ammo.

"Pleasure doing business with you, come back again," the man said, handing him the plain brown paper sack containing his purchase.

Ed nodded and said, "Sure thing."

He rolled the top of the bag down and held it close to his side as he moved quickly to the exit door. Excitement rising from his chest to his head made him feel feverish as sweat dripped down his temples despite the mild temperatures of the month of September. He opened the passenger's side of his 2006 grey Chevy Impala and laid the bag gently on the cloth seat and rushed around to the driver's side. He snatched the door open, jumped in, slammed it closed, and then pushed the button to lock the car. His attention was still drawn to the bag on the seat next to him and although he resisted the temptation to remove the gun from its case, he couldn't keep his hand from running across the surface of the bag that held his new prize possession in a soft caress. He drove the entire distance transfixed as if he were accompanied by a once elusive conquest.

There was no mystery as to why Ed got more satisfaction from a weapon than any woman he had ever been in a relationship with. The reason was born with him. The second son of Laramie and Alta Landauer, he had failed to live up to the legacy of his father as a decorated gunner in the Marines during the Vietnam War, he dimmed in the shadow of his older brother's academic and professional success as civil engineer, and he lacked any distinction other than the title of mama's boy. He had been the soft chubby kid who was bullied and looked over in team sports at school and in the neighborhood. After high school graduation he had no inclination to work in his parent's 'Mom and Pop' store and learn the business that his father had run for twenty-nine years. His hunger for power or authority had yet to be satiated and now he was a man, thirty-four years old. He hadn't been able to earn it so he did the next best thing, he bought it.

***

It was the end of March with only a few months left before graduation. Deshaun was hyped about finishing high school. His plan was to keep it moving, make some extra money, kick it with his homeboys over the summer, and then get out on his own at college in August. He checked the time on his cell phone for the tenth time and clocked out with his four hour shift finally done. He pulled his hoodie on to cover the blue uniform shirt before he walked out into the Gallery to catch the subway home. From his calculations, including today, he should have earned enough on his next paycheck to pay off the balance on his class ring. It was costing him bigtime but he wanted the blinged out one with the extra diamonds on it.

He stepped off the train at Snyder and trotted up the subway stairs two at a time. He felt the cool streams as he reached the surface and pulled the hood of his sweatshirt on to shield himself from the rain. He could have quickened his pace for the long four block walk to his house but the rain didn't faze him. His head rocked to the beat of the rap traveling from his cell phone to his head phones while he contemplated who he was going to ask to go with him on the prom.

His cell phone rang interrupting his jam and his thoughts. He pushed the button to answer.

"Whatsup?"

"Nothing, boy, just checking to make sure you're bringing your butt straight home," Mona said warmly, making him a plate of food before she cleaned the kitchen.

"Yeah, Ma, I just got off the sub."

She looked through the window over the sink.

"It's raining harder, do you want me to pick you up?"

"No way, I can't have my moms carrying me around. I got my hood on, I'm straight."

"I'm not trying to treat you like a kid. I'm making sure you don't miss any days at school or work laying around here with a cold."

"Hold on, Ma. I think there's a car trailing me. It's following me real slow."

"Where are you?" Mona asked, getting concerned.

"I'm up on Shiloh. Now he's driving up beside me and rolling down his window."

"Oh Lord," Mona murmured, "Baby, you need to run across the street as fast as you can."

"It's cool. He's rolling past me, just some weirdo probably."

"Was he white or black?" Mona asked, still alarmed.

"White I think."

"Hold on, I'm sending your Daddy to meet you," she said urgently. "Darren, I need you to go up on Shiloh and Harbor Street and get Deshaun, some nut was just following him."

"What the hell?" Darren asked, confused.

"Just go, honey, it won't take but a few minutes."

"All right, but he'll probably be here before I can get out the door," he said, shaking his head.

Darren walked into the living room and grabbed a jacket and umbrella out of the closet before he headed out of the front door.

"Your daddy is on his way to meet you, keep…"

"Hey, Ma," Deshaun said, interrupting her, "The man in that car circled back around. He's getting out of his car."

"Deshaun, I told you to start running," Mona said with her fear growing.

"Why you following me?" she heard him say. Then she heard the man's voice respond in an aggressive tone but she couldn't make out the words through her panic. "Back up off me," she heard her child shout angrily. Mona listened in horror to the confrontation between them. She heard a grunt and then the phone went silent.

Mona threw the phone down and rushed to the front door. She flung it open and ran out of the house in her bedroom slippers. In the heat of the moment she couldn't feel the chill in the air or rain falling on her dress. The only thing she could think about was her baby was in some kind of danger. She could see Darren up a half-block ahead of her and she ran faster, barely able to hold the sliding shoes on her feet to catch up to him. Her heart was beating at a frenzied pace as her terror escalated.

***

Ed was bored. He'd surfed the channels on TV for an hour and there wasn't anything on that held his attention. Any other time he would have gone to hang out with Jack McCullough, his only real friend, but Jack was probably still pissed from the fight he instigated last weekend while they were at a bar on South Street. He knew Jack would cool down after a while since it wasn't the first time Jack had sworn he wasn't hanging out with him anymore. He didn't know why but there was always some ignorant asshole in every bar he walked into.

He paced across the front window of his house drinking on a beer as the light of day slowly yielded to the night. He looked intently down each direction of the street and across the intersection for any trouble. Being captain of the Town Watch Integrated Service, he was always on the lookout. From what he could see everything was calm. He unlocked the front door with his left hand, still holding the beer in his right, and stepped out on the stoop. It was part of his usual routine to view the length of the street without restrictions. A light rain began to fall and a drop fell on his forehead as he gulped down the last swig of his beer.

Ed stood there for a moment sensing uneasiness in the air, confusing the feeling with his own restlessness. Then on an impulse he hurried back into the house and headed straight into his bedroom. He snatched open the drawer of his night stand, pulled out his holster, and strapped it on. Next he grabbed the gun case and placed it on the bed. He opened it, picked up the pistol, and with one touch of the cool steel within the heat of his hand adrenalin started pumping steadily from his belly to his brain. He slid the piece under his arm into the holster, grabbed a jacket out of the closet, and rushed out of the front door. He locked the double bolt and took the six steps through the rain shower to get in his car.

The street looked peaceful but Ed knew danger usually lurks in the shadows. He started the engine and pulled away from the curb to circle the block. He could hear dogs barking nearby. He cracked the window to figure out what direction the disturbance was coming from. He made a right turn off Humphrey Avenue at the corner onto Oak Street and slowed down. He saw that one of the dogs was contained in a chain-linked fence and the other one was tethered to a pole on the neighboring back porch. They're barking at each other. He pressed his foot back on the gas and made another right turn at the corner of Wolf Avenue onto Shiloh Street. Halfway down the block he spots what he believes is a male figure moving at a leisurely pace.

Ed accelerates until he is just behind him and then he slows down for a closer look. He rolls down the window of the passenger side to clear away the raindrops and sees the face of a young black male beneath the hoodie with hands in his pockets. They make eye contact before he rolls past him and makes another right turn.

"Another black thug up to no good," he muttered, pressing harder on the gas pedal to circle the block and come back up Wolf Avenue.

He reached for his cell phone and pushed in the numbers.

"911, what's your emergency?" the dispatcher asked.

"I just drove down Shiloh Street and there is a suspicious guy over here who looks like he's casing houses. We've had a lot of burglaries around here lately and he fits the description."

"What are your cross streets, sir?"

"I just passed the corner of Harbor and Shiloh but I'm turning around, he's heading towards Harbor Street and I don't want to lose sight of him. Fucking coons," he said under his breath.

"Officers have been dispatched to the area, sir, there's no need to follow him. What is your name, sir?"

"Ed, Edward Landauer. He's starting to run."

"You don't have to chase him, Edward."

"I'm tired of these assholes always getting away," Ed said, hanging up his phone.

He jammed his foot down on the gas pedal and zoomed past the figure in the hoodie, stopped his car in front of him and jumped out.

"What are you doing around here?" he yelled aggressively, pushing up on the young man.

Chapter One

Rain is inarguably the most natural thing on earth; it refreshes, soothes, and promotes life more abundantly. However, changes in the environment can cause this element of renewal to change into a storm when positive and negative charges come together in a flash of lightning and boom of thunder. That's what happened on that rainy evening at 7:15 on Thursday, March 29, 2012. The path of an optimistic young man with a promising future ahead of him was crossed by a cynical man whose life had brought him failures and frustrations. A gun goes off in the darkness with a blaze of light and the explosion of the bullet tears out the heart of the young man, his family, the city, and the country.

***

Mona felt the tight grip of Darren's arm around her shivering shoulders as they stood under the umbrella behind the police barrier, just feet away from where Deshaun lay under the tarp on the wet ground. The Air Jordan's that he'd bought last month stuck out from underneath. They let her know he was lying on his back. For the umpteenth time she wrestled with the impulse to push past the police, pick up her baby, and run back to the safety of their house. He couldn't be dead. He couldn't have been snatched from her so quickly, not while she was talking to him. None of this was real. Mona bowed her head and closed her eyes, she refused to look at this nightmare another second. "I'll wake up and none of this will have happened," she prayed.

Darren stared at the silhouetted figure slumped over in the rear of the police car parked behind the grey Impala. His eyes strained to see the face of the man in the momentary flashes of red and blue light from the squad car. He flexed the muscles of his arms and held on tighter to Mona. She was the only thing that kept him from bum-rushing through the yellow tape, breaking the window on the police car, and killing the shadow of a man with his bare hands. He didn't care what happened to him, they could shoot him too, as long as he took the man to hell with him. His life was lying on the ground with Deshaun. It was for Mona's sake alone that he chose to stay on this side of the grave.

Ed looked out at all the police cars that lined both sides of the street.

"What the fuck is wrong with these assholes?" he hissed in anger.

Silently he asked, "Why in the hell am I handcuffed in the back of a patrol car?" Why were all these people standing around being nosy in their robes and raincoats staring at him like he was some worthless piece of shit? He was the one out here being a hero while they cowered behind their bolted windows and doors. He was the one who started the neighborhood watch. He was the one who had the courage to come out and confront the thieving thugs and drug dealers on the streets and now they were treating him like a criminal. His hands writhed under the metal bracelets making his fingers numb. He couldn't wait until he got a chance to call his father. They would be damn sorry for disrespecting him.

Detectives Maria Rosario and William Carlton, partners for nine years with the Special Investigations Unit of the Philadelphia Police Homicide Division, arrived on the crime scene. Dt. Carlton was tall and built like a longshoreman, he always scanned the overview of the area. Dt. Rosario was small and petite, she always searched for the minute details of the area. After a quick survey of the scene they approached the officer standing by the car with the perpetrator inside of it. Carlton read the name, Daly, sewn on the front of his uniform shirt.

"Homicide," Detective William Carlton said, holding up his badge. "This is Detective Rosario. What do we got here?"

"We've got a 34 year old white male shooter, lives a few blocks over, and a 17 year old black male victim whose parents live two blocks down. The victim was unarmed."

"Did you do a blood alcohol on the shooter?" Dt. Carlton asked.

"Yeah, he had something but he's not drunk," the officer responded.

"What about the kid, any drugs on him?" Dt. Carlton asked.

"No, nothing, he's clean," the officer answered, "Just a cell phone, Septa tokens, and fourteen dollars in his pocket."

Detective Carlton grit his teeth knowing this tragedy was only the beginning of more trouble for the city. He had been on the force for twenty-three years and he knew that a black shooter with a white victim or a white shooter with a black victim always stirred the racial pot. In this case he was sure it was about to boil over.

"I'll ride with you down to the Roundhouse, Officer Daly. Rosario, you carry the parents over with you and take their statements," Dt. Carlton said, walking to the front passenger side door.

Rosario nodded and moved to the edge of the tape where another officer stood beside Mona and Darren.

"This is Mr. and Mrs. Gardner, parents of the…" the officer said, nodding toward the body under the tarp.

"Sir and Ma'am, I'm Detective Rosario. I'm very sorry for your loss," Rosario said sympathetically. "I need for you both to come with me to the station. I have to get your statements about what happened here."

Rosario reached out her arm to support Mona on the left side when she took a step forward. Her awkwardness drew Rosario's eyes down to the mother's feet and she had to take a deep breath to steel her emotions. The sight of her drenched slippers and the rain that had seeped halfway up the hose on her legs was heartbreaking. When they reached the car she took the umbrella that was frozen in Darren's hand, let it down, and helped them into the backseat of her white Ford Taurus. Rosario pulled her vehicle behind the third police car and trailed them. The car carrying Dt. Carlton and Ed Landauer was flanked in the middle.

To Darren it felt like a funeral procession, except the body of his son was still lying on the ground behind them. His chest burned with the acid that bubbled up from his stomach and he felt like he was about to vomit. He had let Deshaun down, he was supposed to protect him and he hadn't done it. Regrets filled his head and heart. They shouldn't have moved down here.

Mona leaned over in the seat against Darren's ribs. Her backbone felt like jelly and couldn't support her. She was conscious that she was in a daze, because that's the only way they could have led her away from her baby's body as he laid on the cold asphalt.

The atmosphere inside of Rosario's car was solemn and quiet as the procession pulled up to 8th and Arch Street where the Roundhouse stood as a remnant to its past glory. The three cars then split off in different directions. Dt. Rosario parked her car below the parking bay and led Mona and Darren Gardner up to an interviewing room where she could take their statements.

The room was about 12 by 12 feet with a long solid table in the middle. There were two wooden chairs on both sides. Darren helped Mona sit down before he took a seat beside her. He could see the weight of the pain on her face and on her body, she was exhausted and near collapsing under the strain of it. All he wanted to do was get her home where she could rest.

"Can I get either of you something to eat or drink?" Dt. Rosario asked kindly.

"Just some coffee for both of us," Darren answered in a low voice.

"Certainly," Rosario said, moving back to the door. She spoke softly to someone on the other side before she came back over to the table. "I would like to tape this interview so that every detail is recorded. Is that all right with both of you?"

"That's fine," Darren answered.

Mona nodded with her eyes closed.

"Normally I would take your statements separately but under the circumstances I'm comfortable with doing them together."

The door opened slowly and a man stepped in with three steaming cups of coffee and set them on the table.

"Thanks, Saul," Rosario said before continuing. "The statement you gave to the police says that you were on the phone talking to your son, Mrs. Gardner. Can you tell me what you were doing and what time you made the call to Deshaun?"

Mona opened her eyes and wiped her tear-streaked face with her hands and took a deep breath before she started to speak.

"Deshaun works at the McDonald's in the Gallery after school to make some extra money for his graduation. He usually catches the sub home but sometimes he goes up to Germantown to hang out with his friends. I called him around 7:00 because that's the time he regularly gets off the train. It had started to rain and I wanted to know if he wanted me to pick him up. He said no and while we were talking he said this car was following him. I told him to run but then he said the car went by. It got me worrying so I told him I was sending his dad out to meet him. Then he said the car came back around and was following him again."

She stopped under a new flood of tears, pounding her fist rapidly on the table in frustration and anger.

Darren began to speak where she left off. "She was still on the phone with Deshaun when she told me to hurry up and walk up the street to meet him. She said some crazy guy was following him. I didn't think too much about it at the time but I went right out."

"I could hear him talking to the guy," Mona said, speaking again. "He asked him why he was following him and the guy got smart with him. He told the guy to get off of him, I could hear them arguing, then a sound like a grunt, somebody getting hit, and then the call was cut off."

"The next thing I know, Mona is running up behind me screaming," Darren interjected. "I slowed down just a little for her to catch up and then we both start running. We went two blocks down Harbor Street and turned the corner onto Shiloh, then we see the police lights flashing. My wife froze right then and I bolted leaving her standing there. I yelled out for Deshaun but when I got close to the cars the police grabbed me."

"They told us that there had been a shooting," Mona whimpered.

"I started shouting, where's my son?" Darren added. "Then one of the cops said, "I'm sorry, you'll have to stand back.""

"I saw his feet and his shoes sticking out from underneath the covering. That's when I realized Deshaun had been shot," Mona cried.

"So you didn't have any contact with the man who shot your son?" Rosario asked directly.

"If I had he would have been laid out there on the ground with my son," Darren said, shifting angrily in his seat.

Detective Rosario turned off the tape recorder.

"I apologize for putting you through this right now, I'm sure you both are devastated under these circumstances. Do either of you need to go to the hospital?"

"No, thank you. What can a hospital do for us?" Darren asked bitterly.

"Is there anyone you would like for me to call or is there any place you would like to go?" Rosario asked, feeling bad for them and wanting to help.

"If you can just take us home, that's all," he answered, shaking his head.

"I'll take you myself," Rosario said, rising to her feet.

***

On the floor below them in Interrogation Room D, Edward Landauer was sitting at a shorter table by himself while Detective Carlton was speaking in a low voice with another officer who was standing just inside the door. Police Chief Mancini stood watching from the other side of the one-way mirror. Ed was getting pissed off. They were holding him there like he was a criminal and he wanted to go home. They had let him make one phone call to his father and that was it.

Detective Carlton finished his conversation with the officer and moved to the table while the officer remained inside the door.

"Okay, Mr. Landauer, do you mind if I call you Edward?" Dt. Carlton asked, taking a seat across from him.

"Ed, you can call me Ed," he answered, irritated.

"All right, Ed. We need to get your statement on what happened out there this evening," Dt. Carlton said, turning on the tape recorder and pulling his note pad out of his jacket. "First I want to let you know that you have the right to remain silent and anything you say can be used against you in a court of law."
"A court of law, what the hell are you talking about?" Ed said with his temper beginning to flare. "I haven't done anything wrong."

"You have the right to consult with an attorney and have him present with you. If you cannot afford an attorney one will be appointed to you," Dt. Carlton continued.

"I don't need a goddamn lawyer, I haven't broken any laws," Ed protested.

"A young man was shot and killed tonight. That's why we're here," Carlton explained. "Why don't you tell us what happened. Start with what you did after you got home from work today."

Edward took a breath to calm himself down. He figured cooperating with them would get him out of there faster.

"There's not much to tell. It was just like any other day," he said, beginning his story. "I was relaxing around the house and when it started to get dark I stepped outside my front door to look around. We've had a lot of robberies in the neighborhood lately. I was standing on my porch when I heard some dogs barking really loud about a block away. I thought I should go check it out so I went back in the house and got the keys to my car. I was driving around the block when I saw this guy in a hoodie who was looking suspicious. I called the cops and told them I was following a suspect."

"What made you think the guy was suspicious?" Dt. Carlton asked, puzzled.

"He was walking slowly and it was raining," Ed answered simply. "It was like he was casing out the houses on the street."

"Why did you feel like you needed to follow the guy or get involved, the police were being dispatched to the area?"

"These guys always get away with the stuff they do. I wanted to make sure I kept him in sight until the cops got there."

"Then what happened, Ed, why did you get out of your car?"

"I just wanted to ask him what was he doing around here and then he pushed me. I asked him again and then he punched me in the face. He started coming at me like he was crazy or on drugs or something so I grabbed my gun to defend myself. Then he tried to take it from me. I didn't have any choice but to shoot him. It was either him or me."

"All right, Ed, thanks for your cooperation," Dt. Carlton said, getting up from the table, "We're going to have to hold you for a bit longer while we continue this investigation."

Ed shook his head. "No problem, whatever I can do to help."

Chapter Two

The bright sun of the morning lit the room and a soft breeze from the narrow opening in the window filled the curtain. Victoria watched it rise and fall in silence. The early hours of the day were the most peaceful and she refused to lose them in a repeat of the same argument. She was tired of hearing Leonard blab on and on about how lucky she was to be his chosen one. She didn't need him to tell her how she should feel, she could think for herself. The news flash he hadn't gotten yet was that their association had run its course. She had struggled too hard to get where she was to let it all go just to be somebody's wife.

"I'm losing my patience, Victoria. You need to stop worrying about your career and get serious about this relationship," Leonard complained. "The little money you make busting your ass every day is inconsequential and right now I need a partner beside me while I take my game to the next level. When you're my wife I'll take care of you."

Victoria made no comment when he threw back the comforter and stomped into the bathroom. That's the reason she always refused to spend the night at his place. She wanted to be on her own territory, independent, not beholden to him for anything. That's the way she had been raised. An only child and a preacher's daughter, she grew up comfortable with being alone while her parents spent the majority of their time and energy focused on the needs and obligations of the church. They were both gone now, praising the Lord on the other side, but they had left her the family house in Yorktown and enough money to finish law school. She had graduated summa cum laude from Temple University's Beasley School of Law and was now an assistant district attorney for the City of Philadelphia's District Attorney's office.

Leonard turned on the water of the shower and shook his head at the peeling caulk around the edges of the outdated tile on the wall. He felt like he was slumming whenever he slept at her place. The neighborhood and the house was so damn middleclass. Why would anybody prefer to stay here than at his home out on the Main Line. He was tired of trying to convince this woman that she needed to get on his train and ride it straight to Washington, maybe even the White House.

The irony was that the things that attracted him to her were the same qualities that stood between them. She was intelligent and ambitious. The woman was driven, a perfectionist, always working long hours in the office law library to prepare the perfect case. Then the clincher, she was super-fine and just as diligent in the bedroom. Despite the fact he had promised himself on many occasions that he was done with the relationship, he was drawn to her like a bad habit.

Victoria got out of the bed, stepped into her slippers as she tied the belt of her robe around her, dropped her cell phone in the pocket, and headed downstairs to the kitchen. She was hungry and thirsty and wanted to get Leonard out of her hair as quickly as possible, she needed some extra time to wash and blow-dry it before work. This was one of the days she wished she had a weave.

By the time she had fried three eggs and microwaved some bacon, the coffee was ready and Leonard had joined her at the table.

"This is getting old, baby," he said, scooping up one whole egg into his mouth. "I'm a winner and I want you on my team."

"You're right, Len," she said wearily, "This isn't working for me either. You're all that but I'm not a team player. I want to win on my own."

This was what Leonard didn't understand. He wasn't interested in trailblazing new inroads on his trip through life. He was satisfied with taking the political path his daddy had paved for him as a former mayor of Philadelphia and pushing it further up the road for his own child. He didn't see the rationale of making things harder.

"You know we're good together," he said, reaching his hand inside her robe.

"In the bed we are," she snapped, getting up from the table.

"That's because you're selfish, Vee," he said, gulping down his coffee.

"I don't even know how you can form your lips to say that, just because I can't put my work on hold every time you have one of your benefits to go to."

"It's because you don't know how to give. You want to be the man and the woman. There's no room for anybody else."

"Whenever a woman wants a successful career of her own she's accused of wanting to be a man. Come on, Len, it's 2012. If that makes me selfish, then so be it. I'm guilty."

"There's nothing wrong with refining who we are. What's the problem with that?"

"This, what we're doing now is the problem. I can't argue in court all day, then come home and argue all night, and again first thing in the morning. That's not the relationship I'm looking for. I don't need an adversary to spar with. I need a man who brings peace to my life."

"I don't see what your complaint is. You're not home cooking and cleaning. I can give you whatever you want."

"I'm never going to be like your mother, Len, and you will never accept that. You want to make me into this ideal woman that only exists in your mind."

"The only thing I'm doing is offering you the opportunity of a lifetime and you are too blind to see it or too ungrateful to accept it."

"Then it will be my loss and I'll have to live with it."

"I'm outta here," he said, buttoning up his suit coat, "I've got things to do. Call me when you get your head on straight."

When Victoria heard the front door close she went behind him and turned the bolt lock. Her phone vibrated against her leg through the robe as she hurriedly climbed the stairs. She pulled it from her pocket and saw it was the office calling. She knew it was Arthur, nobody else called her at home. Arthur Mitchell was her boss, the District Attorney for Philadelphia. She let it ring and waited until he'd finished his voice mail, then she listened to the message.

"Victoria, I need you to get your ass down here ASAP, all hell is about to break loose."

Victoria chewed the side of her jaw while she tried to relax under the flow of the water in the shower. It was going to be one of those days, which seemed to be the norm around the D.A.'s office lately. This wasn't the life she had envisioned for herself when she sat up those late hours studying at Beasley. Even though she had been promoted to the Homicide Unit, dealing with the under belly of the city, the crime, the victims, the misery of it, all had gotten old real fast.

"When was the good life supposed to begin? Where was her penthouse corner office? What clue had she missed?" she thought as she completed her morning routine of moisturization, dental hygiene, and beautification. Never one to give in to her frustration, she pulled her brown tweed Ralph Lauren business suit and a crème colored silk blouse out of the closet, following the mantra of "dress for the success you aspire to be."

Victoria's usual stroll to the subway stop at Broad and Girard was accelerated to a near trot as the message from Arthur replayed in her head. When she got there it caught her by surprise that the assortment of lives that converged daily on the corner ordinarily oblivious to each other were united by an undercurrent of agitation. Normally silent or preoccupied with cell phones, they were speaking at full volume with inflated emotions. Curious, Victoria wanted to linger but the urgency at work demanded she keep moving. Halfway down the steps the familiar stench of urine welcomed her to the platform. Through the turnstile, the train rushed in blowing a force of air around her before the doors opened and she stepped on.

Taking the subway to work was quick and convenient, a straight shot down to Market Street and barely a block over to the Widener Building. It was just across the street from City Hall. That was where she'd met Leonard Sterling two years ago, the only son of Randolph Sterling the former Mayor of Philadelphia, after he was elected State Senator. It was following the announcement of a new crime fighting measure linking local, state, and federal agencies.

Leonard was an open book with dollar signs and success written all over it. She had watched him work the room like he owned everything and everyone in it. It was a sexy look and she was attracted to him. He was brown and bald with perfect teeth, all business except he looked like he could be a running back for the Philadelphia Eagles. Full of swagger, he introduced himself and charmed her like a true politician. She thought Leonard was the man she could partner with, the other half of her power couple, but thinking about their morning conversation she understood that his passion was power. All he wanted her for was window dressing for his campaigns.

With her briefcase in her right hand, Victoria grabbed a pole with her left hand to steady herself as the subway train jerked forward, revealing the understated jewelry and watch she always wore to work. It was then she discovered she was standing in the middle of a spirited three-way discussion. She shifted her body in a ninety degree angle to move out of the direction of the words that flew back and forth across the aisle.

"It's a sin and a shame," an older black woman said to the younger black woman beside her, "A black child can't even walk home without somebody using him for target practice."

"These young hoodlums are always up to no good," a middle-aged black man in a dingy wrinkled suit seated on the other side added, "We might not have the whole story yet."

"It's the same old story, ain't nothing changed," the older black woman said, "White people think that they can shoot black folks down in the street and nobody gives a damn."

"Nobody kills more blacks in these streets than other blacks do," the old man said, rising to his feet to get off at Spring Garden.

"All I know is that the white guy who shot him better not walk," the younger black woman hollered at his back. "If they let him out his ass is gonna catch a bullet."

"Damn," Victoria thought to herself. Messing around with Len this morning she hadn't even turned on the news. Some serious shit had gone down last night and Arthur was sure to meet her at the door ranting and raving. He loved his job and re-election season was less than a year away. She got off the train at the City Hall station, sprinted up the steps, and walked briskly across the intersection to Chestnut Street. She pushed through the heavy glass and brass revolving door and quickly passed through security and caught an elevator to the second floor.

She could see Arthur talking with Detective Carlton in the hallway outside of her office as soon as she turned the corner. He looked at her and then his watch.

Arthur was no-nonsense. He was a redhead born to a working-class Irish-Catholic family in Fishtown, one block away from Kensington and Allegheny Avenue. The noise from the el (elevated train) was the lullaby that rocked him to sleep on the nights when his Pop pulled graveyard duty at a meat packing plant. He still had the paunch he got from the daily meat and potatoes his mother fed him and his two sisters. It was his father's dream that he would join the Fire Department or the Police Department but he preferred to avoid dangerous situations, so he went the college route to get his job working for the city.

"Well, Ms. Perry, so nice of you to join us this morning," Arthur said with each word dripping sarcasm. "By chance have you seen the Daily News or the TV since you have an aversion to using your cell phone?"

"I caught the gist of it on the train, sir," she answered respectfully, hating that she wasn't prepared with the details.

"This case is a powder keg waiting to blow," Detective Carlton said, "We're holding the shooter down at the Roundhouse. He's been questioned and we held him over night. Police Commissioner Mancini hasn't formerly arrested him as of yet. He wants to hear what you advise. He doesn't want to take the heat either way for this one."

"I bet he doesn't with the press all over this like flies on shit. Come on inside Victoria's office and you can tell us what you've got," Arthur said, wanting to speak privately.

Victoria led the way into her office, went behind her desk, put down her briefcase, and took a seat in her burgundy leather chair knowing this was just the beginning of a long day. She motioned for Detective Carlton to have a seat in one of the padded leather mahogany chairs in front of her and Arthur sat down in the chair opposite him.

Detective Carlton pulled out his note pad and began to read, "We have a lone shooter who shot a black kid two blocks from his house and no witnesses as of yet."

"Fill us in on how the questioning went with the shooter and the parents," Arthur urged.

"We've got two contradicting stories," Carlton said, reviewing his notes. "There's the mother who was on the phone with her son, she says that some creep was following him on his way home from work and she told him to run. Then there's the shooter, a Town Watch captain who says he was investigating some dogs barking, saw the kid acting suspicious and followed him. He says the kid attacked him and he shot him in self defense."

"Another reason why we need gun control," Victoria said, shaking her head.

Arthur laughed. "That'll never happen. Guns make a ton of money, Ms. Perry. You can't control money."

"That's not what you say when it's about legalizing marijuana," Victoria said snidely.

"Jails make money too," Arthur said with a smirk.

"Was the kid armed?" Victoria asked Dt. Carlton, ignoring Arthur's comment.

"No, he was clean, and his record is too," Dt. Carlton added.

"Dammit to hell, not this bullshit again," Arthur said, getting wound up. "Was there any evidence of a fight between the two of them?"

"The shooter has a broken jaw and busted lip but we don't have the coroner's preliminary report on the kid yet."

"We need that ASAP," Arthur said. "Get me some background on the shooter, ex-girlfriends, running buddies, bars where he drinks, and where he works."

"I'm on it," Dt. Carlton said before he walked out.

"We have two options, Vicki," Arthur said, standing up, "We can let the shooter go, say the shooting was justified, and hope to hell the fury blows over before election season begins. The other option is to arrest him and charge him with second-degree murder or manslaughter."

"If the case has already gone national, and I'm sure it has, he's got to be charged," Victoria said obstinately, folding her arms and leaning back in her chair.

"The problem is that when whites are killing whites and blacks are killing blacks, nobody cares. Black kill a white or a white kill a black, it's the end of the world."

"He killed an unarmed kid walking down the street, Arthur. Last time I checked there are laws against that aren't they? Besides, he can't use the 'Stand your ground' as a defense for the shooting if the kid didn't have a gun."

"He can still use self-defense if he had a reasonable belief that his life was in danger, and since you feel that strongly about it, it's your case. Get the sworn statement from the officers on the scene and then see Judge Franklin to get the arrest warrant," Arthur said as he walked out of the office.

This was the first chance Victoria got to take off her tweed jacket, it was burning her up. She had felt the dampness of perspiration on her back as soon as she stepped out of the elevator. Picking up a file from her desk to fan herself, she contemplated the issues before her. This case was hot as hell and Arthur didn't want to touch it. Whenever race and guns mixed in the courts it could make or break all of those involved. If she proceeded with charges she had to win or her big dream of a stellar and profitable career was in the toilet. The last thing she wanted was to be branded the black woman that couldn't get the job done because she was out of her league. "Maybe I should let it be," she thought leaning on her folded hands. Being noble only gets you sacrificed and she was too young to die professionally.

She reached for the remote on her desk and turned on the TV. There was a special report airing on a local channel. Standing in the center of a press conference outside of her home was Mona Gardner with her husband, Darren, standing behind her. Victoria turned up the volume.

Mona spoke bravely. "I'm standing here today with a broken heart, in more pain than I've ever experienced in my life. I'm standing here to ask those who want to help, those who care about what happened to my son to stay calm and peaceful. I don't want any bloodshed in my son's name. What I do want today is justice for my son, nothing else matters to me."

Mona stood there trembling, unable to continue to hold her emotions in check. Darren took her by the hand without making a comment and they walked away from the microphones and cameras. The press conference was over. It was in that moment Victoria resolved that she would move ahead to prosecute the shooter. Seeing Mrs. Gardner behave that selfless in the wake of her son being killed, she felt that the D.A.'s office owed it to her to assure that Deshaun got the justice he deserved.

She turned on her computer and drew up the complaint for the warrant to arrest Edward Landauer for the murder of Deshaun Gardner. She put her tweed blazer back on, took the steps down to the vestibule, and walked the half block over to City Hall to the Honorable Harold Franklin chambers.

***

With a reputation of being tough but fair, Judge Franklin was the judge of choice in the D.A.'s office for questionable warrants. He was raised in the Richard Allen Homes during the 1950s, graduated from Drexel in the late sixties, and had worked as a prosecutor in the D.A.'s office for 23 years before he was elected to the first of two terms as a Municipal Court Judge. Now that he was five months past his sixty-ninth birthday and seven months away from mandatory retirement, he was signing warrants one after another like a Philadelphia Parking Authority officer handing out tickets.

"Good morning, Your Honor," Victoria said, entering his chambers. "I need your signature on an arrest warrant for Edward Landauer, the shooter of Deshaun Gardner last night in South Philly. He claims it was self-defense but the kid was unarmed. Based on his 911 call, it seems Mr. Landauer thought Deshaun Gardner was a suspicious person, however, he approached the victim without provocation."

"What is his reason for pulling his weapon and shooting?" Judge Franklin asked casually.

"He says the victim attacked him."

"What's the charge, counselor?"

"Criminal homicide, Your Honor. If we don't set a precedent we're going to have to deal with more Lone Ranger and Batman perpetrators out here thinking they're police enforcers just because they have a license to carry a gun.

Judge Franklin read the complaint and signed it.

"Good luck on that," he said, handing it back to her.

Victoria stepped out into the antechamber and called Arthur.

"Judge Franklin signed the warrant, Dt. Carlton can officially make the arrest. I don't think this case needs to go to the Grand Jury but we can't make any mistakes on this one."

"It's your baby, Vicki. I just got word that Landauer has lawyered up."

"Who's on the defense?" Victoria asked curiously.

"I hear it's Benjamin Madison."

"All right, I've got some work to do before the arraignment," she said, hanging up.

This development changed everything. Victoria knew Benjamin Madison very well. They had gone to Temple together. He was the only one who had eclipsed her, he was magna cum laude. Benjamin was the shit and he knew it. He always made the team, made the grade, got the girl, and got the job. He was a winner from birth. He may not have been born with a silver spoon in his mouth but it was definitely within his reach. His father, the black sheep of a family that had made a fortune in a chain of grocery stores called Penn Pride, had squandered his share of the business, but his brother who had never married or had a family of his own had taken Ben under his wing. There were rumors that this uncle was gay, but he taught Benjamin all he knew about style and the importance of being in the right place at the right time.

"Dammit," she said between clenched teeth when she got back to her office.

This case had more pins and needles than a wild porcupine and Victoria didn't want to get stuck. She leaned back in her chair to weigh the pros and cons. She was well past her three-year commitment to the D.A.'s office. She had been tested in her training, excelled in her stint of misdemeanor trials, the Juvenile Unit, Major Trials, and now she was one of the select few in the Homicide Unit. She had painstakingly built a portfolio of impressive wins for the Commonwealth. Did she have more to lose by leading on this case than she had to gain?

Nonetheless, Benjamin Madison had consistently bested her in law school, grades, mock trials, and in prestigious internships. Right out of the Beasley Law School of Temple University gates he was offered a job at Rosen & Sullivan while she was passed over by all the top firms in the city. He was smooth even back then and time had only served to give him more polish as he shone in the media racking up one high-profile case after another. She knew that Edward Landauer didn't have the money to pay his retainer or fees so she knew this was probably another opportunity for him to step into the spotlight. Nonetheless, this was her turf. She wasn't about to let anybody, not even him, intimidate her into falling back from the challenge. She also figured he had other reasons for taking the case. She was the only unconquered contender that he had pursued in his life.

Chapter Three

A huge crowd of folks had surrounded the outside of the building by the time Victoria got over to the Criminal Justice Center. Some were angry and shouting, some carrying signs, some were just curious looking on, but most were reporters setting up their cameras and testing their microphones. Like kids waiting for a turn to get on the merry-go-round, Victoria joined in the line of people going through the revolving door.

"The circus has already come to town," she said under her breath as she maneuvered through the crowd inside the entrance in anonymity.

The lobby was filled with a cornucopia of lawyers, family members, witnesses, potential jurors, and police officers waiting to pass through the metal detectors. Victoria dropped her crossover bag and briefcase into the shallow plastic container to go through security.

"How are you doing, Rhonda?" she said, greeting one of the security monitors.

"Good afternoon, Miss Perry," Rhonda replied, placing her container on the moving belt. "It's going to be hot in there today."

"So it seems," Victoria said, putting the strap of her briefcase over her shoulder.

She joined the clusters in the vestibule waiting for one of the six elevators to open. Two sets of doors parted and the packs split rushing in opposite directions. Victoria was the last rider to squeeze on and backed up from the closing door.

"What floor?" a young girl with a baby on her hip asked.

"Three please," Victoria answered.

The preliminary arraignment for Edward Landauer in the Municipal Court was now considered to be a high-security case and had been assigned to Courtroom 306. Tempers and anger over the killing of Deshaun Gardner were fodder for a potentially volatile situation. Judge Inez Butler requested the courtroom as a safety precaution.

Victoria looked around the room through the open door and recognized Mr. and Mrs. Gardner from the press conference and news reports sitting close to the front. She walked through the overcrowded gallery and approached the floor-to-ceiling wall of bulletproof glass that separated the counsel tables, the judge's bench, the witness stand and the jury box. Victoria raised her hand to signal for the bailiff to press the button that opened the electronic lock. Stepping on the other side of the door made her feel like she'd just gone over the high peak of a rollercoaster. Her stomach rose up to her throat and she got nervous.

"I haven't had this feeling since my first day in court," she mused, taking a seat in one of the mahogany chairs on the right side at the prosecution's table.

The lock on the glass door clicked again and Benjamin Madison, followed by his young and attractive legal assistant, strode in looking like fresh pressed money. Sharp and Classy in a dark brown Armani suit he made a grand entrance looking like Brad Pitt walking the red carpet of his latest movie premiere.

"He hasn't changed," she thought, glancing over at him "He's still the sexiest white man I've ever seen off or on the big screen."

Benjamin handed his briefcase to his assistant at the defense table before he stepped across the aisle to have a word with Victoria.

"You're looking good, Momi," he said, leaning over and gently touching her elbow.

"Don't start, Ben," she whispered back to him.

"Let's do some business, Vicki. We can put this baby to bed and go out on the town this evening and enjoy ourselves."

"I don't think that's what you want, you get off on something else," she said, staring him in the eye. "I've seen the ecstasy in your face after a win. I could never produce that for you, it's the conquest that makes you climax."

"You surprise me, such insight. All this time while I was looking under your clothes I never knew you had a view of my psyche."

"Cut the bullshit, Ben. If you're looking for a deal on this one, forget about it."

He leaned closer.

"No, Vicki, you got me all wrong. I want the case dropped."

"I hate to disappoint you but that's not going to happen."

"Fair enough, Momi, let's party," he said, squeezing her arm before he released it.

"All rise, the court is in-session, the honorable Judge Inez Butler presiding," the bailiff said, announcing the start of the arraignment.

Judge Butler walked in ahead of her court clerk. She was the youngest of the judges in the Philadelphia Municipal Court and no one was more impressed by her achievement than herself. She wore a smile on her face like Miss America whenever she was on the bench that was sometimes slightly disturbing. Every hair was always in place and her make-up was camera-ready. The only thing overdone was her fingernails. Her tips were way too long and the intricate artwork on each finger served as a distraction. Her colleagues often teased her about having a beauty salon in her chambers.

"Docket number 7631481," the court officer stated, "The Commonwealth versus Edward Landauer."

The side door opened with Victoria and the rest of the courtroom staring. Edward stumbled in wearing dark green baggy overalls being led by a sheriff over to the defense table. His dark brown hair was combed to the back and his full face was lopsided with swelling on the left side. Ben grabbed his hand and shook it.

"Hello, Edward, my name is Benjamin Madison. Your father has retained me to represent you in this case. The charge against you is murder in the second-degree. You don't need to say a word today."

"I can't believe they arrested me, that kid could have killed me," Ed complained.

"Don't stress it, I'll have you out of here shortly," Benjamin assured him.

"Do you waive the reading?" the court officer asked after reading Ed his constitutional rights.

"Yes, we do," Benjamin stated.

"How do you plea?" Judge Butler asked.

"Not guilty, Your Honor."

The room was as quiet and still as a picture in a frame while Judge Butler reviewed the file.

"Ms. Perry do you have any notices?"

"Your Honor, the defendant has shown no respect for the authority of law enforcement and is therefore a threat to the community," Victoria implored, "The Commonwealth asks that the bail be set for $1 million, not only for the safety of the citizens of Philadelphia but for the defendant's safety as well."

Ben interjected. "Your Honor, my client does not have a history of violence or a criminal record and potentially faces more danger while in custody. Mr. Landauer has strong ties to the community and support from his family. He is not a wealthy man, so we ask that the bail be set lower with that in mind."

"The bail is set at $250 thousand with stipulations," Judge Butler declared. "Mr. Landauer, you are not to have any contact with the witnesses to this case or the Gardner family. You are to wear an electronic ankle bracelet to monitor your whereabouts and you are hereby banned from using any firearms, drugs, or alcohol."

"Thank you, Your Honor," Benjamin said, picking up his briefcase.

Two deputies escorted Edward out of the courtroom and the murmurs in the gallery grew to loud rumbles as the pack of spectators spilled out the back of the courtroom. Benjamin Madison walked out as cool and collected as he was when he walked in. Victoria gathered her shoulder bag and briefcase dodging the reporters in the rear and hopped on an elevator just as the door was closing. She stopped short of making her exit at the entrance of the Justice Center. Ben was right outside completely ignoring the dozens of protesters ranting and giving an interview. His confidence oozed from every pore, not cocky, but based on his proven record.

"This is an unfortunate circumstance," Ben said, addressing the throng of reporters, "I have a great deal of sympathy for the Gardner family, however, in due process my client will be exonerated of any charges. Our first action will be to raise the bail and get Mr. Landauer released as soon as possible. His family is anxious to have him back home."

One reporter from the rear pushed his way to the front.

"We just got a report that a fire bomb was thrown into Edward Landauer's house a few minutes ago. Do you have a comment, Mr. Madison?"

"I wasn't aware of that incident, I can't comment on it at this time."

More questions are shouted.

"Do you think you'll need extra security for Edward Landauer after he gets outs of jail? There have been some rumors of death threats toward your client."

"This is a very emotional situation for all involved in this case.

My hope is that we all remain calm and allow the system to do its work."

Victoria watched through the glass as he and his assistant moved swiftly to a waiting car on the curb. She couldn't help but shake her head; he gets to ride back to his plush office while she gets to walk. Barely having taken two steps down from the Criminal Justice Center, an onslaught of reporters blocked her way like an army in attack mode brandishing cameras and microphones to capture her every word.

"Will you be the prosecuting attorney in the case against Edward Landauer?" one of them shouts jabbing his microphone in her face.

"Yes, I will be representing the Commonwealth as we seek justice for Deshaun Gardner and his family," Victoria answered, taken aback by the overwhelming attention.

"Have there been any other witnesses who have come forward?"

"I'm not at liberty to comment on that at this time," Victoria said, wincing from all the questions.

"Do you think you have adequate prosecutorial experience to get a conviction?" an unruly reporter from the rear yelled.

"I have complete faith in our judicial system," Victoria replied, choosing her words carefully. "Mr. Landauer will be judged by a jury of his peers and justice will prevail. In the meantime, you'll have to excuse me, there's much work to be done. Thank you."

Victoria quickened her pace holding her head down in a futile effort to hide her identity from the people who passed her on the sidewalk. From now on Arthur was going to have to provide her with a car to get around in the city. He stood at the elevators waiting for her when she got back from court.

"Looks like the games have begun, Vicki. Come into my office so we can talk," Arthur said, leading her by her left arm.

He closed the door behind them and went over to his shelf

and poured himself a glass of Scotch before he walked over to the window. Victoria dropped into a chair in front of his desk. He gulped half of his drink down and wiped his mouth with the back of his hand.

"The buzzards are beginning to circle, Vicki," he said bluntly, gazing out at the view of the city. "Are you sure you still want to move forward with this case? There's a possibility that the defense may be willing to plea to a lesser charge."

"Now that you've put my face out there in the public as prosecutor I'm not going to back away from the case. I'd be the one responsible for letting that racist lunatic get away with the cold-blooded murder of an unarmed black kid. I'm not going down like that."

"Vicki, you have my full support. I've decided to relieve you of all your other cases until this is resolved one way or another. This prosecution requires your full attention. In addition to that, I'm going to assign someone to assist you on a full-time basis."

"What's the catch? You've never been this accommodating before."

"This is going to be a delicate high-profile case, how you handle it is going to reflect on this office. You're going to need a second chair and I have someone in mind who I think you can work well with."

"I don't get my choice," she asked, surprised.

"This one is a new hire, unassigned. She's a workhorse. Her name is Khloe Luskin."

"Sounds like a white girl with nothing to lose."

"It won't hurt us publicly to be racially balanced, and with all the protests you shouldn't have any trouble with the preliminary hearing. It's already a given that charges have been brought. It's just a formality."

"I agree, and I'm sure with the public pressure that's coming nationally the mayor and the governor are going to want to rush this one through the system ASAP. I may only have four to six months to prepare the case."

"Exactly, so what's your strategy?"

"I need to get to know this Edward Landauer, how he thinks, how he feels, and what makes him tick. I need to interview his girlfriend, his family, his friends, and his co-workers. I have to show his impulsiveness, his temper, and the racist tendencies that made him pull the trigger."

"The race card as a motive is tough, Vicki. It's hard to prove. He'll say he's not a racist and then what."

"I don't intend to make this an argument about race. It has to be about the gun and his rage. This violent gun culture has to be put on trial."

"All that will do is bring the NRA all over us and you can't win against them. Besides, guns don't kill people, people kill people."

"People without guns don't shoot people."

"They're too powerful, Vicki. Go take some time and work on your strategy."

"Thanks for the vote of confidence."

Arthur turned back to the window and Victoria got up to leave.

"By the way, I'm going to need a car and a driver to go to court," she hollered over her shoulder.

"I'll see what we can do," he answered without turning around.

***

Victoria slumped down in her desk chair mentally and physically exhausted. This was the only opportunity she'd had to take a breath since she'd gotten in the office. Leonard had been blowing up her phone all day and she hadn't even eaten any lunch. She kicked off her shoes and reached for her phone hoping Leonard was in the area and wanted to grab a bite for dinner. She pushed his name and waited for him to pick up.

"Vee, it's about damn time," he answered. "I've been trying to get you all day."

"It's been crazy, I haven't stopped all day."

"I saw you on the news earlier. Baby, you need to pass on this case. It's volatile. It can ruin our political future."

"That's your future, Len, not mine."

"Let's not trip, Vee, you love me and I know it."

"I'll admit I love parts of you," she said, joking.

"I'm serious. Does this case mean more to you than our relationship?"

"I can't even think about that right now."

"In that case, call me after you think about it," he said, hanging up.

With that Victoria marked the end of a rough day. She snatched up her handbag and briefcase and turned off the lights on her way out. She took long strides on her walk from Chestnut Street over to Market was about to step on the escalator down to the train in City Hall before she remembered Len saying she had been on the news. She walked to the corner of Broad Street and flagged herself a cab.

Less than fifteen minutes later the cab pulled up in front of her house. From inside the car she could see her neighbor and close friend of the family, Judy B. Baker, sitting in her usual spot outside her door on the driveway. She was a social worker but she had been on disability since she got diagnosed with congestive heart failure. Her daughter, Lanetta, moved back home about a year ago to help out. Miss Judy had been a real close friend of her momma and Lanetta was like a sister to her. Victoria gave the driver a $20 dollar bill and got out.

"All right now, it's our neighborhood celebrity," Miss Judy said, greeting her. Then she yelled out to Lanetta, "Bring out a chair for Vicki."

"Nobody wants to sit out here but you, Mama," Lanetta said, carrying a chair in her arm. "It's nippy out here."

"True or false, that's false. Vicki probably needs some fresh air," Miss Judy said, unfolding the chair.

"What's going on, Miss Judy, how are you?" Victoria said, taking the seat beside her.

"You're the one who's gone Hollywood," Lanetta said, smiling. "You are all over the TV."

"You got your hands full now, child," Miss Judy said.

"Yeah, but I'm not going to let that guy walk away. He didn't have a right to take that kid's life. Somebody's got to stand up and say it's wrong."

"People are already lining up on both sides. Some say they're scared to walk the streets with all these hoodlums robbing and raising hell, that makes it tough on the ones who are trying to do something with their lives," Miss Judy said.

"It don't matter, Mama," Lanetta added, "Cowboy and Indian days are done, you can't run around here like 'Django Unchained' shooting people down when you feel like it."

"Exactly my point, Lanetta," Victoria said, giving her a high-five.

"Anyway, child, have you had your dinner yet?" Miss Judy asked.

"No, ma'am, I haven't had anything since breakfast."

"Now that's a shame, come on in here and eat. We can finish talking at the table."

Miss Judy rises to her feet and goes inside. Victoria folds up her chair and Lanetta folds up her mama's and they follow her into the house. They lean the chairs on the wall inside the door. Victoria sets her things down and goes into the bathroom to wash her hands for dinner before she makes her way into the kitchen. Miss Judy and Lanetta are already sitting at the table blessing the food when she comes in.

"Go on and fix your plate, child. You've eaten here more times than you did at your momma's dining room table."

"I know that's right, Miss Judy. I'm glad I didn't miss this,"

Victoria said, spooning up a large portion of food on her plate. "You make chicken fried rice better than any Chinese restaurant I've been to."

"Tell the truth, child," Miss Judy laughed, "Plus my cookies taste better too."

"Where's your man this evening?" Lanetta asked, "You might need a bodyguard since you getting all famous."

"We're bumping heads right now. I'm thinking I might let it go."

"Vicki, you're crazy as hell," Lanetta said, shocked, "It ain't nothing out here. That man is ultra-successful, upwardly mobile, and he's got solid family roots."

"He's bossy and controlling," Victoria said smugly.

"So what, you are too," Lanetta replied.

Victoria let that slide. "Don't they say opposites attract."

"If you don't want him, I'll take him. I don't have a problem with left-overs. You know they're better on the second day."

"Don't start all of that scandalous talk in front of me," Miss Judy joked, "Show some respect."

"Just show me where the cookies are so I can go home and go to bed," Victoria said.

Judy got up and took the top off of a Tupperware bowl on the cabinet and put three large ones in a plastic bag.

"I got oatmeal today. Take them with you. They'll make you smack somebody."

Chapter Four

It was evident that Edward Landauer had shot and killed Deshaun Gardner. There was no disputing the fact that Deshaun Gardner was unarmed at the time of the shooting. The questions were related to the circumstances of the shooting, whether Edward Landauer was justified in pulling the trigger. Two new witnesses had come forward saying they had seen the scuffle from their windows. One said he peeped out after he heard the car door close and saw Edward approach Deshaun and the struggle between them before the shot was fired. The other had come to the window after hearing voices outside. In the darkness, neither had a clear view of the altercation or heard the conversation between them.

The daily newspapers and the evening news gnawed at the controversy with nonstop coverage of protests throughout the city. Reactions from across the country, interviews with the Gardner family, and commentary from blacks and whites stirred the racial pot. Benjamin Madison had hoped that the heat of anger in the hearts and minds of Philadelphians would begin to die down over time, but against his advice Edward Landauer had decided to forego the preliminary hearing to speed the legal process.

Benjamin, in his frustration had decided to go and have a talk with his client's parents, Laramie and Alta Landauer. It stood to reason that since they had supplied the funds for Edward's release on bail and were paying for their son's defense they may have some influence over the decisions he was making pertaining to the case. Ben couldn't get a handle on his client or understand the friction that he was giving him as his lawyer. He knew he didn't like the guy but that didn't make any difference to him, when he took a case he was in it to win it.

It was a long drive out to the retirement community in Valley Forge where Laramie and Alta had bought a condominium six years ago leaving Edward to himself in the family home. Ben sat in the back of the limo enjoying the peace and quiet without the company of his talkative legal assistant. It gave him an opportunity to listen to his own thoughts. This was going to be a tricky case and even though he was confident that he would win, he knew Victoria wasn't going down without a fight. That's what attracted him to her. He understood her motivation and drive towards perfection. They were like the two Olympic runners in the movie, *Chariots of Fire*, never to be on the same team. He'd asked her out a few times but she never accepted, being in academic competition always got in the way.

"We're here, sir, Patrick Henry Place, number 805," his driver said, bringing him out of his ruminations.

Benjamin got out without saying a word. He rang the doorbell and waited.

Alta Landauer answered, "Come on in, Mr. Madison, we've been expecting you. Laramie is in the living room."

He followed her short footsteps, noticing how petite she was in a shirtwaist dress. Her long hair was in a thick plait that she had twisted into a bun on top of her head. The house was nicely decorated but didn't reflect the level of money that was necessary to pay his fee. The hallway was adorned with pictures of both sons. In most, Edward stood beside his brother who held a trophy, a ribbon, or a diploma.

"Sit on down, Mr. Madison," Laramie said, motioning towards a spot on the sofa. "Alta, get the man something to drink."

Benjamin took a seat on the edge of the sofa and leaned

forward to talk.

"Mr. Landauer, I'm here to learn as much as I can about your son and his upbringing. In order for me to present the best possible defense I'm going to need your cooperation as well as his."

"What do you need to know?" Alta asked, handing him a tall glass of Coca-Cola on ice.

"Tell me about him as if you were speaking in front of a jury," Benjamin said, sitting back and getting comfortable on the sofa, "Help me understand who he is as a man."

Alta spoke first. "When Eddie was born Laramie was still in the service and we changed bases a couple of times from California to Virginia before he finally retired, then we moved to Philly. Eddie had a hard time when he was younger. He wasn't sickly but he was pudgy and the other kids picked on him."

"The only problem Ed had was that you coddled him," Laramie grumbled. "He needed to toughen up. He wasn't like Emerson, his older brother, he was a 'mama's boy' until he went to high school. I never woulda bet that he would have the nerve to shoot anybody."

"He started to take up for himself when he went to high school and he started to make friends easier when Emerson went off to college" Alta added.

"Yeah, it took him a while to figure out what he wanted to do with himself," Laramie sneered. "He wanted to follow in my footsteps and go in the military but he was overweight. Too weak to push himself back from the dinner table."

"I tried to help him lose the weight but he just got frustrated," Alta said somberly.

"Did he want to go to college after high school, what were his goals?" Benjamin asked, eager to hear something redeeming about his client.

"Ed worked in the family store for a few years, but he got bored with it," Laramie said, "He wanted to do something more exciting and he had it in his head that he was meant to be a leader, so he applied to the Philadelphia Police Academy."

"How did that work out for him?" Benjamin asked.

"Without military service he didn't have any of the college credits they required," Alta answered with regret.

"Let's be honest here, Alta, he couldn't have passed the physical fitness test anyway," Laramie interjected. "Ed is my son and I love him no matter what but he's always felt like he needed to compete with his brother. He's always trying to do something that he feels would make us proud of him. That's why he started that neighborhood watch thing to look out for the people around us. Since he couldn't get in the military he still wants to do something honorable."

"That's all he was trying to do out there that night," Alta said with her voice full of emotion, "Except that kid jumped on him and he couldn't defend himself without having to use his gun."

"It's been enlightening talking with you, Mr. and Mrs. Landauer," Benjamin said, rising to his feet and shaking Laramie's hand. "I have a better understanding of how to build my case. I'll definitely contact your other son, Emerson, also. Thank you for your time."

"Thank you, Mr. Madison," Alta said, walking him to the door. "We want our son cleared of all this unbelievable mess."

Benjamin stepped out of the door and walked to his waiting car without looking back. Unconsciously he clenched his jaw during the entire ride back to Center City. He had his work cut out for him. The Landauers wouldn't be the best character witnesses for their own son. He had to somehow camouflage the true image of Edward, from the power-hungry, explosive personality, neurotic, and resentful man who never lived up to his father's expectations, into a hero. By the time the car exited the Schuylkill Expressway it was obvious that he needed to speak with his client. He instructed his driver to get off on Vine Street and take him to the address of Emerson Landauer's house in Olde City. That's where Edward was staying since his release for his own protection.

***

"Mr. Madison, please come in," Emerson said, opening the door. "Ed is in the rec room."

"You must be Edward's brother," Benjamin said, extending his hand, "I'm glad to meet you, aside from the circumstances."

The brothers had similar features but their personalities made them appear very different. Emerson's face was bright with satisfaction like Dr. Jekyll and Edward's was gloomy with discontent like Mr. Hyde. One body represented self-control and the other a lack of will-power.

"I'm relieved to know that we have someone of your competence to represent my brother," Emerson said graciously.

"I'd like to talk with you first for a few moments if I could," Ben said, speaking in a low tone.

"Certainly, there's some coffee ready in the kitchen."

Benjamin eyes roamed around the room taking notice of the collection of fine art and the Italian leather sofa. Emerson was without a doubt the golden child in the family. Benjamin took a seat at the bar of the kitchen. He had to admire Emerson's good taste. The wood was dark walnut courtesy of IKEA, and the pattern of the granite was magnificent in depth and detail. Emerson handed him a porcelain cup of gourmet brew atop a matching saucer and stood before him on the other side of the counter.

"Thank you, the aroma is high quality," Benjamin said, setting the coffee down.

Emerson smiled. "It's a mix of Jamaican beans. Once you taste it you'll be hooked."

Benjamin took a sip and nodded in approval.

"I'd like for you to tell me about your brother, help me get to know him. What was he like growing up?"

"Ed was a good kid. He made okay grades in school. He was kind of husky and a little clumsy so the kids teased him a lot. It bothered him so he stayed in the house watching cartoons most of the time."

"What about when he grew up?" Benjamin asked.

"Ed has always wanted to help people. He wanted to serve his country and his community. That's what he was trying to do the other night. He always tries too hard."

"What about women?"

"He's been close to a few chicks but he has real high standards."

"Do you believe you brother's story about what happened that night?"

"Absolutely, my brother has a strong sense of right and wrong. He did what he had to do to protect himself and the people in the neighborhood."

Benjamin nodded as he took a big gulp of the rich coffee. Emerson would be a strong witness for the defense. He loved his brother and has probably been standing up for him his whole life.

"This is good coffee. I'll finish it while I talk to Edward," he said, standing up with his cup and saucer in hand.

"Follow me," Emerson directed.

From across the rec room Benjamin could tell from Edward's body language that he was pissed off. The leg with the ankle bracelet was propped against the end table and Ed was glaring at it with a scowl on his face. He fists were balled up in his lap ready to fight.

"Hello, Edward, how are you doing today?" Benjamin asked congenially before taking a seat.

"Not as good as you," Ed snarled. "I thought you were going to get these bogus charges dismissed by now. I don't think my folks are getting their money's worth."

"Don't forget I'm on your side, Ed. It was your decision to waive the preliminary hearing."

"What did I need a damn preliminary hearing for, I'm not a

criminal. I'm ready to get this bullshit over with and go back to my life."

"Then my advice to you is to take a plea. The Commonwealth of Pennsylvania has decided that there is sufficient evidence that a crime was committed."

"Hell no, why should I, for protecting myself. What's the case against me?"

"The other witnesses that have come forth are disputable except for the mother's testimony. You might want to reconsider taking a deal. In fact, that option is not off the table. I think I can get this reduced to manslaughter."

"No deal, I'm innocent. He attacked me. I didn't have any choice."

"So you're saying that you were armed with a 9mm automatic pistol and you feared for your life from an unarmed kid."

"That so-called kid was a lot bigger than I am. He knocked me down with one punch."

"We can do this any way you want, Edward, but if I were in your position I wouldn't hesitate to take a plea."

"I don't care what you think, Mr. Madison. If I go to jail, then some other nigger in the pen gets another chance to take me out. They're already calling my phone with death threats and my house has been vandalized. If you're as good as they say you are, I'll take my chances in the courtroom."

"Would you consider an insanity defense?"

"Fuck no, I'm not insane."

"Will you consider a psychiatric evaluation just for the sake of argument?"

"Read my lips this time, fuck no."

"It's your call, Edward. Judge Robert Kelly will be hearing the case, he's a fair-minded man. I just needed to know what cards I'm playing with," Benjamin said as he was leaving the room, "One more thing for you to think about is whether you want the case to be decided by a judge or a jury. Enjoy your afternoon."

"I don't need to think about it," Edward spat. "There are plenty of people who would have done the same thing I did. I want a jury."

***

Arthur hadn't given her a car yet but Victoria knew that her days of riding the subway to work were behind her. This would have been the very day she'd have accepted the ride from Leonard but he hadn't been over since the shooting. The long days that came with this case were already breaking her down and she needed his support, except he had let her know that if she and this case were a package deal he didn't want any parts of it. She called a cab as soon as she woke up to take her into the office, she couldn't afford to be late.

The cab pulled up just as she came down the stairs, perfect timing. Miss Judy was outside sitting in her chair with a bag in her lap when she raced out the door.

"I made you an egg sandwich and I put some more cookies in here too," Miss Judy hollered out. "You don't need to run out of here without eating. Sorry I don't have anything for you to drink except a bottle of water."

Victoria hurried over to her chair, gave her a hug, and took the bag.

"Thanks, Miss Judy, you're a lifesaver."

Victoria could smell the mouth-watering sausage through the paper. She opened the bag and took out the sandwich. It was still warm. She finished it in five large bites and washed it down with the bottle of water just as the cab driver pulled up to the Widener Building. She rolled up the bag with the cookies left in it and put it inside her purse. She dodged the lone reporter watching the government cars and went in the front entrance without fanfare.

She barely had time to make her morning cup of Lipton tea before Arthur burst into her office with a young woman following close behind him.

"Victoria Perry meet Khloe Luskin, she's going to be your special assistant on the case. I have a car for you two but not a driver," Arthur announced, throwing her the keys. "It's parked in the Filbert lot, dark blue Ford Taurus in a reserved space."

Khloe moved forward to shake hands.

"Nice to meet you, Victoria," she said, "This is a great opportunity for me."

"As long as you're not afraid of hard work. With the press all over this case it will take three times the normal preparation," Victoria said, gripping her hand. "Today we interview the Gardners."

"I'll leave you two women to your own devices," Arthur said, walking out the door.

"Time to get rolling," Victoria said, placing the strap of her briefcase over her shoulder. "We have an appointment at the Gardner home at 10:30."

"Do you want me to bring the car around?" Khloe asked.

"No need, we can save time if we walk over together," Victoria answered.

They waited for the elevator in silence and neither spoke until they were outside of the building.

"I can drive if you don't mind," Khloe offered.

"No argument from me on that one," Victoria said happily, "It will help me stay relaxed if I don't have to deal with the road rage."

"I'm from the hills of Richmond, Virginia, I'm used to being behind the wheel."

"So, did you volunteer to assist on this case or were you drafted?" Victoria asked as they crossed the street into the parking garage.

"I was sort of chosen by default but I definitely wanted to be a part of it. It's a big case and it will give me the boost I need. I'm thirty-four years old and I just finished my first year of training in the Juvenile Unit. I need to play catch-up if I'm going to have a career here."

"I can relate, there's nothing like a little incentive to get the job done. You and I are on the same page."

Khloe programmed the address Victoria gave her into the GPS of the Taurus. While she sped through traffic blazing through a succession of yellow lights, Victoria mulled over the questions she had for the grieving parents. She didn't want to add to their pain.

"Do you want to drive past the crime scene?" Khloe asked.

"That's an excellent suggestion. I've only seen it on TV."

There was a large gathering of people standing around the area waving signs with Deshaun's picture on them. Some read, 'We Want Justice.' There was a makeshift memorial on the sidewalk piled high with flowers, cards, candles, stuffed animals, and even liquor bottles. Victoria felt the weight of responsibility on her shoulders as the car slowly cruised down the street with protesters staring into the window. She had to argue in court for these people and for Deshaun's family. The crowd thinned as they approached the Gardner home.

Family members or neighbors stood protectively outside of the front door as Victoria and Khloe climbed the steps to the entrance. Victoria gave polite nods with a demure smile. When she rang the doorbell a man dressed in a suit and bowtie opened the door.

"Good morning, I'm Victoria Perry from the District Attorney's office. This is my assistant, Khloe Luskin. We have an appointment to speak with Mr. and Mrs. Gardner."

"Follow me," the well-dressed man said, leading the way down the hall.

He directed them into the living room where Mona sat on the couch beside an older woman and Darren stood at the window staring out into space. The centerpiece on the coffee table was shaped like a bird's nest decorated with Easter eggs and candy. A phone rang nonstop in another room. Khloe lingered in the background and turned on the small voice recorder she used in law school for long lectures. Victoria sat down on the edge of a chair opposite the sofa and looked into Mona's tear-streaked face that was puffed-up from grief.

"Hello, Mrs. Gardner, we're from the District Attorney's office. I'm Victoria Perry. I'm very sorry for your loss. I will be heading the prosecution for the Commonwealth and I would like to ask you and your husband a few questions if you don't mind."

"Why would I mind, Ms. Perry? I'm burying my son tomorrow. It will be Good Friday but I'll never see him again."

Victoria hesitated and Darren came over from the window, sat beside Mona, and put his arm around her.

"What is it that you would like to know?" he asked.

"It's my job to see that you get justice for Deshaun's murder. I want to get to know your son through your eyes. I need to know what was said in the last conversation you had with him," Victoria said calmly.

"Deshaun was the best part of me," Darren said, taking his arm from around Mona and putting his hands together. "He was real smart and a good guy. He made friends easy, people really like him. He loved basketball, boxing, music, and he had big dreams for himself. He wanted to be a business manager for professional athletes. It bothered him a lot that his favorite player, Allen Iverson, had lost most of his money."

"He had a good head and heart. Deshaun never gave us any trouble. He was my joy," Mona added. "I don't know how to go on."

"It's my understanding that you all have only lived in this neighborhood for about a year. Were there any issues with where you lived previously? Had Deshaun ever belonged to a gang?"

"Deshaun had some friends who got into some trouble but he hadn't gotten involved in any of it," Darren answered. "We moved here to get him away from the dangers of the streets and look what happened. We were better off in Germantown. That's something I have to live with, putting my son in harm's way. I haven't slept a night since it happened. All I think and pray about is trading my life for our son's."

"Tell me what happened that night?" Victoria asked softly, looking at Mona.

"I called him on his cell phone," Mona said slowly and thoughtfully, "I wanted to make sure he was coming straight home. I told him I would pick him up since it was starting to rain but he said no. Then he said somebody was following him. I asked my husband to go and meet him. Then he said this car had come back around. I heard words between them and then the call was cut off. I ran out to help my son but by the time we got there he was gone. The police wouldn't let me near him."

Mona collapsed against the woman sitting next to her and closed her eyes.

"It would be a great help to our office if you could give me the names of Deshaun's close friends," Victoria said to Darren. "We'll be speaking with his teachers at school and co-workers on his job. The defense will probably try to attack Deshaun's character so I'll need witnesses to speak up for him."

"The Gardner's have a lawyer who has collected that information, I'll have him contact your office," the well-dressed man interjected, hinting that the interview had come to an end.

"Again, I'm sorry for disturbing you at this time and I thank you for your cooperation," Victoria said to Darren before they followed the gentleman out of the room.

"They'll be excellent witnesses," Victoria said when they were back inside the car. "We'll need as many as we can get. Undoubtedly we'll have to fight the typical defense used when the victim is a black male."

"What's that?" Khloe asked without a clue.

"That he was a no-good thug and deserved what he got," Victoria answered matter-of-factly.

Chapter Five

"How did things go with the family this morning?" Arthur asked when Victoria and Khloe got back to the office.

To Victoria it seemed that he spent half of his time lingering outside of her door.

"Their emotions are running high but I think they will be good witnesses," Victoria answered.

"I need you two to meet me in my office in ten minutes. We need to get our ducks in a row before the pre-trial conference with Judge Kelly. Detective Carlton is going to bring us up to speed on his investigation with the other witnesses."

"There goes lunch," Victoria said with a sigh, "Just enough time to use the restroom."

"I'll order up some sandwiches, City View delivers," Khloe responded.

Khloe was on the phone while Victoria made some notes on the organizing chart she designed to manage the strategy of her cases. She knew Benjamin practiced a similar approach. It was going to be an old-fashioned game of Battleship and both were determined not to be sunk.

Victoria knew Benjamin had the advantage, all he had to do was provide a reasonable doubt, but she had to prove that Ed Landauer shot this kid in cold blood.

Detective Carlton was already seated at the oval table inside of

Arthur's office with his partner Detective Maria Rosario. Arthur sat in the big chair at one end. Victoria and Khloe took seats opposite the detectives. Victoria put her legal pad on the table. Khloe turned on the recorder in her lap.

"All right, people, tell me something good," Arthur said, clasping his hands together.

"Well, I've interviewed the shooter's ex-girlfriend and from what she told me he's got a temper," Carlton started, "There's one domestic call on his record. His best buddy says he can be a hothead when he's had a few under his belt."

"His neighbors are supporting him," Rosario added, "They feel like he's been invaluable in organizing their Town Watch program."

"That's ridiculous," Victoria interrupted in frustration, "The guy is just a vigilante-wanna-be who shot an innocent kid."

"I know you're emotionally hyped from visiting with the parents, Vicki, but you've got to keep your personal feelings out of it," Arthur warned. "If there is any inclination of this being about race or prejudice we're toast."

"Sorry, I'll keep my professional face on," Victoria said with cynicism

"So, detectives, what have the new witnesses brought to the table?" Arthur continued.

"Basically we have two credible witnesses, one white female and one white male," Dt. Carlton said, looking at his notes. "The guy is Bradley Schrader, blue collar, married with two kids, daughters. He says he heard the car door and then he looked out saw the shorter one approach the taller one in the hoodie. He said they argued for a few seconds then the taller one pushed the shorter guy, they struggled, punches were thrown and then he heard the shot. He says they were real close so he didn't see the gun pointed."

"That could go either way, what about the female?" Arthur

asked.

"Ariana Angulate, she's 45 years old, divorced, with one grown son," Dt. Rosario replied. "She lives alone. She heard the voices and the confrontation but she didn't look out until she heard the shot. She said she heard someone call out for help."

"Let's review the Medical Examiner's report," Arthur said, opening up the file on his desk.

Dt. Carlton opens his identical file before he speaks.

"The shot was close range through the heart. He was killed instantly. No gun residue on the victim hands. No visible scratches or bruises on the body from a struggle. There were swollen knuckles on the right hand, presumably from the punch to the shooters jaw."

"What were the injuries to the shooter?" Victoria asked.

"He complained that his jaw was broken and was taken to the hospital but it was determined to be a minor fracture. No other treatment was needed," Rosario added.

"It must have been a pushing and shoving match until the kid threw the punch, then the shooter pulled his gun," Carlton postulated.

"We don't know that's what happened. The shooter may have gotten out of the car with his gun already drawn," Khloe added.

"It doesn't matter, it's still a man with a gun against an unarmed kid," Victoria said.

"This guy is short and pudgy. He says the kid was beating his ass. He says he had to shoot before the victim killed him."

"How much of an ass-whipping can you get in a couple of minutes at best?" Victoria asked sarcastically. "He was itching to shoot the kid."

"That's what you have to prove," Carlton said, closing the file.

"Not much help with the evidence, Vicki, iffy at best," Arthur said shaking his head. "This case can go either way."

"If you went to a restaurant and got sick, food poisoning, do you think they should be held responsible?" Victoria asked.

"Naturally, they served it," Arthur answered.

"Even though they had no intent to make you sick?"

"Certainly."

"What is the difference in this case?"

"It doesn't matter, Vicki. See if we can put together a deal before the pre-trial conference."

Arthur swiveled his chair around to face the window signaling that the meeting was over. He had to lean heavily on Victoria, juries seemed to like her from the impressive list of convictions she had won. Arthur accredited it to her good looks and amicable disposition.

Detective Carlton drummed on the table with his fingers before he got up and walked out with Detective Rosario following close behind.

Victoria took a deep breath, then did a quick nod of her head to the side and mouthed the words to Khloe, "Let's go."

The sandwiches had been delivered and were sitting on the small round table when they got back to Victoria's office. She grabbed two Jamaican ginger ale bottles from the small refrigerator behind her desk and joined Khloe at the table.

"Corn beef or Italian?" Khloe asked.

"Give me the corn beef," Victoria answered, passing her one of the ginger ales.

"So what's the plan?" Khloe asked, unwrapping her hoagie.

"I'm not against making a deal even though he's guilty of murder in the second. I would consider it a win for the good guys. My offer is manslaughter, voluntary. But if I know Ben Madison, and I do, he'll want involuntary. Personally, I feel I was more than generous in the second degree charge."

"Are you saying you won't accept involuntary manslaughter?"

"I would have to defer to Arthur on that. We can't come out of this empty-handed, all hell will break loose."

"I can get you the numbers on convictions of non-gang civilian shootings across the country."

"I'll need that, and we'll need to set up a meeting with Dr. Roland Gregory, he's the psychiatrist who consults with the department."

"I'll get the interviews transcribed and I'll get them to you tomorrow," Khloe said, finishing up her sandwich. "Will you need me for anything else?"

"No, good work, thanks," Victoria said, swallowing a large gulp of the ginger ale.

"Till tomorrow then," Khloe replied politely, taking the trash from her lunch with her.

Victoria wrapped up the other half of her corn beef hoagie and walked over to the window behind her desk to stretch her legs. Watching the activity on the street and the people below, as they hustled from one direction to another on their individual tasks, she pondered the legal conundrum before her. On one hand the case was simple, cut and dry, murder or self-defense. However, on the other hand there were many angles to consider, including the element of a hate crime and even the prospect of premeditation. She kicked her shoes off, sat down at her computer, and spent the next three hours reviewing similar murder cases. At 6:30 she packed up her notes and the leftover portion of her sandwich, caught a cab and went home.

Miss Judy was sitting out front in her usual spot. The brightness of the day had dimmed and so had her facial expression. Her ever present smile was absent.

"They burying that boy tomorrow," she said sadly.

"I know," Victoria said, pausing for a minute, "I talked with the mother today."

"Are you going to the funeral?" Miss Judy asked.

"No, the press will be all over it and I don't want to be a part of any disrespect. I'll watch it on the news."

"Okay then, baby. Go on in and get you some rest, you look tired."

"You have a good night, Miss Judy," she said before she closed the door.

Victoria didn't sleep well. The heaviness from the Gardner's household smothered her like a thick blanket and she couldn't breathe. Tossing and turning through the night she thought about Leonard. If he were there they could have rolled around together until she passed out, except she hadn't seen or heard from him since he gave her the ultimatum about taking the case. She got up the next morning feeling worn out and discouraged.

After a long hot shower, she searched through her suits for something bright colored to lift her spirits. She found a deep peach ensemble with a jacket without a lapel and a pleated skirt. Hopefully the bounce in the skirt would transfer down into her feet. For breakfast she made herself two pieces of toast topped with butter and strawberry preserves to soak up the huge cup of coffee she poured from the pot. She was about to call for a cab when there was a knock on the door. She could see through the glass that it was Khloe.

"Good morning," Victoria said hesitantly.

"I thought you might need a ride to work and I have the car," Khloe said, holding up the keys.

"You are officially my new best friend," Victoria said, relieved. "I'll get my things."

They rode in silence except for the radio playing on an all news channel. This was one of the rare mornings that Victoria wished she lived further away from work. The early drive with the fresh air blowing through the open window had refreshed her. There were no reporters in front of the Criminal Justice Center when they passed it, probably all at Deshaun Gardner's funeral. Victoria hurried through the front entrance of their building while Khloe went to park the car in the lot. She took the elevator to the

2nd floor and reached her office without having to speak to anyone. She closed the door behind her and turned on the twenty inch TV that sat in the center of her large bookshelf and took a seat as the services were about to begin.

This was the third funeral she had attended on TV, the first was Michael Jackson's, and the second was Whitney Houston's less than two months ago. In a way they all seemed like family. The inside of the church had reached full capacity and mourners stood out on the steps and lined the streets in an air of solemnity and calm, an eerie contrast from the previous days of conflict and protest. Seeing all these people there in love and support of this young man reminded Victoria of how much she missed going to church and the refuge you could find there. As a child she never missed a Sunday beside her momma and growing up she had never attended any other church than her father's. When he died she stopped going, she doubted that another man of God could fill that void in her life.

Soft music played in the background and the camera focused on the long line of attendants greeting Mona and Darren Gardner. Mona wore a hat and dark glasses to shield herself from the photographers hoping to capture her grief. Darren hovered at her side dressed in a black suit. There was a slide show flashing on the big screen on the side wall of the church. Pictures of Deshaun as a baby, pictures of him in his mother's arms, playing catch with his dad, graduation from junior high school, and him hanging with some friends on the block, showed the happy childhood of a young man with his whole life ahead of him. Now it was over.

The speakers were warm and sympathetic, the music and soloists were soulful and soothing, and Rev. Julius Monroe's eulogy was comforting and insightful, but the sight of the young body laying up there in the center of the ceremony was utterly heart wrenching. It was painful to watch the misery of the family and friends. Death is always hard to swallow, but in this instance, like so many others, senseless and without reason, it's even more difficult to stomach.

When Victoria reached her emotional limit she muted the volume and leaned back in her chair gazing at the ceiling as her thoughts drifted back to her own memories, the carefree times with her mom and dad, walking along the Boardwalk at Atlantic City licking a custard ice cream cone with her pockets stuffed with salt water taffy. It had been their favorite place to go. She loved to walk between them while the sea gulls squawked above their heads searching for food. The sound of the waves and the feel of the warm bubbly water over their feet were like heaven coming down to earth. She longed for the simplicity of those days.

A wide lens followed the casket as it rolled up the aisle with Mona and Darren walking slowly behind it with bowed heads. More photographers flashed cameras and reporters pushed microphones into the faces of the grieving family and friends as they were shuffled into the limousine parked behind the hearse. Their suffering was a crime, an injustice of the highest form, a family devastated by the hands of another without cause.

The newscast switched to a panel of self-important political pundits and attorneys vying for attention as they debated the issues surrounding the shooting of Deshaun Gardner. They were all clamoring for a seat at the trough to get a piece of the national spotlight. This was no longer about the stolen life of a young man. It was about who would win in the end and all the players were jostling for a better position.

Chapter Six

"Alta, I don't mean any harm but please turn that crap off," Laramie said, coming into the living room after his morning walk.

"I feel sorry for them, they lost their only son," Alta answered with irritation. "The whole thing is tragic."

"What's tragic is the small fortune I'm having to pay to keep your son out of jail. That boy is just one less nigger on the street causing trouble."

"The truth is Ed was probably the one who caused all the trouble," Alta said sadly, changing the channel.

"I don't doubt it, that boy never could do anything right to save his life," Laramie said, sitting down in his favorite chair in front of the television and lighting a cigarette.

Alta left the room and went into the kitchen, she couldn't stand to hear him talk about Ed like that. She thought that maybe if he hadn't made the boy feel so useless all the time he wouldn't have to prove he was worth something. Suddenly the phone rang making her jump.

"Hey, Mom, how are you and Dad doing?" Emerson said on the other end.

"We're fine under the circumstances. What about you and Ed?"

"Him staying here is not working out. He's pissed off all the time and my neighbors are getting antsy. They're afraid the protests will come around here if the press or anybody else finds out where he's living."

"I'll speak to your father about it, honey. We'll work it out. Let me talk to Ed for a minute."

There was a pause while Emerson went to give the phone to his brother.

"Hello," Ed griped.

"How are you feeling, Eddie?" she asked.

"How do you think, Mom? I'm stuck up in this house like a prisoner. These assholes on the TV keep talking about me like I'm crazy or something. I had a right to protect myself."

"I know, son. Be patient, we'll get everything worked out soon."

"Right, Mom," he said angrily, hanging up the phone.

"Emerson called," Alta hollered out from the kitchen, "He wants to know if Ed can come out and stay with us until this thing dies down. He's getting complaints from his neighbors. They don't want any trouble."

"Neither do I," Laramie responded, "We moved out here to get some peace in our lives. Tell Ed to find himself an apartment or go to a hotel and I guess I'll have to pay for that too."

***

Benjamin pushed the remote and shut off the newscast of the kid's funeral. He was glad that it was done. Now he could go to work in good conscience. Winning this case with Ed Landauer as his client meant it would have to be won outside of the courtroom. He had no choice but to try it publicly using the media as his co-counsel and he had to do it before jury selection. Race was his biggest opponent in this case. He couldn't erase that but he could minimize its effect with a black man on his side. Benjamin didn't have to think twice, that man would be Thomas Clancy, the first token black at the firm of Rosen & Sullivan.

Thomas Clancy was the darkest black person he had ever met with all the facial features of a West African, large nose and full lips. The dichotomy was that Thomas fully embraced his inner white man. He was a straight-up Republican conservative who only dated white women and was always overcompensating for the shame he felt for being born black. Benjamin suspected he would jump at the opportunity to distance himself from the black community.

He pressed the button for his legal assistant.

"Gayle, give Thomas Clancy a buzz, I need to see him up here ASAP."

"Sure thing, boss," Gayle answered, smiling to herself. She was a certified paralegal and had worked for Ben Madison long enough to know how his mind worked. His every move was calculated and this one was transparent to say the least.

Thomas Clancy was in his office with the door closed. He hadn't been included in the office chitchats about the controversial case. No one wanted to offend him or be politically incorrect. The call from Ben Madison's assistant was divine intervention as far as he was concerned. He dashed up the three flights of stairs to the twenty-first floor, too eager to wait for the elevator.

"Go on in he's expecting you," Gayle directed after he entered the office suite.

Thomas made an effort to contain his enthusiasm as he walked through the door. If his assumption for being summoned to Ben Madison's office was correct this chance would certainly help him move up in the firm.

"Hello, Thomas, come on in and sit down," Ben said warmly, standing up at his desk to greet Thomas with a handshake. "Can I offer you something to drink?"

"No thanks, Ben, I'm fine," Thomas answered, taking a seat close to the large desk.

The whole office was impressive, three times the size of his, and impeccably decorated with bronze sculptures of the 'Old West' by Frederic Remington. He watched Ben pour from a bottle of

Badoit, French sparkling water, into a crystal glass filled with ice.

"I'm sure you're aware that I'm the lead counsel representing Edward Landauer in the shooting case of Deshaun Gardner," Ben said casually.

"Yes, I am," Thomas replied.

"The rodeo is about to begin and I would like you to consider assisting me as co-counsel."

"There's nothing to consider, I'm in," Thomas said, ready to bounce out of his seat.

"Good deal. I don't have to tell you that this won't be child's play. We need to start putting up our defense now. I want the pictures of Edward Landauer's swollen jaw and busted lip out there on TV, in newspapers, and on the internet. I need interviews with Deshaun's best friend, Jamaal, all over TV. He's got a substantial criminal record and he looks like a thug. We've got to change the subject of the conversation to crime on the streets of Philadelphia and citizens fighting back."

"I'll get public relations working right away," Thomas said excitedly.

Ben relaxed and rotated his chair to the side to take in the beauty of the city view behind him, confident that Gayle was already working on the things he'd mentioned to Thomas. The man was a paper-pusher, not a litigator, he lacked presentation skills. It wasn't a problem for Benjamin, he only needed Thomas for window dressing.

***

Khloe walked into Victoria's office holding two cups of coffee just as the phone rang. Victoria saw it was Arthur calling and put him on speaker.

"Heads up, Victoria," Arthur said sternly, "The pre-trial conference with Judge Kelly is scheduled for Monday morning, nine o' clock sharp. I need your 'A' game on this."

"I'll be ready, Arthur, don't worry, we're on the right side of this," Victoria assured him.

"Do you need me to work on anything specific before the conference?" Khloe asked, handing Victoria a cup of coffee.

"I have all I need for the pre-trial meeting. After that, the concentration will be on preparing our list of prosecution witnesses. If this goes the way I think it will, the trial date will be in ninety days or less. Take the weekend and have some fun. It will be serious next week."

"I'll keep my phone on," Khloe said on her way out.

Victoria organized her talking points for the conference during the rest of the afternoon. By early evening she felt like a taut spring stretched to its limit. All of her muscles were tense, beginning at her jaw line and reaching down to her neck and shoulders. Even her arms were flexed and her core was tight. Her whole body sensed the fight ahead and was already preparing for combat. It was all a bit premature though since it was just Friday evening, more than forty-eight hours before the pre-trial conference.

"I've got to relax," she said, pulling her notes together and packing the ever-thickening file inside her briefcase.

She shut down her computer, turned out the lights, and made her exit. Outside in the cool evening she took a deep breath and raised her arm to hail a cab. The weekend had arrived and she didn't have any plans. Leonard was still missing in action. Then it dawned on her what she wanted, a place where she could kick back and take the edge off. It was Warm Daddy's. Some soul food and some live jazz would be the perfect combination to de-stress.

Going out for an evening by herself was Victoria's second choice for a great night. On any given day she usually had more social interaction than a Septa bus driver and sometimes it got to be too much. That's when she preferred going alone to restaurants or clubs that have live music. She could savor a delicious meal without too much conversation and allow the flavors to speak to her. Being alone she could get into the vibe of the music instead of trying to talk above it.

Traveling down Spring Garden Street was a straight shot to Columbus Blvd. Victoria walked into the restaurant right before the $15 cover charge began and got a table near the right front of the small stage in front of a window. Her full days had run together all week and she couldn't remember if she'd even eaten lunch. She ordered the low country catfish, collard greens, yams, and cornbread.

Thankfully the waitress got her food without much delay. It smelled so good that she took a few seconds to relish the aroma before she began to eat. The first bite of the collard greens removed the edge she had been feeling and she ate slowly, gazing around the room as if she's watching a show at home in front of the TV. Then the band began to play.

The sound of his horn captured her attention before she saw him. He blew bold and strong, even piercing at moments speaking volumes with each held note. Victoria sat up in her chair and listened intently to every tone and inflection and the emotion that exuded from the melody. He owned the stage.

"Who is he?" she thought, checking him out. He was about five-foot-ten, milk chocolate brown with a light beard and long dreads, about 180 pounds, and wearing dark shades. She hadn't seen him there before. By the end of the set she wanted to know more about this man who had been 'killing her softly with his song.' She wasn't sure if it was the glasses that shielded his eyes that made him interesting and mysterious but she would soon find out.

Several of the members of the band including the horn player went to the bar for a drink between their sets. Victoria put her handbag and briefcase over her shoulder and headed to the restroom. She always carried a toothbrush and toothpaste wherever she went. She learned early about the depth of first impressions. Once she cleaned her teeth, applied fresh lipstick, and combed through her hair, she wasted no time getting to the bar.

"Gentlemen, I enjoyed your set very much," she said, "I haven't seen you all here before, are you local or visiting the city?"

"We're out of Baltimore. We play here a couple times a year, except for Dupree," the guitar player said, nodding towards the saxophone player. "He's calling Philly his home now."

"I try to sit in whenever they come to town for a gig, we all went to school together at Morgan State," Dupree said, being friendly.

"That's real cool. I'm glad I got a chance to hear you guys play. I was moved," Victoria said, stepping back. "I'll give you my card and you can call me when you're in town again."

"I play three nights a week at The Blue Note, Tuesday, Thursday, and Saturday," Dupree said, "Come by anytime."

"I'll do that," Victoria said on her way out of the restaurant.

***

Victoria lay awake for most of the night with Deshaun's funeral replaying in her mind. She needed to speak with Mr. and Mrs. Gardner before Monday. She knew Arthur would love for this case to be settled out of the courtroom but she felt a personal obligation to the family to let them know that a plea would most likely be on the table. The minutes passed like hours while she waited for a reasonable time to make the phone call.

Darren answered the phone on the second ring and agreed to let her come by for breakfast. She showered, put on a jogging suit, and tucked her hair in a baseball cap. She put on a pair of sunglasses with a thought to the horn player last night and fast-walked up to Broad and Girard to catch the subway. One step down she remembered it might be wiser to catch a cab instead.

It was ten minutes before eight when Victoria's cab turned

onto Shiloh Street. The dirt of the street had begun to cover the makeshift memorial of stuffed animals, cards, and flowers. The crowd of protesters had diminished down to a faithful few from yesterday due to the early hour. There was still a small group that guarded the stoop of the Gardner family's home. Victoria took off her cap and shades and they parted and let her pass.

Their attorney, Christian Booker, who she'd seen on the news, met her at the door.

"Good morning, Ms. Perry, we can talk in the kitchen," he said cordially.

"Thank you," Victoria said, following him closely as he led the way.

She didn't notice the first time she was there that the house was very similar to her own. Family pictures lined the walls along the hallway and she breathed in the faint smell of vanilla from a plug-in air freshener. In the kitchen, copper molds hung above the cabinets and a collection of salt and pepper shakers sat on a shelf. There were two older women bustling around in the room with Mona and Darren, one cooking and the other washing dishes.

"Good morning, Mr. and Mrs. Gardner, I apologize for disturbing your breakfast but I want to keep you informed on the details of the case," Victoria said, standing beside the table.

Mona looked up at her. "I cannot describe to you the unbearable, unspeakable, unimaginable pain to bury your only child. He was ripped out of my life while I was talking to him."

"Please sit down," Darren said, pointing to an empty chair on his right.

"Would you like some breakfast?" the woman standing at the stove asked.

The comforting smell of sausage and biscuits wafting in the air was tempting.

"Just some coffee please," Victoria answered politely, taking a seat at the table. "The pre-trial conference is scheduled for Monday morning with Judge Kelly. I didn't want you to be blindsided from the results of the meeting. I'm very sure that the Mayor and the District Attorney want to close this case as quickly as possible. A plea will certainly be offered."

"So what charges can they expect?" their attorney asked.

"Voluntary manslaughter may be an option, although I'm not sure what the defense will be seeking. They may ask that the charges be reduced all the way down to aggravated battery.

"My son was killed in cold blood," Mona said slowly, her voice barely above a whisper. "Shot down in the street for no reason except for being a young black male. His life was worth more than that."

"So far we have trusted the system to do the right thing. I hope that trust hasn't been misguided," Darren added, getting up from the table.

Victoria took two large swallows of coffee from the cup before she said, "I want this case to proceed. I'm prepared to take this case to trial. It would not be my choice to allow him to walk away with a short reprimand. I just felt like you had a right to know what's going on. I want justice for Deshaun."

"We thank you for that consideration," Mr. Booker said, "We don't have any choice but to put more public pressure on the D.A. and the mayor's office."

Victoria excused herself and followed Christian Booker to the door.

Before he opened it he said, "I hope you are prepared, Ms. Perry, because whichever way this goes, you're being set up to take the heat for it."

Victoria didn't need a newsflash to let her know that those with power would always cover their asses while the ones put out in front would be left out in the cold. She had consented to be on the frontline but that also meant you were expendable. You would either perish or come out a hero. She was risking a lot, and time and time again she had come in second behind Benjamin.

Victoria twisted her hair back under her hat and put her shades back on to catch the subway being that her cab driver had decided not to wait. She jogged along the route that Deshaun must have taken so many times, bowing her head when she passed the makeshift memorial. On the train her stomach growled under the background noise of the rumbling along the tracks making her wish she would have accepted the breakfast offered to her, but in her mind that would have been unprofessional. She thought about stopping somewhere but she didn't want to take the chance of being recognized.

When she got to the house Miss Judy was out front soaking in the mild morning rays of the spring day sun.

"Did I miss breakfast?" Victoria asked playfully.

"I've got some pancake batter left in there if you want to eat," Miss Judy answered.

"I'm starving, point me to the skillet."

"Lanetta is in there, I'll be done in a few minutes. I need a little bit more of this Vitamin D."

Victoria went inside and saw Lanetta sipping a cup of hot tea and relaxing in the den watching reruns of 'Good Times' on the TV.

"What's up, sister girl?" she asked.

"Enjoying my two days off," Lanetta said, looking over her shoulder.

"You're blessed, I'm working seven days right now," Victoria said, washing her hands before she turned up the heat on the skillet.

"You better, if that white boy walks on this it's going to get real hot before the summer is over. People are getting tired of black boys being shot down and nobody going to jail."

"I hear you on that, but it's a lot of black boys doing the shooting. As a prosecutor I have to keep my eyes open to all of the killings," Victoria said, retrieving the container of pancake batter out of the fridge.

Lanetta swung her lay-z-boy chair around and responded angrily.

"There's a difference between that gang war bullshit and an innocent brother being shot down because he's black. The hate is getting out of control."

Victoria poured three circles of batter in the hot skillet and watched them swell and bubble.

"The problem is there are too many hot heads out here armed to the teeth. Nobody wants to have an old-fashioned beat down anymore," Victoria said, flipping the pancakes. "You remember how we used to say it, 'can't get along get a fair one going.'"

Lanetta laughed releasing the tension in the air.

"You reached way back for that one, girl."

Victoria had to laugh too as she scooped her pancakes onto a plate and smothered them with butter and syrup. She poured herself a cup of orange juice, sat down at the kitchen table, blessed her food, and took a large bite.

"You didn't lie," Miss Judy said, coming in the door. "You were hungry, baby. Did you go for a run this morning?"

"No, I went to visit Deshaun Gardner's family."

"How are they doing?" Miss Judy asked, concerned.

"It's real hard on them but they have a lot of support from family and friends."

"What about you? I haven't seen Mr. Leonard Sterling around here lately?"

"That's right," Lanetta chimed in, "Where's our future brother and governor been lately?"

"I had to make a choice, him or the case," Victoria said, shifting the food in her mouth to speak.

"That's deep, Vick," Lanetta said, "I can't believe you let that fine thing go for a case."

"I didn't go to school all those years to be somebody's housewife. I'm too overqualified to be cooking and cleaning."

"I don't know about that," Miss Judy laughed, "You got on that stove real quick. Don't forget women get hungry for other things too."

"Uh-oh, Mama's getting ready to preach," Lanetta said, swirling around in her chair.

"These career women always trying to act like they don't need anybody but I know better."

"It's not that, Len is cool but he's just not me, I'm not feeling him anymore. Somebody else has my attention."

"And who might that be?" Lanetta asked curiously.

"There was a musician at Warm Daddy's last night who blew my mind with his sax."

"Did you say with his sex?" Miss Judy teased.

"No, Miss Judy, you are over the top, his saxophone," Victoria laughed.

"Okay," she said, holding her chest, "You almost gave me a heart attack."

"Anyway, you saved my life again, thanks for the pancakes," Victoria said, rinsing the plate and putting it in the dishwasher. "Now I've got to get back to work."

"Let me know when you go back to hear what-his-name," Lanetta shouted behind her. "I'm going with you."

"I'll do that," Victoria said, closing the door behind her.

Chapter Seven

Victoria had been in the office for an hour before Arthur arrived. He had called her late Sunday to inform her that he was going to be the lead attorney in Ed Landauer's pre-trial conference with Judge Kelly and she would serve as co-counsel. If he could work out a plea bargain with Benjamin Madison he would come out of the meeting with no damage done, looking fair and impartial, with a boost to help him in his re-election campaign. Arthur wanted that third term before he made his next move.

Victoria sat beside Arthur in the back of his Lincoln Town Car deep in thought while he talked nonstop handling office business on his cellphone. They could have walked the block and a half to City Hall but Arthur had earned his chauffer driven car and he always used it. It was only after they got into the waiting elevator that he put away his phone. They stepped out on the third floor just when Benjamin Madison and Thomas Clancy exited the adjacent elevator. Victoria and Arthur trailed the two of them down the hall to Room 372, the chambers of the Honorable Judge Robert Kelly.

Benjamin nodded in recognition with a well-mannered half-smile as they approached the office. He opened the door and held it for Victoria and Arthur to enter first. It was exactly 9:00.

Nancy Morrow, the judicial secretary greeted them.

"Good morning, counselors, the judge is ready to see you."

She led them to the door opened it and closed it behind them.

Judge Kelly was a stickler for staying on schedule, moreso his personal schedule. You could set a clock by his movements, he came in and departed his office at the exact same times daily and he ate his meals at the exact same times throughout the day. He was also obsessed with drinking 10 glasses of water and walking 10 thousand steps each day.

"Excellent," Judge Kelly said, sitting straight up in his huge chair when they walked in. "Everybody is here, now we can get down to business. Take a seat or stand, whichever makes you comfortable. Let's try to get this settled out of court, shall we."

Victoria sat down first, then Benjamin, and Thomas followed suit. Arthur put his briefcase down but remained standing.

"Mr. Mitchell, it seems you have the floor," Judge Kelly said pleasantly.

Arthur began to put forth his argument.

"The circumstances of this case are polarizing and it has garnered national attention. A young unarmed black teenager was gunned down two blocks from his home. Minutes before, Edward Landauer called 911 to report him as a suspect. Against orders from the police dispatcher, he approached Deshaun Gardner, there was an altercation, and he shot him once in the chest. Witnesses haven't been particularly helpful to either side of the case, Your Honor. The evidence is not complicated, it was homicide without premeditation, Mr. Landauer was charged with second-degree murder."

"That sounds reasonable, Mr. Mitchell," Judge Kelly said, glancing at Benjamin.

"Your Honor, Edward Landauer had no other choice but to use deadly force to protect himself from Deshaun Gardner," Benjamin explained. "My client approached the young man simply to speak with him but Deshaun reacted violently. Mr. Landauer undoubtedly feared for his life and it became self-defense at that point."

"Excuse me," Arthur interrupted, "It was your client who

created the situation from the beginning and escalated it by brandishing his gun."

"My client made the police call with the belief that Deshaun Gardner was about to commit robbery," Benjamin argued, "He was trying to prevent a crime not commit one."

"Gentlemen, those are arguments for the jury," Judge Kelly said impatiently. "We're here to come to an agreement. I'd like to see us all come out of this without dirt on our faces. Mr. Mitchell, what are you offering?"

"Our office is confident that we can get a conviction on murder two, but we are making a more than generous offer of voluntary manslaughter with a minimum sentence of 15 years."

"Mr. Madison, what is your position?" Judge Kelly asked, looking over his glasses.

"It's undeniable that my client's action resulted in a death, however it was unintentional, involuntary manslaughter at the most," Benjamin stated.

"That's a misdemeanor is this state. In this heated atmosphere, he can't walk away without consequences," Arthur protested, "You're talking about less than 18 months on good behavior."

"What we had in mind is five years of probation," Benjamin said coolly.

"If you're not interested in a realistic compromise, this meeting is over," Arthur replied, dropping down into a chair.

Everyone in the room was still, hushed, as if they were all holding their breath.

Then Judge Kelly spoke. "It looks like we're going to trial." He looked at the calendar on his computer. "I'm looking at ninety days, around July ninth. Mrs. Morrow will contact you with the exact court date. Good day to all of you."

Mrs. Morrow gave them all a cheerful smile as they filed out of the office. Benjamin led the way with Thomas walking proudly close behind him. Ben walked to the end of the hallway for privacy and paused at the window to make a phone call.

"Three, two, one," Benjamin said after he ended the call. "It's blast-off time, my man."

Thomas looked at him puzzled and asked, "What's going on?"

"This trial has officially begun. We are going to make this case every day until jury selection. We are going to appear on every major talk show, national news channel, and on the front pages of newspapers and magazines."

"I'm here for whatever you need," Thomas said with confidence. "When can we spend some time coordinating the points we want to hit?"

"Not necessary," Benjamin assured him, "All I need for you to do is stand or sit beside me on my right when the cameras roll."

Thomas's shoulders fell and rounded like a balloon losing air. It just occurred to him why Benjamin had handpicked him to assist on this case. It was the first time in his life that being black had ever gotten him anywhere. His stomach turned in disgust. He had worked his ass off to minimize his blackness and now it was the only thing that mattered to Ben. He swallowed the bile that rose in his throat determined to use this circumstance for his own benefit.

Victoria and Arthur rode the elevator down grateful they didn't have to share it with Ben Madison and Thomas Clancy. Once they moved past the construction outside of the building they saw a cluster of reporters standing between them and Arthur's waiting car.

"We aren't making any statements," Arthur murmured to Victoria, moving toward them.

"Did you make a deal?" one reporter yelled.

More shouted questions. Their voices blended together into a roar while cameras zoomed into their faces. The driver opened the door and Arthur dived in and Victoria hopped in behind him. His driver pressed the accelerator and sped away from the curb and the chaos.

"It's only going to get more intense, Vicki. Are you prepared for the spotlight?" Arthur asked while he checked messages in his phone.

"I'm going to try this case as I would any other, being under the microscope of the media won't make a difference to me," Victoria answered.

"That's the first time since you've worked in the D.A.'s office that you've allowed your naiveté to show. Best to keep your ass covered when the whole country is watching."

"How do you propose that I do that?" Victoria asked, interested.

"Benjamin Madison is a big mean dog who won't hesitate to bite you. Announce your press conference for tomorrow and don't embarrass yourself or my office."

Arthur answered a call on his cell and Victoria took the opportunity to send a text to Khloe telling her to come to her office in ten minutes. When the car dropped them off in front of the Widener Building, Arthur got out first, still talking on his phone and never looked back. Victoria felt like she couldn't get to her office fast enough. She took the stairs after she got through security. Khloe was outside the door waiting with lunch and coffee.

"If you don't want coffee my feelings won't be hurt, I could use both cups," Khloe said as Victoria approached.

"At this juncture I'm not turning down anything," Victoria said thankfully, unlocking the door. "We've only got a few hours to get camera ready."

"I figured as much, Ben Madison has been all over the airwaves," Khloe said, setting the take-out bags down and turning on the TV.

Victoria reached her hand out blindly to find a chair with her eyes glued to the screen. CNN was replaying an interview with Benjamin on the steps outside of City Hall. He stood there handsome as hell spewing the seeds for his defense. He started off giving his sincerest condolences to the Gardner family before he moved on to play up his client as the victim.

"Nothing has changed, my client will plead not guilty to second degree murder charges."

He described the broken jaw that Edward Landauer had suffered and stated that his client felt that if he hadn't used his gun he would have been killed. Then he went further to say that his client had refused to accept a plea bargain because he had committed no crime. He wore a faint smile when he advised the public not to rush to judgment, to allow his client due process. The criminal justice system will have the last word.

"Dammit, he's always one step ahead of me," Victoria blurted in frustration, "And he's parading around with their firm's house nigger to let us all know this is not about race. Not a problem for me, Ben," she said, talking to the TV. "I have no intentions of stirring the racial pot. It never comes out the way you want it."

"Fascinating," Khloe said jokingly, "Here, I was thinking this was going to be a 'boys against the girls' kind of fight."

Victoria didn't want to but she couldn't help but laugh, "Let's eat, I do my best thinking over good food. What's in the bag?"

"Ham and cheese on round rolls with pickle and barbecue chips."

"That will work, girl," Victoria said, opening up her sandwich. "By the way, my mouth may get out there sometimes so I apologize in advance. I hope you aren't sensitive."

"I used to be, but law school cured me of that affliction."

Victoria's mouth was full so she put up her hand for a high-five. She took a few more bites and crunched on the chips before she paused.

"My foundation for the prosecution is that those of us who have not decided to carry arms in our everyday activities need to be protected from the impulses of those who do. There is another side to the second amendment argument."

"So you need the stats for the number of innocent people killed by firearm fanatics."

"Exactly, but first let's get through this press conference. I need you to call Mr. and Mrs. Gardner to let them know what's going on, and then I want you to notify Dt. Carlton and Dt. Rosario that I want them there with us in the morning."

"You want me to stand beside you and be the token white woman to show we are fair and balanced," Khloe chuckled. "Seen but not heard."

"It wasn't my plan but it works out perfectly, except I won't keep you silent."

"You mean we're a team."

"I want to win and this case is too big to be an individual sport. I'll need you to consult with experts to select as witnesses for the trial on those stats. I need to go over the medical examiner's report about the angle and distance of the shot."

"Do you want the pictures of Edward Landauer's injuries?"

"I want everything we can get but I won't discuss it in the press conference. I know Ben Madison very well. I can't show any of my hand or its game over before we hit the courtroom."

"So he's as good as his reputation?" Khloe asked, intrigued.

"Better, I went to school with him," Victoria answered casually.

"Maybe you can hook me up, I'm available."

"That's an idea," Victoria giggled.

Khloe made the calls to the media announcing a press conference by the District Attorney's office in the morning. Ben's statement after the pre-trial conference served as sound bites on all of the major networks and he appeared in a spot on the Fox network. Victoria worked late into the evening until the alarm she set for 10:00 went off. She wanted to get a good night's sleep so she would look her best in front of the cameras. Ben may have jumped out of the gate before her but she was very much still in the race.

***

Public reaction after Benjamin's appearance all over the

networks was unequally divided. He had his supporters and they felt more comfortable speaking out against the rampant crime in Philly and how they had to take the streets back, but the larger side outraged over the death of a young unarmed black teenager were back out protesting in full force again. She knew Ben's strategy was to try to humanize his client but his announcement had turned up the heat on the simmering melting pot of Philly making it bubble and boil.

Victoria got out of the bed early the next morning ready to make her national debut. She chose a gray sheath dress and a lavender blazer to mix the edge of authority with femininity. Bold silver earrings and necklace gave her the stylish flair to match Ben's. Khloe picked her up at home and they rode in early to grab some coffee and join up with the detectives. They walked quickly through a line of protesters holding signs that said, "No Justice, No Peace." Arthur called as soon as they got in her office to let her know that Police commissioner Mancini would be on hand to field any questions for the Police Department about the latest eruption of protests.

Victoria walked into the media room at the District Attorney's Office filled with reporters and took center stage at the podium. The lights from the cameras brightened the room and the flashes blurred her vision.

"Good morning, everyone, I'm Victoria Perry, Assistant District Attorney and prosecutor for the Deshaun Gardner case. This circumstance has heightened the passions of this city, the state, and the country making it one of the more challenging cases of our office. Nevertheless we have a job to do. The District Attorney's office is committed to justice for Deshaun Gardner and Edward Landauer. We are not motivated by the protests of the community but by the laws of the Commonwealth of Pennsylvania. Outside of this building there are signs that read "No Justice, No Peace." I want everyone to rest assured that there will be justice in this case. We ask for your continued support and prayers in this prosecution. Now we'll take some of your questions."

A slew of hands flew up in the air.

"Yes, ma'am," Victoria said, pointing to a reporter on the left.

"Has there been any additional evidence to justify the murder charges against Edward Landauer?" she asked.

"The standard by which we determined the charge of second-degree murder have been met by this case," Victoria answered, taking another question from a man in the back. "Yes sir?"

"Ed Landauer's injuries included a broken jaw. Did Deshaun Gardner have any injuries besides the gun shot?" he asked.

"We can't comment on the evidence of the case, it will all be discussed during the trial, that's what the courts are for," Victoria answered, nodding to a woman on the first row.

"Are civilians allowed to carry guns as Town Watch members?"

Victoria stepped aside and yielded the microphone to Dt. Carlton.

"I can't emphasize this enough. Crime fighting is the job of the police. We cannot have citizens taking the law into their hands no matter how good the intention. All suspicious activity observed has to be reported to the police."

Dt. Carlton backed away from the podium and Victoria said, "We'll take one more question."

A man in the back stood up and asked, "Did Mr. Landauer have a license for 'open carry' of his gun, and in the case where there are limited witnesses, why does the accused have to prove his innocence?"

"To my knowledge, Mr. Landauer did not have an 'open carry' license for his gun," Victoria stated. "Foremost in my mind is that of the more than 8000 firearm criminal homicides in this country last year, less than 3 percent were found to be justified.

In this case a homicide was committed and the District Attorney's office works in conjunction with law enforcement to assure that the constitutional rights of all the people are protected. It is our obligation to prove the case beyond the shadow of a doubt. Thank you all."

Murmurs grew louder in the room as Victoria and her group filed out of the room.

"We're out," Dt. Rosario said, leaving. "Just pick up the phone if you need anything."

"Thanks," Victoria said, throwing up her hand.

"Good job," Khloe said, patting Victoria on the back.

"This is only the first. I'll let you handle some if you're ready. Do you think you'll feel comfortable in that environment?" Victoria asked as they waited for the elevator.

"I think so," she answered pensively.

"Good, the next thing is we need to get a solid list of character witnesses. Ben's only defense is to vilify the victim to make it appear justified."

Victoria dropped down in her chair and kicked off her heels before she took a deep breath of relief. She was pleased with the way the press conference had gone. Arthur wasn't blowing up her phone so he must be satisfied as well. She swiveled back and forth a few times organizing her thoughts and then her office line buzzed. She saw it was Leonard and swiftly picked it up. She knew they fussed half the time they were together but she hadn't seen him for over a week and she missed him. Her bed had turned cold and lonely.

"Hello, stranger, it's about time," she said, happy to hear from him.

"I caught your press conference," he said sullenly.

"What's the matter? You didn't think I did a good job."

"Victoria, I asked you not to take this case. Everything you say and do are a matter of public record. For me it would cause serious political ramifications. One of your statements can be construed to say you support gun control."

"I don't have a problem with that, I am for gun control. So what?"

"Gun lobbyists are very powerful. I have to be neutral on that issue."

"So be neutral."

"You don't understand, Vee. I've been trying to tell you that for us to be together we have to be a team. You can't do anything that would keep us from winning."

"You mean you from winning."

"That's the nasty game of politics, baby. Anything you say can be used against you."

"So I'm a liability."

"You're suffering from a limited upbringing. You're thinking small. Why can't you see the big picture? Michelle did it for Barack."

"Are you serious?"

"Not everything has to be about you, Vee. You're spoiled."

"What's the problem with that, you should want to spoil me."

"We all have to give. Relationships are not a one way street."

"I don't know what you're talking about. You're the one who wants my life to revolve around you. I don't think you're sure what kind of woman you really want."

"I don't think you know what the hell you're looking for."

"Truthfully, I'm not even looking for a husband right now. I just want somebody to love me. If you can't do that without me becoming someone else then we need to part ways."

"I don't want to hear any more of your fantasy bullshit. I asked you to back off this one for us. I can't jeopardize all that I have accomplished."

"This can be a game changer for me. It's the chance for me to get out of public service and into private practice."

"I wish you the best, baby," Leonard said, hanging up the phone.

"Damn," she whispered, "I can't win for losing."

****

The plainclothes officer assigned to Victoria for the press conference dropped her at home just after 6:00. Miss Judy wasn't sitting outside so Victoria knocked on the screen door.

"Come on in," she sang, sounding cheerful and tired at the same time.

"Hey there," Victoria said, walking through the unlocked door. "Are you having a slow day?"

"I had two doctor's appointments today so I'm out of it. I haven't even cooked anything. Lanetta went to get me some wings from Reading Terminal. She should be back in a minute."

"That ought to fix your situation."

"You got that right. We saw you on TV earlier. I'm so proud of you, child. I know your momma and daddy are too. You have come a long way."

"Thanks, Miss Judy."

"Hey, Hollywood," Lanetta said, bursting in the door.

"Is there anybody more dramatic than you?" Victoria asked with a laugh.

"You're the one on all the news channels so it must be you."

"How did I look, girl?" Victoria asked, holding her hand out for a slap.

"You were banging from head to toe."

"You know I had to come correct."

"Do you two mind if I get something to eat?" Miss Judy interjected, feigning upset.

"I'm sorry, Mama, don't have a hissy fit over these wings," Lanetta joked, fixing her a plate of food with some aloe vera water.

"You better have some, Vicki, you know they're good," Miss

Judy said.

"I'll take a couple but I can't get too full, I'm going out tonight," she replied.

"Uh-oh, what do you have up this evening," Lanetta asked curiously.

"I'm going down to the Blue Note to hear a man blow."

"Would you like a chaperone since you're a celebrity now?" Lanetta asked.

"Can you be ready in a half hour and do you mind driving?"

"I can handle both of those, honey."

"All right, I'll be back in a few," Victoria said, taking her wings with her.

***

Victoria and Lanetta strolled into the Blue Note one hour later, looking good and smelling good. Victoria had let her hair down, changed into black leggings, a sequined top, a short red jacket, and some strappy red sandals. She knew it might be a little much for a Tuesday night but who cared, Leonard had officially broken up with her and wearing red always made her feel better. Lanetta was wearing a colorful hug-every-inch dress and six-inch heels. Whenever she went out she didn't play.

A Grover Washington CD played in the background at the Blue Note and the walls were decorated with paintings of Jazz greats from Duke Ellington to Wynton Marsalis. It was still early and the band wasn't playing yet but the club had a nice crowd. A host met them at the door dressed in a tuxedo.

"How many are in your party?" he asked.

"Just two, and we'd like a seat close to the band," Lanetta instructed.

"This way, please," he said, strutting around tables until they were in the second row of tables. "Is this acceptable?" he asked courteously.

"It's fine," Victoria said before Lanetta could complain.

"Your waitress will be here shortly," he said.

"That brother is sweeter than I am," Lanetta said, sliding down in her chair.

A waitress came over to the table, gave them menus, and then recited the specials for the evening. "We also have a two drink minimum," she added.

"I'll have a red zinfandel and a small plate of veggie lasagna," Victoria said, ordering first.

"A vodka Collins for me and the fried crab cakes plate with a spinach salad," Lanetta said, handing her back the menus.

"I'll be right back with your drinks," the waitress said, smiling.

They sat without talking while Lanetta scoped out the place and Victoria checked emails in her phone.

Then Victoria said, "Leonard and I broke up today."

"So what else is new, you two are always breaking up."

"I told you before, he said it was him or the case. I chose the case. It's done."

"Wow, that's deep. Just in time," Lanetta said when the waitress brought their drinks over. "Are we getting drunk tonight?"

"Nope," Victoria said, sipping her wine as the lights dimmed and the band came on stage, "We're here to see another man who has captured my interest."

"Here's to you, Vick," Lanetta said, holding up her drink, "I want to be just like you when I grow up.

"You are super silly, girl."

"No, I mean it. You're my hero."

"You can stop, I've got the check," Victoria said when their food came.

"Let's party then. Another vodka Collins for me," Lanetta told the waitress.

"This lasagna is really good," Victoria said with her mouth full.

"I'm enjoying the food but that's not the reason we're here is it."

Victoria eyes were drawn to the front as the band got situated on stage. The MC walked up and stood at the microphone. In a seamless and effortless transition the band began to play softly blending with the recorded music. The back ground music faded as the Voyagers took over raising the volume. It was impressive and the applause spread across the room in admiration.

The band paused and then the MC spoke.

"Ladies and Gentlemen, The Blue Note welcomes you to a smooth melodic cruise this evening with the Voyagers."

More applause and whistles from the crowd filled the air. The band slid into *All Day Music* an old tune by War. All the tensions of her day faded as Victoria was absorbed into the groove of the music. The lyrics played out in her mind and she threw her hands up over her head like Mother Williams did when she caught the Holy Ghost on Sunday morning at her daddy's church. The fashionably dressed and composed audience jumped to their feet when the band did a medley of Con Funk Shun, Cameo, and Zapp. Even Lanetta got caught up and did her wiggle at the side of the table. The band gave them a reprieve when they slowed down playing Kem's *Love Calls*. Dupree moved to the front and the mellow sound of the saxophone soothed all that ailed Victoria. The sweet notes circled and swelled around her until she was drowning.

"Which one is he?" Lanetta asked, bringing her back from the brink.

"He's the sax player."

Lanetta nodded in approval. She thought he was nice-looking, fit and trim, sexy with dreads, and he could play the hell out that instrument.

"I know you're not going to try and get with that?" she said warily.

"Oh yes, I am."

"I can't believe you. He doesn't look like your type. You must be under too much stress with the case and Leonard."

"Did you forget I'm grown?"

"Ooops, enough said, girlfriend."

Lanetta downed her second drink and Victoria ordered a second glass of wine. Growing up together they knew when to let each other have their space. They slid back into the groove of the music and had a good time.

When the band wrapped up their first set Lanetta asked Victoria, "Don't you have to get up in the morning?"

"Yeah, I do, give me a minute," she answered, getting up from the table.

Lanetta watched her go over to the table in the back where the band was taking a break. Dupree stood up and walked her over to the bar.

"Victoria, I'm glad you came out," he said, smiling.

"So am I, it was a pleasure. The show was great."

"Thank you. Are you going to stay for the second set tonight?"

"No, I can't. I have an early morning and a long day in front of me."

"I saw you on the news today."

Victoria nodded and looked away. Suddenly, the fact that she probably couldn't go anywhere without someone recognizing her bothered her. She hadn't fully contemplated this part of the deal.

"Relax, it's okay," he said.

Victoria didn't know how to react. Her life and her job had always been completely separated. Now she was at a loss for words.

"I'd like to take you out to dinner?" he said.

"I probably need to stay low-key for a while."

"I could cook dinner for you sometime."

"Now that is a better idea."

"Let me see your phone," he said.

Victoria pulled out her phone and handed it to him. He called his phone.

"Now I have your number and you have mine. I'll be in touch, soon."

Victoria put her phone back in her purse and Lanetta caught up with her halfway towards the exit of the club.

"Well, what happened?" Lanetta asked. "What's the rush?"

"Nothing, he recognized me and that threw me off."

"You might as well get over that. Your face is going to be a regular in the news until the trial is over. You knew that was going to happen didn't you?"

"I hadn't thought about that. I just figured it would be the platform I needed to show how good of an attorney I am."

"That's what you have, Vick."

"So I see."

"What about Mr. Dupree?"

"He says he wants to cook dinner for me."

"Boom, that's what you wanted."

"Yes, it is," Victoria said, recovering herself.

"Good, now you're going to have to take the wheel. That vodka must have splashed in my eyes because I can't see straight."

They both laughed and joked all the way home. Victoria changed into a long t-shirt, curled up in front of an episode of Wendy Williams with a bowl of ice cream and fell asleep.

Chapter Eight

Benjamin Madison sat in his office watching Headline News. Darren and Mona Gardner and their attorney, Christian Booker, were guests on the Jane Valez-Mitchell Show. Mr. Booker was explaining that their son, Deshaun Gardner, was yet another victim of racial profiling, that basically he was shot because he was black and because he was wearing a hoodie.

"Simply put, if Deshaun were white and wearing a denim jacket he would still be alive today," Mr. Booker said to Jane. "There is a serious problem in this country with all young black men being viewed as hoodlums and drug dealers."

"I think we can safely say Mr. Landauer felt that way," Jane commented. "Recordings of a number of his phone calls to 911 show that he assumed all the suspects of the robberies happening in his neighborhood were black."

"That's right, Jane. From the 39 phone calls that he made to the police, all of the individuals which he referred to as suspicious were black."

"How do you feel about that, Mr. Gardner?" Jane asked.

"It's hard for me to describe. As a black man I have had people react negatively to me more times than I can count but I wanted better for my son. To have him killed because he was a young black male is simply devastating to me. I only wanted to keep my boy safe."

"What would you like to say, Mrs. Gardner?" Jane asked, turning her attention to Mona.

"If we allow this to happen without justice for my son, then no black man is safe walking the streets," Mona said, holding back tears.

"That is the most important thing to remember in this case," Christian added. "This child was stalked and confronted, Edward Landauer was the aggressor. The United States Declaration of Independence says we all have the right to life, liberty, and the pursuit of happiness. That means we should be able to freely walk the streets in our own neighborhood, even young black men who wear hoodies."

Benjamin pushed the off button on the remote. The media reports were disturbing. He needed to change the tone of the discussions ASAP. He hated to have to resort to trying the victim instead of defending his client but he didn't have much choice. He had just received Ed's police record from the background check he ordered and it wasn't anything to brag about. He had been charged with assaulting a police officer and resisting arrest, and had a restraining order against him by his old girlfriend. He had also been ordered to attend anger management classes.

His intercom buzzer interrupted his thoughts.

"Thomas Clancy here to see you," Gayle said.

"Sure, send him in," Ben answered.

"Come on in, Thomas," Ben said, welcoming him into his office. "We're going to have to get some help on changing the perception of this thing. The protests and conversations have heated up again and we need to switch the subject. I want Ed's injuries on the front page. The topic has got to be crime in the streets of Philly and citizens who are courageously fighting back."

"What are you proposing?" Thomas asked half-heartedly.

He didn't see the sense in him making an effort to contribute to the case if all Ben wanted from him was his black skin.

"The parents are doing the rounds, the kid is looking like an angel and Ed's the evil villain."

"I don't think we want to put our client out there," Thomas said doubtfully.

"Definitely not," Ben said, "Even still we need a positive image of our client to be a part of those discussions."

"Who do you have in mind for the job?"

"I want his brother, Emerson, doing interviews. I need his neighbors doing interviews."

"We only have one neighbor who'll consent to appearing in favor of our client."

"Where are we on co-workers? Anybody there want to speak for him?"

"Not any that you would want to use as character witnesses, seems his temper has a hair-trigger too. He's gone postal on at least two of them."

"Fuck. I'm going to need a parade of good white people and a few blacks to swear that he's a kind-hearted peacekeeper to get him acquitted. Right now he looks like a crazy hot-head who runs around in the night playing policeman games."

"You'll be lucky to get three in that crowd besides his mama," Thomas smirked on his way out of the office.

Benjamin pushed his intercom and said, "Gayle, clear my schedule for the rest of the day, I've got to go meet with someone.

***

Victoria sat at her desk reading a text from Dupree. "Glad you stopped by last night, want to see you soon. Thoughts of you kept me awake late and woke me early." She saw it as a romantic gesture and was still smiling to herself when Khloe walked in. Quickly, she texted him back, "I'll be there tonight."

"Looks like you're having a good morning," Khloe said, noticing her smile. "You must have had a good night."

"Not bad, and I think they'll be getting better," Victoria said, putting down her phone.

"So what's the plan for today?" Khloe asked, taking a seat.

"I've been working on an outline for the prosecution and I want to go over that with you."

Khloe took a seat, got her iPad out of her bag, logged in, and waited.

"After the opening statement I want to establish the character and temperament of the defendant. I want his background and history out there."

"You want to show he's an asshole. What witnesses do you have in mind for that?"

"Co-workers, old girlfriends, neighbors, we'll have to do some interviews to choose the ones that have had clashes with him."

"I'll call Dt. Rosario and see if she has some names for us."

"We'll need to establish the frame of mind he was in."

"How are we going to do that if he doesn't testify?"

"We're going to have to get expert witnesses, forensic psychologists, at least two."

"We only have one consultant on staff. I'll get references for someone else."

"Then we have to go through the whole process again with Deshaun Gardner, his character, his teachers, and of course his parents."

"What about his friends?"

"That's touchy. His best friend, Jamaal Taylor, has a record and looks gangster. If we put him on the stand Deshaun will be a thug by association. Get me a girlfriend if you can and other relatives."

"You're leaving the actual crime committed for the final argument?"

"Yeah, we'll go through the facts of the shooting, first the officers at the scene, the arresting officer at the Roundhouse, and then Dt. Carlton and Rosario."

"If you wrap up with the medical examiner in the argument it might be a cold end."

"That's true; I'll end with Mrs. Gardner, she was the last to speak with Deshaun. What I really need to cement a win is for Edward Landauer to take the stand."

"I can't see why they would let him testify. He's short-tempered."

"If I can attack his character enough I think he'll want to testify."

"How are you going to get it out there in the media?" Khloe asked

"I don't want it in the media. I don't want the jury to have a chance to digest it. I want them to be shocked and disgusted."

"Are you sure you want to wait? They're already talking about how Deshaun ran with a rough crowd of juvenile delinquents in Germantown."

"Give a call to Christian Booker, I need him to keep Darren and Mona Gardner out there defending their son."

Their conference was interrupted by a knock on the office door. They gave each other a questioning look. Victoria shrugs her shoulders and Khloe goes to answer the door. She opens it and there stands Benjamin Madison. He's flawless as usual. Khloe is clearly smitten even though he doesn't notice her.

"Would you please excuse us?" he asked, never taking his eyes off of Victoria.

Victoria turned toward Khloe. "It's okay, we'll touch base later on today."

Khloe gathered her notes and iPad and took another glance at Ben before she left the office. Then he walked over to Victoria's desk.

"You haven't reached out, Victoria, so I decided to pay you a visit."

"Is this business or pleasure?" she asked.

"I'm at your service, whatever you want."

"Ben, you are so full of shit," she said, shaking her head.

He laughed. "Not completely."

"Sit down, counselor, tell me why you're here."

"Come over and sit on the sofa with me. We're old friends. We can talk for a minute."

Victoria hesitated before she stood and moved from behind her desk and sat on the sofa in front of her bookshelf. Benjamin smiled and sat down beside her. His eyes leisurely scanned around the room before he said anything.

"How are you, Vicki, how have things been since our Temple days?" he asked casually.

"I've been good, a few complaints but I'm all right."

"You know you're better than this," he said, looking at the walls and ceiling of her office.

"I think you were about to tell me why you're here," she replied, dismissing his remark.

"You know this thing is going to get ugly before it's over."

"It already is. Your client committed murder."

"I would like to spare Mr. and Mrs. Gardner as well as my client from any more of the unpleasantness of this circumstance."

"I think we're way past avoiding that."

"This isn't the first time an individual shot an unarmed person, unfortunately it happens every day. The media is attracted to incidents where race can be seen as an issue. Moving forward I don't want this to be seen as race related."

"You can't dodge the facts, Ben."

"Sure there was profiling but he didn't go out there to kill anybody."

"I'm not the one you have to convince. If people are not able to control their tempers then we have to control the ease of which guns can be purchased."

"Americans love their guns so that's not going to happen."

"Maybe not, but it's my job to put the bad guys away."

"I'm trying to keep a good one from being wrongly convicted."

"Do you really believe that?"

He grinned. "Attorney client privilege."

"Are you here shopping a deal for him?"

"Is there one for sale?" he asked deviously, insinuating something underhanded.

Victoria jolted up from the sofa outraged. "Ben, I don't have time for the bullshit."

"Don't trip, you're being overly sensitive," he said, grabbing her hand. "You always did take everything too seriously. I'm not trying to mess with your head before the trial."

"Like that is something you are above doing."

"I play dirty if I have to, but I'm neither ashamed nor proud of what I do to win."

"You don't have to tell me, I got to know you pretty well."

"That's the point, you didn't. If you did you would know that I was and still am attracted to you. From the first day I saw you in our Contracts class. I couldn't stop staring at you."

"Yeah right, it was more of you wanting to keep a close eye on the competition."

"You were sharp without a doubt, but you were cute. You have a brilliant mind, that's the center of my fascination with you."

"You don't know anything about me."

"I know all I need to know."

She nodded her head. "More games."

"No games. Say you'll go out with me when we're done fighting."

"Another man who cares more about his success than me, no thank you."

"That shouldn't be a deal breaker, you can relate can't you," he said, bending over and looking her in the eyes.

"Maybe I am guilty," she said, glaring back at him.

Benjamin laughed deep from his gut and stretched his arms out to call a truce.

"None of this is personal, Momi. We don't have to fall out of the bed on this."

"This has been an interesting experience going down memory lane with you, but that's not why you came here," she said, moving back behind her desk. "So let me be clear, I'm not about to make a deal with the devil today."

"Well, you know how to reach me," he said, walking out of the door.

***

Victoria lost track of time researching murder cases between unknown parties. Her brain was on overload and her eyes were red and strained. It was time to join the mad dash of the city, go home, and regroup for another day. She could hear the noises of rush hour coming through her open window. She'd just stood up to stretch when Khloe blew through the door like a hurricane.

"What's up?" Victoria asked, wondering what other surprises were left in the day.

"It's the national evening news report, pictures of Deshaun and some of his friends in his old neighborhood are all over the wire. They're suggesting that he ran with a gang and his BFF, Jamaal Taylor, gave an interview looking totally hood and hinted about revenge if the shooter doesn't go to jail."

"Ahh hell, here we go," Victoria, feeling the direction of the media storm turning.

"When it rains it pours," Khloe added, "The medical examiner's toxicology report was released today and it says that Deshaun had traces of THD in his blood."

Victoria raised her hands exasperated.

"It's nothing new. They do it in rape cases all the time. Demonize the victim until people feel like they deserved what they got."

"Are you going to stay with your initial strategy?"

"The press never gets tired of race baiting, it sells papers and pumps up ratings, but it can backfire with a jury."

"So what did Cary Grant's long-lost son want?"

"Everything, as usual."

"There's nothing wrong with white meat, Vicki," Khloe said teasing her.

"Go for it, I'm not in the market."

Khloe licked her lips. "I just might do that."

The phone rang and Victoria answered it on speaker.

"Drop the case, dumb-ass nigger bitch," a female screamed and then hung up.

"Perfect ending to a perfect day," Victoria said.

"You want a ride home?"

"Yeah, I'll meet you downstairs in a half hour."

The latest reports on Deshaun caused the rage of the black community to shoot up like a fever. A crowd of several hundred protesters was growing larger as people joined from varying directions circling City Hall demanding justice and holding their 'No Justice: No Peace' signs. A few stood on the walls and a few on top of bus shelters. The number of onlookers grew larger too as people stopped to watch the procession. Some opposed to the protest shout curses at the demonstrators. One man yelled out, "Justice was already done."

Camera crews stood by filming while roving reporters held their mics in the faces of those spewing their anger about the latest reports on Deshaun Gardner. Cops stood anxiously around the perimeter of the peaceful demonstrators waiting for any act of violence to give them a reason to put an end to the march.

Victoria took a deep breath and darted out the entrance of the building. Recognized by reporters, they blocked her way and jabbed microphones in her face demanding a statement on the case. Victoria pushed through the melee dodging questions to the end of the sidewalk where Khloe waited in the car.

"You sure you don't want to call Mr. Madison back and take him up on that deal," Khloe asked, speeding away from the curb.

"I should have thought about that before I stuck my neck out. There's no graceful way to get out of the gutter."

***

Miss Judy was outside getting some air when Khloe dropped Victoria off in front of the house.

"Long day, child?' she asked.

Victoria nodded as she turned the bolt lock on her door.

"One of the longest."

Victoria stared out the window at the moon for most of the night unable to fall asleep. She felt vulnerable and she didn't like it. Being somewhat of a control freak, the uncertainty in her life and career was agonizing. When the sun rose she rolled out of bed determined to get a tighter rein on the wild horse that she had chosen to ride. The plan was to get her independence back. Used to coming and going on her own, she was tired of being chauffeured around town.

Still in her pajamas she headed out on the driveway to uncover her daddy's prize possession, his 1996 Toyota Avalon. He called it 'Old faithful' because it had never given him any trouble from the day he drove it off the lot. It was in pristine condition despite being almost 16 years old. Victoria took care of it just like her daddy did. She had it detailed twice a month while she went to the beauty salon to get her hair done. It didn't require much cleaning because she only drove it when she was going to Jersey or doing some heavy grocery shopping. That was changing as of today, she needed to be able to move around freely. Besides, driving it made her feel like her daddy was riding shotgun.

After Victoria was dressed for the day ahead, she packed a bag with a change of casual clothes and a hat to help conceal her identity in public since more people were recognizing her. She drank a cup of coffee to wash down the blueberry bagel with butter and poured the rest of the pot into a thermos to take with her. She planned to revamp her schedule and lighten up on her research.

Her cell phone rang after she tossed her overnight bag in the trunk of 'Old faithful.'

"Do you want me to stop by for you on my way in," Khloe asked, cheerily, sounding as if she'd gotten the good night's sleep that Victoria had missed.

"No thanks, I'm driving my daddy's car in today," Victoria replied. "I'll meet you in your office this morning, "I'm going to shadow you on your cases in the morning sessions. I don't want to get stale being out of the mix for months until the trial."

She didn't mention that getting away from all the prank phone calls coming into her office was the main reason for her motivation.

"You know how municipal court is, I don't mind if you don't mind."

Victoria was seated beside Khloe as the daily docket was cleared but her mind was someplace else. Arthur had called to tell her that Mr. and Mrs. Gardner would be in his office that afternoon and he wanted her there. It was safe to assume they didn't care for the latest news reports. The greater part of her preoccupation was with Dupree, he had asked her to come to the club after work. It was Thursday and his band would be playing. She couldn't think of a better place to relieve the pressures of her day than The Blue Note.

Back in her office after watching Khloe work through almost fifty cases, Victoria took off her blazer and shoes to eat the Cobb salad she ordered in. She had to slow down on the hoagies and cheesesteaks before they accumulated on her waistline, she hadn't done a real workout since Arthur handed her the Gardner case. She turned on the TV and punched channel six on the remote.

She wanted one more look at Action News before the meeting with the Gardners. It wasn't encouraging. They were doing a segment about hoodies, referring to them as thug attire. They were replaying comments from Geraldo Rivera that said that it was reasonable for Edward Landauer to be suspicious of a black guy wearing a hoodie. Deshaun Gardner's lack of a criminal record was inconsequential.

At 1:45 she slid her feet back into her pumps, touched up her make-up, and put her blazer back on before she headed to Arthur's office. She got there just as Christian Booker was arriving with his clients.

"Hello, Mr. Gardner and Mrs. Gardner," Arthur said, welcoming them into his conference room. "Good to see you again, Mr. Booker. Please have a seat. Can I get you anything?"

"No, thank you, Mr. Mitchell," Christian said, "There's no need for pleasantries, why don't we get right to the business at hand."

"All right," Arthur said, leaning forward at the long table. "What can I do for you?"

"Mr. and Mrs. Gardner are very displeased with the way that their son's character is being assassinated in the media," Christian said. "We aren't seeing any counter attacks by this office or at least some pushback on Edward Landauer."

"Controlling the media is beyond our scope," Arthur replied.

"You and I both know these kind of attacks poison the jury pool," Christian complained.

"I know that it is hard to hear people use the media to denigrate your son and try to justify the shooting but that's not out fight. Our job is to deliver a vigorous prosecution for the Commonwealth," Arthur stated sympathetically.

"Our son's name is being drug through the mud. He never belonged to a gang," Mrs. Gardner said with tears in her eyes. "They're out there defending that killer and nobody is defending my son. What they're doing is an injustice. It's all lies."

"The only trouble he ever got into was being late or skipping school a couple of times," Mr. Gardner said in exasperation.

"The media has a free hand, they can talk all they want. This office is held to a higher standard," Arthur explained.

"Mr. and Mrs. Gardner," Victoria interjected, "The accused doesn't have a clean record and that will be brought out in court. If I blow all my ammunition now, I won't have much to fight with when the trial begins."

"I know that this situation is extremely difficult but you are able to defend your son in the media better than anyone else. Don't hesitate to speak out at every opportunity," Arthur urged, standing up.

"Don't worry, we intend to," Christian said, leading the Gardners out of the office.

Arthur dropped down heavily in his chair.

"Why couldn't that loser have taken a plea and spared us all of this shit. Just today we got another nut threatening to blow up the building."

"I got another prank call myself," Victoria added.

"The sooner we get this case settled the better," Arthur complained. "The whole thing has set off a chain of arrests with protesters breaking shit, antagonizing the police, altercations in restaurants, and even on the bus stops. The whole city is working overtime and the mayor is having a fit about all the money it's costing."
"Whenever race gets in to the mix, it's going to bring hostilities to the surface. That's why we need to be worried about all the guns on the streets. We all can't get along in this country and probably never will, but we can't resort to behaving like this is the Wild Wild West where everybody is packing."

"I pray that you are ready for this showdown because all eyes will be on this department. No matter how it goes down somebody is going to be fucked. If we can't put him away at least make it look good."

Victoria gathered her note pad and left. Walking back to her office it was now clearer to her why she had been given the case so easily with all the attention it received and a second chair attorney with no experience. Arthur didn't necessarily want to win the case, and with her being black there wouldn't be any notion of ethical impropriety. For the politically vested it wasn't about justice for some young black kid murdered in the streets, it was about keeping the status quo, re-election, and maintaining power.

More than ever Victoria was determined to show them all that she wasn't to be taken lightly. She thought about the hurt in Mona Gardner's eyes. Nothing could take away the pain, but locking up the man who shot him might give her some peace.

Chapter Nine

Victoria locked the door to her office, relieved to call an end to another long day. She had been looking forward to taking a break and seeing Dupree again. She closed the blinds for privacy while she changed her clothes. She put on the pair of white skinny jeans, a long turquoise flowing blouse, and the flat sandals that she'd brought with her in the overnight bag. She combed her hair down, topped off her outfit with a small bibbed straw hat, and then added a pair of shades before she tipped out on South Penn Square. Daylight savings time had begun and the sun was still up, hopefully she could get to The Blue Note without being recognized.

So far so good she thought as she pulled into the parking lot of the club. She pulled her phone out of her purse and texted Dupree that she was on her way in. The door swung open just as she approached it. When she saw it was him holding it on the other side she couldn't help but smile for the first time that day.

"Glad you came out, it's good to see you," he said, ushering her inside with his hand lightly around her waist.

"It's good to see you too," she said, still smiling.

"You look amazing. Are you hungry?"

"Oh yeah, I haven't had a decent meal in days."

"That's so sad, I'll get you something special," he said, leading her to a secluded table.

"This is kind of far from the stage."

"I thought you might appreciate a little privacy."

"You're right, I forgot about the outside world for a minute."

"How about a glass of wine, it'll mellow you out."

"Thanks, that sounds great."

Dupree patted her on the shoulder on his way to the bar. Victoria took the opportunity to give him a long look. His long dreads were neatly pulled back into a ponytail. He was dressed in faded jeans, loose but not baggy, and a button-down panama jack shirt with pictures of blue water and palm trees all over it. She wished she could get lost in the island on his back. She watched him talking to the bartender, noticing his mannerisms, and the ease of his movements. He was as smooth as the music he played.

He walked back over to the table moving with the grace and confidence of a lion.

"White wine okay?" he asked.

"Certainly," she answered, taking a sip.

"I ordered us a large pizza pie, but tomorrow you have to let me cook for you."

"That's an offer I can't refuse."

"So tell me some things about yourself, and I already know you're a lawyer."

"Let's see. I was born in Philly, an only child. My father was a preacher and my mother was his first lady. I went to public schools and graduated from Temple a couple of times. I've never been married and I don't have any children. I like to travel, eat good food, and listen to good music. I have a thing for designer shoes. I live for sweets, especially lemon pies and peanut chews."

"Intriguing," he said, extending his hand to shake, "I'm happy to get to know you."

"Now it's your turn."

"All right, I'm the youngest of three brothers and I was raised in Baltimore. My dad worked in an auto assembly plant for General Motors and my mother worked the second shift as a nurse. I started playing the sax in junior high. Unlike my brothers, one went to jail and the other to college, I went on the road. I was married once, she had a son when we met, but I don't have any children of my own. I'm not very religious," he added with a smile. "Music is my passion. I smoke ganja, it brings out my creativity, and I love to cook."

Victoria nodded. "That's interesting, you've peaked my curiosity."

"That's a mutual thing. I really liked your vibe when we first met."

"It looks like we can start our own mutual admiration society."

"I'll be the president. I know you probably don't want to talk about it but I admire the job you're doing on the shooting of Deshaun Gardner."

"You're right. I don't want to talk about it but I thank you for that."

The waitress brought a vegetarian pizza out to their table with two plates. Victoria slid a large slice on her plate and took a bite. Dupree watched her for a few seconds before he did the same. The tables in the room filled up as the clock moved closer to the hour the band would take the stage.

"I guess it's time for me to go to work," Dupree said, checking his watch and standing up. "Will you be around after the second set?"

"I wish I could but it has been a crazy day and I have to get up in the morning. Maybe you should give me the grocery list for what you want to cook for me tomorrow."

"I've got it covered," he replied, stepping behind her chair and whispering in her ear, "The first song is dedicated to you."

Victoria ate another slice of pizza before she went back to sipping her glass of wine. Enjoying the ambience of the club, all the stress of the day disappeared. The DJ turned up the music as the band came out. The song changed to Stevie Wonder singing *Golden Lady* and the band joined in, the CD faded out when Dupree's saxophone solo began to play. The sound of his horn rolled over her like warm water in a shower. It soothed her muscles as they relaxed and her body swayed and rocked with the lilts and rising of the notes. She let it take her on a magical ride. As long as they were playing nothing was wrong in the world.

When the set ended Victoria knew it was time to get back to reality. She sent Dupree a text saying she loved the set and her address before she eased out of the door.

*****

The morning went by quickly in the municipal court for Victoria and Khloe. The cases on the morning docket were rapidly disposed of with agreements being tossed out like cards by a casino blackjack dealer.

"Another day's work in the justice system," Khloe said on their way out of the courtroom.

"Sometimes I wonder if I'm fighting on the right side," Victoria said.

"Why's that?" Khloe asked pushing the down arrow on the elevator.

"Most of the perps are black and they're probably in here due to profiling."

"Don't let history or your emotions cloud your thinking. Some of them are real bad dudes. They aren't in the system for nothing."

"That may be true," Victoria snapped, "Except black people aren't the only face of crime, they just get caught more often than anybody else. We can't deny there's a reason for that."

The elevator doors opened and both were glad it was empty.

"When you asked me to get the numbers on shooting deaths of unarmed victims, you only wanted the facts, Victoria. Aren't we in the business of facts not public opinions? We have to let them speak for themselves whether we like what they say or not."

"That's easy for white people to say. The laws of nature have proven the relationship between 'cause and effect.' Victims of criminal behavior many times become perpetrators, and it's not based on race. You can't argue the fact that black people have had a long history of oppression. White people disregard it as a factor to absolve themselves of their contribution to black crime."

"You should probably be on the other side of the aisle, my friend. At what point are we responsible for our own actions?"

The elevator doors open and they step out.

"On that note, I rest my case, Khloe. Ed Landauer is responsible for his own actions. A young black guy walking down the street wearing a hoodie did not provoke his own death."

"You owe me a drink after subjecting me to that. I thought you were going to go Malcolm X on me for a minute."

"Look who's being sensitive," Victoria laughed. "Walk me to my office. I've got a bottle tucked away."

"I hope you have some food in here too," Khloe said as they walked in.

"I only have cheese and crackers. I'll order you a Rueben sandwich and you'll calm down."

"Yeah, you had me going there for a minute."

"That was one strategy I've been thinking about using to change the direction of the jury's thinking. It may not be the right angle for the white members of the jury; I got you on the defensive. I don't want that reaction."

Victoria put down her briefcase, opened up the cabinet on her bookshelf, and took out two glasses and a bottle of cognac.

"Since we're talking without filters, you need to know most white people are leery of black people, black men in particular."

"That may be true, however, don't forget that most law-abiding folks of every color are scared of hoodlums and thugs regardless of their race."

"Probably so, but you can't make blanket statements about white people. It's unfair. We don't all feel the same about race."

"That much is clear. Look at the epidemic of 'jungle fever' affecting so many white women. They love black men."

"You are so wrong for that, Vicki."

"I couldn't resist it," Victoria said, handing her the glass.

***

Victoria left the office early to clean the dust out of the kitchen before Dupree arrived. When she finished running the dishwasher and putting away the dishes she had about an hour to catch her breath and get refreshed. She slipped into a pair of leggings and a long sleeveless top. She heard the knock on the door right after she put on her lipstick.

"Good evening," she said opening the front door, "Welcome to my home."

"Thanks for accepting my invitation," he said, stepping inside and giving her a quick kiss on the cheek before checking her out. "You look nice and comfortable."

"I should be, I'm at home," she joked. "Follow me, I'll take you to the kitchen where you can get this show going, I'm hungry."

He set down a backpack he was carrying on the floor beside one of the end tables.

"I like your house," he said, admiring all of the Afrocentric art on the walls.

"I grew up here, it was my parents' house."

"That's all right. It's good when black folks can leave something back for their kids."

Victoria stopped at the entrance to the kitchen and paused for Dupree to go in.

"Make yourself at home and let me know if you need anything like pots and pans or seasonings to work with."

Dupree walked in and placed his other bags on the counter

while he looked around.

"How about some glasses, I want to pour you some wine to sip on while I cook."

"Definitely, that's a good start," Victoria said happily.

She went in the dining room to get two large stem glasses from her mother's breakfront. Victoria watched him remove the cork from a bottle of Chablis and pour the wine.

"Here's to new friendships," he said, raising his glass.

She clicked hers against his.

"To new friendships," she added before she took a large drink.

Dupree put his glass down and began an inventory of the cabinets.

"I like the selection of cookware. I didn't think you did much cooking.

"I don't. They were my mother's, she liked to cook."

He nodded his head without commenting.

"So what's for dinner?" she asked.

"I don't eat pork or red meat, so it will always be chicken or fish on the menu."

She took another long swallow of the wine.

"I don't mind, I like it all."

"Good, I'm making red snapper stuffed with crab dressing and green beans with walnuts and dried cherries. I put it all together earlier so it just needs about thirty minutes to cook."

Victoria watched as he removed the food he brought from plastic containers. He wrapped the stuffed fish in foil and put it on a tray. The green beans were placed in a double boiler to steam.

"You didn't mention that you were a chef."

"I like to experiment with recipes. It's an extension of my creativity."

"I must tell you, I'm a sucker for bread and butter."

"I've got you covered," he said, pulling out a long loaf of French bread.

"You are so impressing me right now," she said facetiously.

"And you are a closet comedienne."

"I have my moments."

"Why don't you give me a tour of the house while we wait?"

"Really?"

"Yes, I want to see how you live. It tells a lot about you."

"Okay," Victoria said, getting up from her chair. "You passed through here on your way in, this is the living room."

"Whose room is through that door?" Dupree asked, pointing to her parents' bedroom.

"That's my mom and dad's."

"I'd like to see it if you don't mind."

"I don't mind," she said, leading the way and opening the door.

It was still the way they kept it when they were alive. It was the largest bedroom in the house but Victoria still felt like it belonged to them. She could never sleep in it. There was no way she could do any unholy things in the room they shared.

"You haven't change it have you?"

"No, I couldn't bring myself to do that. I guess I would feel alone here if I moved their things. The way it is I feel like they're close to me somehow."

"You don't have to explain, I get it."

Victoria showed him the den downstairs and the garage.

"So where do you sleep?" he asked casually.

"My bedroom is all the way upstairs," she answered.

"I'm right behind you," he said.

Victoria climbed the long flight of stairs and pointed to her room. Dupree went inside. It was meticulously kept, everything was in its place. He looked at the display shelf that held a worn out doll and a set of Grimm's fairytales. There were medals from various honor societies and a trophy from the badminton team at William Penn High School. He looked at all the diplomas that hung on the wall among art prints by Leroy Campbell and

John Holyfield. The comforter on the bed was paisley, a mix of turquoise, jade, burgundy, and gold, neatly covered with shams and pillows.

"You like a lot of vibrant colors."

"I guess I do," she said, looking around the room.

"I'm surprised."

"Why is that?"

"You're an attorney. I thought your world would be black and white."

"I've learned that nothing is completely black or white."

"So you're saying there are gray areas."

"I'm saying that all things are colored by a variety of factors."

He smiled and nodded. "You're deeper than I thought."

"Now you've come all up in my crib and insulted me, why?" she asked inquisitively.

"Show me your closet."

Victoria opened her closet and stood back. "Is the answer in there?"

"Yes. Look at all the labels in here."

"So what, I like nice clothes."

"In my experience, women who are decked out in designer shit all the time are basically shallow. Everything about them is superficial."

"That is a prejudicial statement, Dupree. I thought musicians were more objective and broadminded. Could your limited experience with hardworking women have made you biased?"

"Ouch, touché, you brought a knife to a fist fight."

"I don't play. I'm a litigator, baby."

"Let's go back to the kitchen, the food is probably ready. I don't want you to have me up on charges if I burn it," he teased.

"You're a very quick study."

Victoria set the table, lit some candles, and refilled their wine glasses while Dupree put the finishing touches on the meal. When he brought the serving dishes in and sat down she grabbed his hand and said a short blessing over the food.

"I should probably remind you that I'm not a particularly religious person," he said, buttering up a slice of bread.

"I've missed more than a month of Sundays myself," she replied before she put a forkful of snapper in her mouth, "However, I always bless my food."

"It's a little more than that for me. I can barely remember going to church as a child and I've never gone since."

Victoria looked at him, stunned for a moment. Her whole childhood had revolved around her daddy's church. It was the foundation for her whole life.

She swallowed and said, "This is all so delicious. You can really cook."

"My mama was a good cook. I guess the deacon liked her cooking."

"Excuse me?" Victoria said, confused.

"My mama ran off with a deacon at the church when I was eight years old. All I know is his name was Brother Earl. My daddy raised us by himself after that. We never stepped into the doors of a church again, not even for my Grandmama's funeral. He never trusted women after that. He never brought another one in the house as far as I knew."

"Wow," Victoria said, taking a large gulp of wine, "That's a hard story. Did your mama ever get in contact with you again?"

"Nope, that's a closed book."

They ate in silence for a while enjoying the meal until the awkward moment passed.

"Thanks for preparing such a lovely dinner. I'm stuffed," Victoria said, gazing down at her empty plate. "Time for me to do the clean-up."

"It can wait," Dupree said. "Take some time to relax."

"Sounds good to me."

They went into the living room. Victoria turned on some music before they sat down.

"Put your feet up, lean back, and close your eyes," he directed.

She obliged him and he began rubbing her temples. His hands were strong but not calloused. Her head fell further back as her tensions dissolved under his hands. His hands moved down to her neck and into her shoulders.

"You have gifted hands. You make music, you cook, and you give a great massage."

"I also identify with the Rastafari way of life."

"So you smoke your share of ganja."

He kneaded deep into the muscles of her back.

"I do."

"Do you want to light some up now?"

"I wouldn't feel comfortable smoking ganja in the preacher's house."

"It's my house."

"Why don't you let me finish your massage upstairs? I have some oil I'd like to use and I don't want to get it all over the fabric of your sofa."

He grabbed the backpack he brought in.

Victoria chuckled, and then she stood up and walked up the steps. She wasn't sure what else Dupree had on his mind but the massage had her in a different state of mind.

"Why don't you undress before you lay down, it'll make it easier.

She gave him a look that questioned his sanity. He gave her a look of impatience.

"Don't worry, even in my limited experience I've seen all of the parts before."

"Is this supposed to be your technique of seduction?"

"No, I'm giving you a massage. If I was trying to get my body next to your body I would take your clothes off for myself."

"Okay, Marcus Garvey, do your thing."

Victoria nonchalantly undressed as if she were in the room by herself. She hung up her jeans, put her shoes into the closet, and put the other clothes in her bathroom hamper. Then she laid down on the left side of the bed and closed her eyes. Dupree rubbed her body down from her shoulders to the little toes on her feet. When he finished she was in a deep sleep.

***

Victoria woke up around 6:00 the next morning. She saw a note on the nightstand. It said, "Visit me at my place and I'll give you a private concert." She smiled to herself. It had been an interesting and pleasant evening, no pressure and no arguments. She got up and showered feeling as refreshed and content as a newborn baby. She put on some shorts and a t-shirt to clean up the mess from dinner but when she got downstairs the kitchen was immaculate. She walked into the dining room and it was spotless. Dupree had cleaned up before he left. He was an enigma to her, much different from any other guy she had spent time with. She was as guilty as he was in his judgment of her, she had assumed he was an easy-going carefree musician but he was as complex and full of deviations as a Rubik's cube.

Full of energy following a good meal and a good night's sleep, Victoria grabbed a baseball cap and a pair of sneaks out of the front closet and dashed out of the door for an early morning jog. It was peaceful during this time on Saturdays. Only a few in the neighborhood had ventured out for the mandatory walking of their dogs. Victoria jogged up the block towards Master's Street. She preferred to run in the opposite direction of traffic, it made her feel more secure. When she got to Columbia Ave, which had been changed to Cecil B. Moore Ave, she turned left and ran up to Broad Street. The whole atmosphere was totally different from the days when she held onto her momma's hand as she shopped.

Temple University had gradually engulfed the area over the years. The memory made her mouth dry as if she would choke. She made another left that would take her back in the direction of home for water.

Miss Judy was standing supported by her walker outside of her door when Victoria came running down the block.

"How are you this morning, Miss Judy?" she asked, approaching her door.

"Glad to see you in the land of the living," Miss Judy said.

"What do you mean?" Victoria asked, coming to meet her.

"I saw some strange man come out of your door in the middle of the night."

"That was Dupree. He made me a home-cooked dinner yesterday."

"You might want to let me know when you're having company. I was worried with you being on that case now. Lanetta stopped me from calling the cops."

"I'm sorry about that. Could I get a drink of water before I pass out?"

"Come on in, I was about to scramble some eggs, you can make the toast."

"Yes ma'am," Victoria said, holding the door for her.

Lanetta was lounging in the sitting area off the kitchen watching a re-run of the Jamie Foxx show when they walk in.

"Oh hell no," Lanetta chuckled, putting down the lift of the lay-z-boy chair and leaning forward. "You're out jogging this early after getting your groove on. What does that mean? It was either fantastic or pitiful."

"Have some respect," Miss Judy said, washing her hands at the sink.

"It was neither so stop tripping," Victoria remarked. "He cooked us a very nice dinner, massaged my neck, washed the dishes, and went home."

Lanetta stood up to help with the breakfast.

"Oh shit, that is amazing." she said, shaking her head in disbelief.

Miss Judy busied herself cracking the eggs while her skillet warmed up. Victoria washed the sweat off her hands and got some butter out of the refrigerator before she dropped four slices of rye bread into the toaster.

"What's so incredible about that?" Victoria asked. "We're getting to know each other. He's a real interesting guy."

Lanetta got out the plates and poured them all some orange juice.

"I thought this was a 'hit it and quit it' type of thing."

"First of all, I don't roll like that, I like him," Victoria said, buttering the hot toast.

"He's fine and all of that but he's not relationship material," Lanetta replied.

"You know he's a musician, they're rolling stones just like the Temptations sang," Miss Judy said, putting the steaming eggs on the table. "Music is his first and only true love and that's how that will be. He doesn't want anything more, no obligations, no attachments, and no responsibilities. Believe me when I tell you."

"How can you say that, you don't know him?" Victoria argued.

"Oh I know him all right," Miss Judy continued, "I lived with a man just like him when I was a senior in college. I was crazy about him. I even thought I wanted to marry him but he didn't have any ambition. Working a regular job was out of the question. All he cared about was his music, and it wasn't paying the bills."

"Wait a minute, Mama. I didn't know anything about this," Lanetta said, surprised.

"That goes to show, you don't know everything," Miss Judy said, bowing her head for grace.

Chapter Ten

By the Friday before Mother's Day, the storm in the city had reached an ebb. The protests around City Hall had dwindled some each day until there was just a handful remaining on Saturday mornings. The primary election was over and the attention of the press had shifted to the more scandalous Sandusky rape trial. However, the relief in the Mayor's office was short-lived after the release of the 911 tape to news outlets. The public heard the voice of Edward Landauer say the suspicious guy was black three times. They heard him say that he looked like he was on drugs. They heard him refer to him as an asshole. They heard the dispatcher tell him to wait for the police.

On Sunday, Mona Gardner was in the grips of despair, enduring her first Mother's day after Deshaun's death. Unable to get her out of bed Darren laid beside her. He turned on the TV to break the painful silence only to hear the recording of the man's voice who killed their son speaking to a dispatcher during the minutes he stalked him while they showed the street memorial that continued to grow for Deshaun. The horror of it paralyzed Mona for a moment before she could react.

She screamed at the top of her lungs. "No more!"

Darren shut the TV off but the damage had been done. He watched helplessly as her body twisted and contorted in agony.

"I'm sorry, honey. I'm so sorry," he said over and over again.

"Why do they have to keep torturing us?" she yelled painfully. "My son is dead."

"Let me take you to church, sweetie. I need to get out of the house for a while."

"For you I'll go but there isn't any peace left for me in this world."

"Don't say that, baby. We have to fight for Deshaun. We can't give up yet."

His words sobered her.

"You're right. I can't rest until that bastard is beneath the jail or six feet under."

The anger overpowered her sorrow and she swung her legs to the side of the bed and got on her feet. Darren breathed a sigh of relief. They would make it another day.

They walked into the sanctuary at the Christian Heart Interdenominational Church hand in hand just after 10:00. Several members stood up and greeted them as they walked up to the pew where they regularly sat midway to the front. Seated beside their pastor, Rev. Julius Monroe, was the ever-expedient Civil Rights representative, Rev. Lee Johnson. He smiled in satisfaction once they had arrived. He was anxious to make their acquaintance and be of service to them and the Philadelphia community in yet another fight against injustice. He felt sympathy for the loss they had suffered but like so many other instances, this was a chance to make tremendous gains, notoriety for his movement, and increased political leverage.

The choir sang "Precious Lord" and there were few dry eyes when Rev. Johnson walked to the pulpit and asked the congregation to join him in a march on City Hall. Rev. Monroe stood up in support, then Darren Gardner stood up and clapped, and the rest of the church followed suit. Rev. Johnson raised his hands and closed his eyes, thanking God for yet another opportunity.

***

By Monday morning the storm precipitated by the shooting had regained its strength and intensified with its eye over City Hall. Rev. Lee Johnson had made his presence known all over the city recruiting several thousand to march in protest of the injustices against the black community. His success had also served to generate a large number who had come to represent the opposing side. Marchers circled the center of town in a circumference of nearly four blocks. Anxious policemen armed to the teeth holding riot shields patrolled on all sides to contain the volatile situation. Eight park police wearing helmets were mounted on horses in a line like jockeys poised for a race.

The conglomeration of demonstrators corresponded to a number of gripes. Some held signs that blamed the police for slow response time, others wanted gun control, more wanted the Mayor to do something about the level of crime in the city, and others took issue with the Criminal Justice Department for not bringing first degree murder charges.

Parking was so far away from downtown that Victoria decided to take her daddy's car back to the house and catch the subway into work. She took off her Hugo Boss pantsuit and changed into a sundress with a straw hat and sunglasses. She put her files and iPad in a large flower print bag she threw over her shoulder. She slipped through the doors of the train just as the doors were closing. Outrage was the theme of the overlapping conversations that filled the train. Some praised Edward Landauer for his courage in patrolling his neighborhood. Most felt he was some type of creep with a mental problem playing cop.

"He stalked that boy, plain and simple," somebody hollered out.

"He shouldn't even be out on bail," another added.

"The dispatcher spent too much time talking, he should have

sent the cops right away, if he did the boy might still be alive."

"I'm sorry he shot that boy, he was a good kid, but it's the niggers out here raising pure hell that we need to hold responsible. They the one's got everybody scared to come out," an old black man sitting with his wife said.

If it wasn't for his age, the old man's words might have bought him a beat down, but that and his meek looking wife next to him gave him a pass.

Victoria filed off the train and mixed in with the crowd, thankful that no one had recognized her. Before she made it through the block to her office she had to show her badge five times. Arthur was standing outside of her office when she got off the elevator.

"Casual Friday at the beginning of the week," he smirked, noticing her outfit.

"It's my disguise for catching the train," she replied, opening the door to her office.

"Ingenious, I hope you have an equally clever plan to switch self-defense to murder."

She put down her things and sat at her desk.

"I don't have to, it was murder."

"The odds aren't in your favor."

"What do you mean?" she asked, baffled.

"The talk shows are saying he's not a criminal, just a pro-active member in his neighborhood looking out for the rest."

"Whose side are you on? Anyway, the people will have their day in court."

"Historically, when black goes against white in the courtroom, white usually wins."

"Thanks again for the vote of confidence."

"I know you're going to do a skillful prosecution, I just don't want you to take it personally."

"It's not personal, Arthur, it supposed to be justice."

Feeling a chill on her sleeveless arms, Victoria turned up the thermostat and opened her window. All of a sudden they heard the sound of breaking glass from the street below. Then sirens began to wail. Arthur rushed to the window beside her. The orderly march had given way to chaos, damn near a riot. Punches were being thrown between rival protesters and police encircling the pockets of violence were swinging their billy clubs with reckless abandon.

"I liked it better when they looted and burned up their own neighborhoods," Arthur said before turning and walking towards the door.

"Check yourself, your prejudice is showing," she called out to his back.

She watched the scene at the window for more than a half hour while the police struggled to subdue the crowd. The daily sparring matches between public and private mouthpieces had just begun. Still two months from the trial, the attacks were likely to become more vicious.

***

The partners of Rosen and Sullivan sat around the long walnut table in the conference room after a meeting with several of their senior attorneys. Benjamin Madison sat near the head with Thomas Clancy seated beside him.

"Gentlemen, is there anything else pertinent that we need to discuss before we adjourn?" Frederick Rosen asked.

Short glances were exchanged along and across the table.

"What about the Landauer case, Ben? That seems to be a lightning rod for controversy," Silas Sullivan asked curiously.

"It has started a media blitz and I don't see that subsiding for quite some time," Ben said.

"Looks like it woke up a lot of sleeping dogs in the camp," Rosen remarked. "They kill each other every day and nobody says a word. When a white man kills one, it's the end of the world."

Thomas Clancy shifted uncomfortably at the comment.

Ben responded. "Crimes between black and white are inflammatory and divisive. The skirmishes on City Hall this morning confirm that there is definitely a like-minded audience for our client."

"It's a shame we can't bill him for all the free publicity he's getting," Rosen added.

"He's not a celebrity so he really doesn't care for it," Ben said, thinking about Ed's attitude.

"Well, he'll be infamous just the same, whether he likes it or not," Rosen said.

"He'll love it if he comes out smelling like a rose," Sullivan said.

"I don't see how that's possible," Thomas interjected.

No one spoke for a moment. Had Thomas Clancy actually said something that could be interpreted as support for an African-American position or was it a lack of confidence in Benjamin? Thomas felt the air grow thick in the room around him and regretted his slip of the tongue. If only he could fade into the background of the woodwork and disappear. He tried to do damage control.

Thomas cleared his throat and said, "Mr. Landauer seems like a very private person."

"I understand," Sullivan said, nodding his head. "At any rate, I'd like to see you out there a bit more, Ben. After all, you are the pretty face of this firm. If your client doesn't want the publicity, we certainly do."

Rosen stood up. "If nothing further, I'm sure you gentlemen have plenty of work to do."

The room cleared quickly with Ben hanging back and touching Thomas's shoulder when he leaned forward to stand.

"Two things," Ben said. "First, I know you have been at this firm long enough to have developed very thick skin. Second, race doesn't interest me. I only care about winning. I hope we are on the same page."

"If that page says that I'm the co-counsel because my skin is black, then I understand completely," Thomas said tensely.

Ben stood up and patted Thomas twice on the back. It wasn't personal. That was just life as far as he was concerned. Nobody had the choice of cards they were dealt at birth. If you're dealt a bad hand, then you just have to learn to play your cards better than most. He felt Thomas needed to become comfortable playing the race card. To him it was kind of sad when a player refused to use his trump.

***

It was a tough week for the city. There were three more shootings, all gang-related. Newspaper headlines read "Murder Epidemic" and "Kill-adelphia" with sensational articles about the latest rash of homicides running through the Badlands, Fishtown, and West Philly. Police Commissioner Mancini escalated the unpopular 'stop-and-frisk' policy as his answer to public pressure and criticism. The jail and the courtrooms were jammed but Mayor Turner had spoken with Arthur Mitchell and insisted there would be no delay in the Commonwealth v. Edward Landauer. Jury selection would begin in seven weeks as scheduled.

The protests had quieted down after Rev. Lee Johnson left town and the media tide had turned. Emerson Landauer was making the rounds on TV news talk shows on behalf of his brother. He was a likable guy and pretty convincing in his arguments that Edward would never intentionally hurt anybody unless he was in grave danger. Ben Madison had been on all the major national networks including CNN, HLN, and FOX doing interviews about the insufficient efforts of law enforcement in fighting crime. Victoria sat in her office watching his latest. She had to give him props; he was making a persuasive case defending the frustrated public.

The prank phone calls to the office had become a regular occurrence. Criticism of the D.A.'s office grew and some even wanted the case tried by a state prosecutor. Editorials in the paper showed Victoria looking like a 'black Betty Boop' and Ben looking like Superman.

Chapter Eleven

"What are your plans for Memorial Day weekend?" Khloe asked while they stood waiting for the elevator at the end of the day.

"Having dinner with a friend," Victoria said, smiling. She could certainly use another home cooked meal and a massage after the week she'd had. "What about you? You've been working like a slave. Let it all go for a few days."

They stepped onto the elevator when the doors parted.

"How, I don't have a social life to speak of," Khloe complained, "I've been living here for almost a year and I haven't been out once."

"You're kidding."

"I'm not. The only men I've met are those here at work and the others who harass me on the way to the sandwich shop. All of them are off-limits."

They got off the elevator and walked through the lobby with Khloe griping.

"Stop, Miss Lonely, you're bringing tears to my eyes," Victoria laughed. "I'll hook you up. There's a big charity event that supports FIRST CHANCE, a foundation that sponsors the brightest and most talented students in the city on June fifteenth. It's a huge gala; all of the Philly's most eligible will be attending. We're going."

"Thanks, I guess I have to keep fantasizing about Ben Madison until then."

"You're breaking my heart, Khloe. If I didn't have a fine man waiting on me I would take you to happy hour."

"Have a good time," Khloe said, walking ahead out of the exit. "I'm good, I'll pick up some fresh batteries on my way home."

Victoria laughed all the way to her car. She put Dupree's address in the GPS of her phone, put in her *Who is Jill Scott?* CD, and drove out of the parking lot. She thought about stopping by the house when she turned onto Girard Avenue but she already had a change of clothes in the car. She sang along to *The Way* and caught a string of green lights and made it down to I-95 in less than ten minutes. She got off on Bridge Street which turned into Bustleton Ave, then drove past Roosevelt Blvd up further in the Northeast for several miles. *Brotha* was ending when she turned off onto Panorama Drive and up to 8023, the address he gave her.

When she saw the quaint single home with the detached garage and manicured lawn she rechecked the address before she got out of the car. She knocked on the door with hesitation. Her arm had barely reached her side when Dupree opened the door.

"Are you always waiting at the door?" she asked with a smile.

"Not always. Glad you made it," he said, giving her a welcome hug before he shut the door behind her. "I love your dress."

"I don't turn down free meals," she said, admiring the fireplace and hardwood floors. It wasn't at all what she had expected. She followed him into the modern kitchen with an island and through a back door to a deck where a barbecue grill was smoking. "This is a very nice spread you have out here."

"It belongs to a fellow musician friend of mine. I stay here whenever I'm not on the road. He's touring Europe playing with a rock band for the rest of this year."

Victoria sat down in one of the cushioned wicker chairs around a glass top table.

"Smells good, I hope it nearly done."

"We're going Jamaican today. I made you some jerk chicken, rice and peas, and cabbage and carrots. For dessert we're having dark gingerbread."

"I'm in heaven."

"Not yet, but I hope to take you there," he said with a hint, pouring her a rum and coke.

"Is a massage on the menu?"

"Without question, ma'am."

Victoria chuckled and lifted up her glass in a salute before she drank some.

"Hmm, that hit the spot," she said, beginning to unwind.

"You don't mind eating outside do you?" he asked, taking the food off the grill.

"Of course not, this is a great set-up."

Dupree made two plates and brought them over to the table.

"So how was your day?"

"It was crazy. I don't want to even think about it right now."

She said her grace then dug into the chicken with one hand and a fork in the other.

"It looks like you spent the whole day preparing this."

"Not really, cooking relaxes me."

She nodded and smiled. "Eating relaxes me."

Her cell phone rang but she ignored it. Dupree finished and watched her eat.

After a while he said, "I'd like you to do something for me."

"What is it?" she asked nonchalantly.

"Would you turn off your cell phone? I want your full uninterrupted attention this evening."

"Sure, I can do that."

Victoria reached in her bag for her phone and pressed the off button. Dupree held up a long thin cigar.

"Do you mind if I smoke?"

"Go ahead, you're at home."

He smoked in silence while Victoria enjoyed a slice of the gingerbread. She could smell the pungent ganja as it permeated the air around them. The sun was setting and the sky looked magnificent. She leaned back in her chair with her glass of rum and coke. He put down his cigar and lifted his sax out of its case next to him.

"Are you ready for your private concert?"

"I'd love it but I couldn't ask for anything more after that dinner."

"Yes you can. I'm here to serve at your pleasure."

"Like I said, I'm in heaven."

Dupree played a medley of romantic tunes of old school mixed with neo-soul. He did some Luther Vandross and Sade, and some Erykah Badu and Maxwell. Victoria kicked off her shoes and closed her eyes and she could almost feel the music circling in waves with the light winds around her. The emotion-filled notes transported her to a place where nothing else existed. It was probably due in part to the contact high she got from Duprees's cigar and her second rum and coke. She was so absorbed that she wasn't aware when the music stopped.

"How do you feel?" he asked, gently rubbing his hand along the side of her arm.

"I told you I'm in heaven."

He grabbed both her hands and lifted her up from the chair.

"Come inside with me, I want to join you."

He held the back door and she walked into the house. He took her by the hand and led her to his bedroom. The music never stopped, it flowed throughout the house. His room was like an island retreat. The walls and ceiling were light blue, the throw rug was a thick shag of aqua, and large tropical flowers filled the corners. There wasn't a headboard on the bed, just a pile of pillows in varying shades of beige and brown.

He pulled her close in his arms and kissed her mouth gently and affectionately like she seen him do to the mouthpiece of his sax.

"Sit down, I'll get the oil," he said.

He lit several candles and the room began to glow like hot coals. Victoria watched him pull off his shirt and untie his hair. He came over to the bed and pulled the sash on her dress, it unraveled and he slipped it off of her shoulders. He poured the lightly scented oil in his palm and rubbed his hands together. He started at her temples.

"You're a very beautiful woman," he said in a low voice, "I noticed you when you first walked in the door at Warm Daddy's."

"You captured my attention when you played. It's intense."

His hands moved down her neck and back. He took off the rest of her clothes and rubbed her entire body. Victoria was enthralled, almost hypnotized by the rhythm of his touch. She didn't even realize when his tongue had finished the job his hands had begun. In ecstasy she climbed on top of him and their bodies danced to the music.

"Now I'm in heaven," he said, kissing her again.

***

For a moment Victoria didn't know where she was when she woke the next morning. Then Dupree walked over to the bed fully dressed with his hair pulled back in a ponytail.

"I ran you a bath. Get it while it's hot," he said, smiling.

Victoria was stunned. This was a first. Nobody had drawn her a bath since she was five years old, and that was her momma. She slid out of bed.

"That's another invite I can't turn down but you didn't have to do that."

"It's my pleasure. Do you need some clothes?"

"I have a bag out in the trunk."

"I'll get it."

He handed her a towel and left the room.

"Wow," Victoria whispered, easing down in the hot water.

It was puzzling to her that a man who said his mother ran off would be this attentive and caring for women. He was almost too good to be true. When she got out of the tub her bag was waiting in the bedroom. She put on the jeans and a t-shirt.

"So what are your plans for the day?" he asked when she found him out smoking on the deck. "I've got to play tonight but we can spend the day together."

"I've got some things to do around the house," Victoria answered, feeling a little awkward.

"Come with me to South Ninth Street first and then I'll drive you home."

"Okay, let's do it."

Victoria got her bags and met him at the front door. He locked it, took her overnight bag and put it in the trunk, and opened the passenger side of the car for her. It was with much trepidation that she got in. He walked around, got in, and started the engine.

"This was my daddy's car," she said sternly.

"I can see that he took great care of it."

"Nobody else has driven it besides him and me."

"If you're uncomfortable we can take my car," he replied, considerately.

"No, it's all right, just be careful."

He patted her on the leg.

"I intend to."

Victoria let the window down and inhaled the fresh morning air. She was thankful for the silence as they drove. It gave her time to hear her inner voice. It was asking her the same questions that Lanetta had asked. How far was she going with Dupree? Was this the end of her escapade with a sexy saxophone player or was it the beginning of a relationship?

When they got to South Philly he stopped at Global Crepes and Local Shakes. Victoria got a smoothie and Dupree ordered a Nutella latte and a crepe with hummus, feta cheese, olives, and dried tomatoes.

"I enjoyed your company last night, Vicki."

"It was a great evening," she replied.

She studied him in the natural light while he ate. The undertones of his skin, the shape of his hairline, the smoothness of his lips, even the way he held the fork.

"Have some?" he asked politely.

"No, I like watching you eat."

When they were done he paid the check and they strolled up one side of South Ninth and then down the other. Dupree brought spices, coffee beans, and some fresh fruit. Walking behind him, Victoria's thoughts went back to the many Saturdays that she strode just behind her mother's heels along the same streets, stopping at the same corners and stores along the market. Her mom would hunt for bargains for hours, only giving up the chase when they couldn't carry another bag. Not much had changed. The fresh fish in barrels and the slaughtered cows and pigs hanging in the windows still fascinated her. It was the idea of something that had once been alive had been killed and prepared as food to cook and eat. It seemed barbaric in some way, but she had never been moved enough to become a vegetarian. The thought of depriving herself of the taste of meat would be cruel and unusual.

Back in the car, Dupree drove down Fifth Street to avoid the downtown traffic. The morning had gone quickly and she had a long list of things she had to do before the weekend was over. He pulled into Custis Place and right away Victoria could see something was wrong. 'Old Faithful' had barely stopped when she threw the door open and jumped out. She stood there dazed. Then it hit her like a punch in the stomach. Her legs turned to rubber and she crumpled to the ground. Miss Judy and Lanetta came out as soon as they heard the car. Dupree helped Lanetta lift Victoria to her feet but her eyes were transfixed on the front picture window of the house. It had been shattered and the French sheers her mama had ordered just before she died were hanging out and blowing in the gentle breeze.

"It happened last night," Miss Judy said. "I tried to call you."

Then Victoria remembered that her phone was still turned off.

"We heard the glass break and then the sound of a truck speeding away," Lanetta added.

Miss Judy took her hand. "Come on in the house for a minute and sit down, child. I'll get you a glass of water."

Dupree followed the women inside. Victoria sat down in the nearest chair. Dupree stood behind her rubbing her shoulders while Miss Judy poured her a glass of cold water.

"I used our key to get in the house. I found this on the floor in the living room," Lanetta said, bringing a brick into the kitchen. "It had this note attached to it with a rubber band."

Victoria took the wrinkled piece of paper and silently read the words haphazardly written on it. "Leave it alone, nigger bitch, or the next one will be upside your head. Landauer better walk or this place will burn."

Dupree took it out of her hands and read it.

"Do you want me to call the police, Vicki?" Miss Judy asked.

"What can they do?" Victoria wondered out loud. "No, I'll report it when I get to work on Tuesday. I've been getting some prank calls at my office too."

Dupree finally spoke. "It's only going to get worse as the trial gets closer and then who knows how the crazies will react."

"It's just to intimidate you, Vick," Lanetta said furiously. "They just want that white boy to walk. We're not having it this time. You know I got you covered, sister."

"I'm not going to let it worry me but you two are my family, I don't want to put you in the line of fire," Victoria said softly, still upset.

"I want you to stay with me for a while, at least until you figure out who's fucking with you," Dupree said firmly. "More police around here is only going to draw more attention, then it could get seriously dangerous."

Victoria's brain was congested, there were too many thoughts speeding in every direction. The other voices around her were only adding to the confusion. What was her next move? It wasn't in her character to act on impulse. She needed some time to think and clear her head. There were too many people in the room.

"Give me a minute," she said, standing up. "I'm going to check on the house."

Dupree followed her to the door. "I'll go get something to fix the window."

"You can get some plywood at Kessler's up on Girard," Miss Judy shouted behind him.

Victoria slowly opened the front door and walked in. She saw the broken glass on the carpet before she reached the top of the short flight of stairs. Glass was splattered over the sofa and the coffee table where she kept the magazines displayed just like her momma liked them. Nothing else had been disturbed. The kitchen was just as she left it. She got the broom and dust pan and swept up the glass. One thing was already clear in her mind. She wasn't going to jeopardize her momma and daddy's house or the only family she had left next door. She would stay with Dupree for the time being.

She sat down in her daddy's chair and tried to think of what he would say to her. She closed her eyes straining to hear his voice. Was this case worth the trouble it had cost her so far? Arthur wouldn't fight her if she made a deal or passed it to someone else. What about Deshaun, the talented kid robbed of his life? She had given her word to Mona Gardner. Then she got mad.

She was nobody's puppet. She never allowed anybody to

manipulate her. She had already made up her mind weeks ago. Some fool trying to scare her wasn't going to change that.

Dupree came through the door with a piece of plywood to board up the window.

"I'll pack some things to take with me," she said, going up the steps.

He nodded his head, relieved. "Okay."

Dupree put the two large suitcases in the trunk of 'Old Faithful' while Victoria went to talk with Miss Judy and Lanetta.

She wrapped her arms around Miss Judy. "I don't know how long I'll be away but I'll keep in touch." She gave Lanetta a high-five and walked towards the car.

"Do me a favor and leave your phone on, child," Miss Judy called after her. "My heart can't take all of this drama."

***

"I heard what happened. How are you?" Khloe asked frantically, bursting into Victoria's office on Tuesday morning. "What did the police say?"

"Calm down, I'm fine. There wasn't anything to go on and nobody saw the truck. They've put a monitor on my office phone to see if they can trace the calls."

"Do you want to stay at my place or do you want me to stay with you?"

"It's not necessary. I'm staying out in the Northeast with a friend."

"Would that be the same friend who cooked dinner for you on Friday?"

Victoria couldn't hide her smile. "Yes, that's the one."

"Sounds like you're not too upset about it."

"I'm just rolling with the punches, Khloe."

"That's good because another witness has come forward saying he saw Deshaun punch Edward Landauer in the face."

"Why did he wait so long to come forward?"

"It's a woman, she says that she didn't want to get involved before. Supposedly, now her conscious is bothering her."

"Have Carlton or Rosario talked to her yet?"

"They're meeting with her this morning."

The phone rang and they both froze. Victoria looked at the caller ID.

"Who is it?" Khloe asked nervously.

"It's Ben Madison."

"He probably wants to talk a deal. What are you going to do?"

"I'm going to let it ring."

Chapter Twelve

The trial was just over a month away when Victoria stood in the lobby of the Criminal Justice Center filled with her colleagues, judges, and numerous community leaders for the ceremony re-dedicating and re-naming the Criminal Justice Center building after Justice Juanita Kidd Stout. She was the first African American woman to serve on the Pennsylvania Supreme Court. To Victoria she was the hero who had paved the way for her and so many other black attorneys.

Over the next two weeks, Victoria's days at work were challenging to say the least. She practically felt like she was bipolar. Between the high volumes of cases coming in the office, she spent her time doing research and fielding phone calls from Ben Madison, the Gardners, their attorney, Christian Booker, reporters, and pranks. Her nights were effortless with Dupree providing her with delicious meals, serenades, massages, and all the loving she wanted.

Last night it flipped, she and Dupree had their first disagreement and it caught her by surprise. Generally, he was always willing to do whatever pleased her. She didn't think it was a big deal, but as far as he was concerned it was non-negotiable.

When he came home from the club she was lying in bed reading. She closed her book and mentioned the FIRST CHANCE gala that was coming up on the weekend.

"Babe, I was thinking it would be nice if you rented a tuxedo to wear on Saturday."

He took a breath. "I didn't realize that you expected me to go with you. I was planning on going with the fellas to a gig in Baltimore."

"Of course I was expecting you to go with me. Who else is going to be my date?"

"I'm sure there will be quite a few of your colleagues there."

"I want us to go together."

"It's not my scene, Vicki."

"It's a cause and an event that is very important to me."

"Then go and have a good time."

"I would like to have a good time with you there. I don't have a problem hanging out with your musician buddies. Why can't you give me the same consideration?"

"There's not much I wouldn't do for you, but I draw a line with that bougie crowd. I'm not an actor so why should I spend an evening pretending."

Victoria was tired and didn't feel like arguing so she turned her back and went to sleep.

***

"What do you wear to a gala, I might need to buy a dress," Khloe asked after her Wednesday morning case load.

"If you don't have a formal gown, girlfriend, it's time to go to Lord & Taylor's. You'll need to look red carpet ready with hair and make-up glam. All the 'Who's who" of Philly will be there putting on some serious airs."

"It sounds serious. I'll need all of Friday to pull myself together."

"Do what you have to do and come correct. You might see an eligible bachelor."

"Are you bringing your mystery man?"

"Unfortunately not, you'll be my only escort. I usually share a table with some old college friends of mine."

"I can't wait to see how the other half lives."

Victoria had to laugh. "I don't think its half, try 10 percent."

She had to shake her head when she thought about Dupree's objections to going with her to the benefit for FIRST CHANCE. What was the big deal? It was three days away and she was looking forward to it. She had been keeping a low-profile for more than two months and she wanted to get dressed up and go out for a night of socializing. She needed to forget about all the pressures and responsibilities that had become her constant companions since she was assigned the Edward Landauer case. With all the hats and disguises she was using to sneak around town she needed a hair and spa treatment to look like herself again. Moreover, she had a great dress she bought on sale after Christmas last year that begged to be worn.

***

Dupree got up early on Saturday morning, the band was leaving to play for the summer festival in D.C. before their night gig in Baltimore. Victoria had finally accepted his decision and was happy to have some time to herself to get ready for the evening. She left the house right after him, driving 'Old faithful' back to North Philly to her familiar stomping grounds. She didn't care who might recognize her or what they might say, she needed a manicure and a pedicure and the Dominican shop on Girard Ave across Broad Street was the only place she trusted to fix her hair for this occasion, they always worked magic.

After two and a half hours of beautifying, Victoria pulled into her driveway at Custis Place. Positioned in her favorite spot, Miss Judy greeted Victoria when she got out of the car.

"You're looking good, child. It's good to see you back home," she called out.

Victoria walked over for a minute to talk.

"I missed you two. How are you feeling?"

"You know me, I'm not going to let anything hold me down. You look pretty, are you going to the benefit ball?"

"Yes ma'am. I'm not going to let these crazy people keep me locked down."

"Now that's the Vicki I know talking. You don't need to stay way out in East-Nowhere under that man. I can look out for you myself, right here."

"I know that, but for now he takes my mind off of work."

Miss Judy smirked. "I bet he does."

"Where's Lanetta this morning?" Victoria asked, changing the subject.

"She went to Atlantic City for the weekend."

Victoria smiled. "That's something I haven't done in a while."

"Well, when you get done with the trial, you and I are going to take that ride. They have a bunch of money up there with my name on it."

"I'm going to hold you to that one," Victoria said, moving towards the steps.

"Please do," Miss Judy said, "In the meantime go on and get ready for you night out."

***

Victoria gazed at her reflection in the full length mirror. At first, she had questioned whether she should wear the red gown, but the woman looking back at her removed all her reservations. It definitely made a statement. "Why shouldn't she stand out in the crowd?" She didn't need to blend into the background, she hadn't committed any crime. Her cell phone beeped at 7:30. In a quick glance she saw it was Khloe texting she was outside. Quickly, she put on the ruby earrings that Leonard had given her for Valentine's Day and tucked the cell phone in her evening bag and tiptoed carefully down the stairs and out the door in her five-inch satin Manolos.

Victoria could see Khloe was radiant in a soft yellow gown when she opened the car door.

"You know you are allowed to ring the doorbell and come into the house," Victoria joked as she got her dress situated in the passenger seat. "You're making me feel bad."

"Don't, I'm only saving my feet," Khloe said.

"That's the price of beauty, lady, sore feet. Anyway, you look gorgeous."

"Thank you, and you look hot in that red."

"That's the idea, it's my power color."

Khloe pulled out onto 12th Street.

"What's the best way to get to the Rittenhouse Hotel?"

"Drive down 15th Street all the way to Walnut Street and then make a left on 19th Street. Tonight we're not sparing any expense, use the valet parking."

It was just before 8:00 when Khloe drove into the front entrance around the statue of the girl in the water fountain of the hotel and handed the valet her keys.

"This is definitely first-class," she said, tucking away the small ticket in her sequined bag.

"Five-stars, baby. This is how the 10 percent live," Victoria said, leading the way through the golden doors to the reception area outside the ballroom.

Their steps were silent across the dense carpet in the atrium and the deep yellow ceiling emitted a glow. The soft music from a classical jazz quartet grew louder as they got closer to the ballroom. All of the hosts in the reception area were dressed in black trousers, white shirts with a black vest, and white gloves. One of the hosts offers them a glass of champagne from his tray.

"I feel like Cinderella," Khloe whispered.

Victoria held up her glass for a toast.

"Have yourself a ball because tomorrow we wake back up in the real world."

They sipped from the tall flutes while Victoria pointed out the mayor and his wife, the CEOs of Cigna, Sunoco, and Comcast, the leading partner at Fox Rothschild, and Will Smith's parents. She searched the atrium for another familiar face and nearly dropped her glass when she saw Leonard across the room with Simone Moore, a popular stage actress in the city. Suddenly the burnt orange walls with gold-toned oriental rugs made her feel like she was on fire.

"Let's go in and find our table," she said abruptly, placing her half-filled glass on an empty tray outside of the ballroom.

"I'm right behind you," Khloe replied, following suit.

Victoria made her way to the table she shared with her college cronies, some had done well for themselves, and the others were still benefiting from the success of their mamas and daddies. There was Marvin Campbell, she had known him since elementary school, he grew up around the corner from her and played basketball at Temple. Now he warmed the bench for the 76ers. He always brought his girlfriend of five years, Tamika, who he had no plans of marrying. There was Angeline Irving, they had been roommates in her sophomore year. Her parents were part owners of the local Coca-Cola Bottling Company. She had married one of her father's colleagues, Gerald Davis, who was seventeen years older than her. Then there was Joshua Blackmon, they met in their freshman year, he had started his own software company and sold it to a division of Microsoft. He married Hannah, his white trophy wife, three years ago. They were all there munching on hors d'oeuvres. Only two seats at the table remained empty.

"Hello, hello, ladies and gentlemen. I haven't seen you uppity niggers since Christmas," Victoria said boisterously.

"I wasn't sure if we were going to see you tonight," Angeline said, smiling.

"You should know I would never miss an opportunity to see you all," Victoria said, taking a seat. "This is Khloe Luskin, a new attorney in the office."

"Welcome, Khloe," Hannah chimed in, "It's so nice to have some company at the table."

They all laughed, introduced themselves, and spent the next few minutes catching up while the hostess refreshed their glasses. Then Khloe noticed Ben Madison at the buffet table.

"Vicki, why don't we get some food to soak up this champagne?"

"That's a good idea," she answered, rising from the table.

At the beginning of the table they picked up crystal plates and small forks. Victoria was trying to choose between smoked salmon, tempura lobster, and baby lamb chops when she heard a familiar voice and felt warm breath on her neck.

"Good evening, counselor," Ben said pleasantly, "You look beautiful as always."

"Good evening, Ben, and thank you. You're looking very dapper as usual."

"I've been wanting to speak with you, can we meet sometime next week?"

Victoria had no intentions of meeting with Ben outside of the courtroom. He could weave a spell like a magician and she needed her wits about her.

"You remember, Khloe, she's my co-counsel," Victoria said, stepping to the side. "You can contact her about any concerns you may have."

Khloe turned around eagerly and said, "I'd be happy to meet with you, Mr. Madison."

Victoria chose some baby lamb chops and hurried back to the safety of the table. She wasn't ready to bump into Leonard and his new lady.

The music stopped and Leonard walked over to the podium to introduce the mayor. Victoria could feel stares from around the room, and the eyes at her own table were glaring at her as he spoke and it gave her chills. She focused on the small bones on her plate and listened as the mayor came forward and gave the history of the FIRST CHANCE foundation. The program continued with the amount of funds that had been raised, the success stories of students who received grants, and ended with awards to new scholarship recipients.

The music began again and they were served a three course meal of cauliflower soup, roasted quail or filet mignon, and pistachio mousse cake. The hostess served coffee after the tables were cleared. Some of the older couples in the room had gotten up to dance to the smooth jazz before the dee-jay came on at 10:00 to get the party started.

"Come on, Khloe," Hannah said, standing up, "I want to introduce you to some of my white associates that are here."

They all laughed again.

"It's about time," Joshua said. "Now we men can go out and have a smoke and a real drink."

The men excused themselves from the table.

"Now we women can talk," Tamika said with her eyes on Victoria.

Angeline spoke up next. "What is going on Vicki? You didn't tell me that you and Leonard had broken up."

"It wasn't a big deal. We both were really busy and just drifted apart. He realized that he didn't want a woman with her own career."

"I can see that," Tamika said sarcastically, "That bitch hasn't had an acting part in two years."

"You should have told me, girl. I have somebody I want to introduce you to," Angeline said.

"I'm seeing someone right now," Victoria replied.

"Have you lost my number?" Angeline asked curtly. "You know I'm your BFF, and I haven't heard about any of this."

"This shooting case is occupying all of my time right time. I've been out of touch."

"Not with everybody," Tamika added.

"Give us the news," Angeline demanded.

"His name is Dupree. He's a musician, I met him at the Blue Note. He plays the saxophone in a band called the Voyagers," Victoria said.

Angeline was taken aback. "Are you for real? A musician. He's below you, girl."

"He's there for me. He handles everything I need taken care of, he cooks, cleans, and takes me wherever I need to go," Victoria said in his defense.

"He sounds like he's more of a woman than a man," Tamika blurted out.

Victoria was insulted. "Don't get it twisted, he's all man. I don't need anybody to lead me or dominate me. I'm financially stable. I'm content, I'm happy."

"But he doesn't have anything else to bring to the table," Angeline fussed.

"I don't need anything else," Victoria explained.

"You're going to let a total package like Leonard go for a musician?" Tamika asked, wondering if Victoria had gone crazy.

"I'm not going to lie, it gave me the vapors to see him with somebody else," Victoria admitted, "But I'm cool now."

"Come on, Vicki, we all want that knight in shining armor," Tamika said,

"Only those of us who still believe in fairytales," Victoria chided.

"Okay, we'll leave it alone for now, it's not serious enough to ruin the night over," Angeline said. "We came here to have a good time."

Victoria breathed a sigh of relief.

The quartet stopped playing as the lights dimmed. The dee-jay pumped up the volume with an old-school tune just as Marvin, Gerald, and Joshua made their way back to the table.

"Don't even think about sitting down, old man," Angeline told Gerald.

"That's why I'm here, I know you're ready to get out on the floor," Gerald responded.

Marvin stood behind Tamika's chair. "We're going to have to cut out early on you guys, I've got an early plane to catch to Miami in the morning."

"Come on Marvin, the 76ers are not in the playoffs," Joshua kidded.

"I can't miss game one of the finals, man," Marvin said, bumping his fist.

"I heard that," Joshua said, looking around the room for Hannah. "I don't know where my wife wandered off to."

"She must be at a private party with some of her white people," Tamika said, standing up to leave. "Give me a call sometime, Vicki."

Then Khloe came back to the table alone.

"I think I need to find that party," Joshua said, following Marvin and Tamika out of the ballroom.

"Are you having a nice time?" Victoria asked Khloe.

"Absolutely, I just came to give you the keys to the car. I'm going upstairs with my prince."

"Oooh, Khloe, I had no idea you were so…, how do I put it politely, so progressive," Victoria teased.

"I'm horny, so what. I hope you haven't had too much champagne to drive your own ass home."

"I'm fine, go on and handle your business, the batteries deserve a rest tonight."

Khloe dropped the keys on the table and disappeared into a large group mingling together. Victoria sat alone at the table watching the crowd dance and groove in unison to the cupid shuffle. Hypnotized by the steady beat of the music her mind drifted to another place. She was drawn out of her reverie when Leonard sat down beside her.

"Do you want to dance?" he asked.

"No, I was just getting ready to leave."

"By yourself?"

"Yes, tonight I am."

"I heard you were seeing somebody."

Victoria changed the subject. "What about you, have you finally found you first lady?"

"I thought I had but she wouldn't cooperate. Now I'm still looking."

"Stop it, Len, how could I stand by you if you wouldn't stand by me. Your passion is power, I was just a fixture."

"It wasn't that, Vee, I was concerned about our futures and I'm sorry if I didn't articulate it in a better way."

"In any case, you're safe out of the line of fire with a new woman on your arm."

"You know I'm still here for you. Word is you've had some threats and some problems at the house. I want to help. Talk to me."

"I can't think of anything to say, Len."

Leonard didn't know how to respond. In the midst of the only quiet spot in the room, Victoria scooted her chair back so she could stand, picked up the keys and her evening bag and walked out of the Rittenhouse. She drove back to her house and got in her own bed.

* * *

Victoria was back in the Northeast when Dupree came home on Sunday evening. She was happy to see him but the mystique that surrounded him when they first met had begun to dissipate. He wasn't her musical magic man there to grant all of her wishes. He was imperfect, a mortal man of her own world.

Chapter Thirteen

The latest bout of turmoil in the city had begun to subside. Victoria hadn't gotten any of the crazy prank calls in four days and her apprehensions about her safety had steadily waned. Dupree was still protective and attentive but she spent most of her time at the office researching and preparing for the trial.

A week before the court date, photo journalists and reporters from all over the country returned to the scene of the crime, Harbor Street. They were doing interviews with people in the neighborhood about their thoughts on the upcoming trial. Some were glad that the whole drama would be over soon. Some expressed that there shouldn't even be a trial. There were rumors that the gang Jamaal belonged to had sworn there would be revenge for Deshaun's murder. Mayor Turner upped his profile and was seen on all the local channels making a plea for peace and patience, asking the city to allow the justice system to do its work.

Alta and Laramie Landauer spoke to Nancy Grace in an interview.

"What are your feelings as the trial approaches?" Ms. Grace asked.

"We are very hopeful that justice will prevail and Edward will be able to go on with his life," Alta Landauer said with sincerity. "Eddie is a good person. He never set out to hurt anybody. The truth will set him free in the end."

Nancy turned her attention to Laramie. "Mr. Landauer, many

people and protesters have called your son a racist killer. What do you have to say to them?"

"My son is not a racist. I raised my boys to treat everybody as equals."

"From what I've seen of him during the preliminary hearing, he seems angry or entitled," Nancy said, digging for a stronger reaction.

"That's my fault. I was a military man and I raised my sons to shield their emotions, particularly in public. He is very upset, he has been a victim in all this."

"Deshaun Gardner's parents have lost their son. What would you say to them?"

Alta spoke up quickly. "I am very sorry for the pain they have had to endure. I wish none of this had happened. I keep them in my prayers every night."

More interviews with Darren Gardner, and their attorney Christian Booker, were seen on the major channels as well with him expressing the nightmare that his family still lived in daily. He talked about his wife, Mona, how she was currently in the hospital close to a nervous breakdown. He said he was anxious to see Edward Landauer found guilty.

Ben Madison with Thomas Clancy by his side, did his final rounds on the talk circuit. Benjamin was getting the bulk of the invitations from the networks; he had the looks and the charisma that the camera loves. They seemed disinterested in Ed Landauer, he didn't draw ratings, but they all couldn't get enough of Benjamin Madison. He was a top-notch attorney, played a mean game of tennis, and he was the most eligible bachelor in Philly.

***

It was Saturday night, the weekend before the trial was to begin. Victoria was sitting out on the patio with Dupree. They had just finished a light dinner. He was leaning against a maple tree smoking while she lounged on a chaise sipping on a rum and coke. She had made a decision after the FIRST CHANCE Ball but she hadn't shared it. She watched the smoke from his blunt curl and rise in the air and disappear into the atmosphere. It calmed her nerves and reminded her of the times she would sit beside her daddy and watch the fish swim in their 50-gallon tank.

"Dupree, there's something I want to talk to you about."

He tapped the blunt against the tree to kill the light.

"What's up?"

"Jury selection begins on Tuesday. I truly appreciate you opening up your space to me but I've decided that I want to stay at my own house during the trial. Mentally it's better for me to be in my own element, it's my foundation."

"I can understand that, but I don't think it's actually safe for you right now."

"That's a risk I'm willing to take. I believe it will pay off for me in the long run."

"I'd like to come and stay with you if that's not a problem."

Relieved, she stood up and wrapped her arms around him.

"It's definitely not a problem."

On Sunday night she packed up her suitcases and they drove back to North Philly.

***

For so long it seemed like this day would never come. Victoria had felt she was ready to try the case two months ago, now she wasn't so sure. She had spent all of Monday afternoon listening to the 911 call that Edward Landauer had made. She stood in the shower praying to God that he would give her the wisdom and words to win this case. She wished she had gone to church on Sunday to demonstrate her faith and worthiness for her prayer to be answered. Her daddy would have advised her to ask for blessings before she went into this battle. But she didn't want to be a dark day member, the ones who only come to church when they want something or when things have fallen apart. She could see her mama shaking her head in dismay.

She scanned the closet for the perfect opening day ensemble, something conservative but fashionable, confident but not arrogant. To match the seriousness of the day she chose a black sheath dress with a matching tan jacket trimmed in black. She slid on her tan and black spectator pumps and added her mama's pearl necklace and earrings for the finishing touch.

Dupree had made her an omelet for breakfast. She ate it for energy even though her head and stomach felt like she had a bad case of sea sickness.

"To be on the safe side, I'll drop you off today," Dupree said while Victoria reapplied her lipstick. "I think you should catch a cab home, I'm gigging at Warm Daddy's this evening."

"That's cool. Khloe can drop me home at the end of the day."

Victoria kept all of her files and notes with her in her briefcase. She was prepared to go straight to the courtroom. She texted Khloe to meet her there. Then her phone rang while it was still in her hand. It was Arthur asking her to stop by his office when she arrived.

No parking signs were strung for more than a block away from the Justice Center. Protesters with signs held high that said, "No Justice, No Peace" marched in silence along the sidewalk. Another group stood across the street with signs that said, "We're Fighting Back."

After a quick goodbye kiss and a deep breath on the corner of Penn Center Square, Victoria stepped out of Dupree's car onto the curb. When she got to Arthur's office his secretary greeted her with a compassionate smile as if she were going off to war in a foreign country.

"Go on in, he's waiting for you," she said caringly.

Victoria walked into his office and he motioned for her to take a seat.

"Good morning, Victoria. I wanted to tell you that I have total confidence in your ability to try this case. You have my full support. Don't hesitate to ask for any assistance that you may need over the course of this trial."

"Thank you, sir, I appreciate that."

Victoria rose to her feet and shook his hand on her way out. She wondered what all the formality was about. It made her even more nervous. Arthur had never given her a pep-talk in all the years she had worked in the D.A.'s office. On impulse she took the stairs down to the first floor hoping it would burn off some of her anxiety.

On the north side of City Hall, Victoria walked into the frenzy of reporters. Police wearing riot gear were positioned outside of the chain-link fences that had been put up against the concrete barricades that surrounded the building. Flashing her ID, Victoria pushed her way through the mass of people at the entrance. A cacophony of questions were shouted at her from the left and right crashing against her head like cymbals.

She kept repeating herself as she moved forward.

"No comment. No comment."

The entrance to Courtroom 1105 was blocked by an overflow of spectators, reporters, and security. Cameras were being excluded from the jury selection process. Without a word spoken, a path opened for her to enter. She felt a pat to her shoulder from someone but she looked ahead not making eye contact. She walked up the aisle of the gallery and through the swinging gate. Khloe was already seated at their table on the right.

Victoria had barely taken her seat when a roar of combined voices at the rear of the courtroom stunned them all. She turned around to see Ben Madison stroll in like a model on the runway with Edward Landauer just behind him on the left, followed by Thomas Clancy, and in the rear his legal assistant. He gave a polite nod towards Victoria and Khloe. A few steps behind them were

Alta and Laramie Landauer and their son, Emerson. They sat on the first row behind the defense table. Then a quiet filled the room that was deafening. Victoria turned again to see Christian Booker escorting Darren and Mona Gardner into the courtroom.

Every seat in the courtroom was taken when the bailiff came in and announced, "All rise! The Common Pleas Court is now in session. The Honorable Eugene Kelly presiding."

Judge Kelly walked in at 8:59 without looking into the gallery with his court clerk, Mary Brigman, walking in behind him. He eased into his chair and only then faced the courtroom. He and his clerk are a contrast of images, he's pale, tall and gaunt, with a thick head of curly gray hair, and she's a short plump black woman with a long straight weave with blonde streaks.

"Docket number 7631481," the court officer stated, "The Commonwealth versus Edward Landauer."

Judge Kelly instructed the bailiff to bring in the panel of jurors. There were forty-seven in the group, a diverse mix of men and women, white, black, and Hispanic.

Victoria had spent hours speculating on the preferred juror for the prosecution. Ideally they would be black and under 55 years old, the rest were questionable at best. The potential panel of random jurors sitting in the crowded courtroom had viewed the orientation video and completed the questionnaire stating they were U.S. citizens, over 18 years of age, and could read, write, and speak English. They had been given badges and assigned juror numbers for the voir dire process.

The court clerk, Mary, read the swear to the jury panel.

"Do you, and each of you, understand and agree that you will accurately and truthfully answer, under penalty of perjury, all questions put to you concerning your qualifications and competency to serve as a trial juror in the pending matter before this court?"

They answered in flurries of yes, I do, and we do.

Then the jury was addressed by Judge Kelly.

"Are you all US citizens and residents of Philadelphia County?"

After confirmations, Judge Kelly went through with the formality where he told the potential jurors about the case that would be heard and the names of the persons involved. When he asked them if there was any reason why they couldn't be fair or impartial there was no response.

"The Commonwealth may begin its examination of the panel," Judge Kelly said.

Victoria had decided that Khloe should begin the questioning. She rose, smoothed the fold in her dress, and moved closer to the jury box. She introduced herself and started with some general questions. When she asked if there was anyone who did not wish to serve, juror number eight, a young Hispanic woman who looked like she was in her mid-twenties raised her hand.

"I work at two restaurants, seven days a week," she said, "It's a big problem for me to be here today, there's no way I can serve as a juror and pay my rent."

Seven more hands shot up wanting to explain their personal situations. One had to pick up a child at 3:00 every day. Another was caring for a sick parent. After they were done speaking, six jurors had been excused because of what they described as extreme hardships.

Khloe continued. "Has anyone here served on a jury before?"

Five hands were raised. Khloe asked each of the five a few questions about the cases they served on. None of them had served in a murder trial before. She moved on. How many people had read about the case in the newspaper? How many had watched it on the television news. All hands had been raised in answer to those questions.

"What news channels do you usually watch, CNN, CBS, ABC, or FOX?"

Khloe strategically pointed to several to hear their preference and Victoria took notes.

"Has any one of you or a member of your family been a victim of a crime?"

An older black male in the back raised his hand.

"Was the perpetrator black or white?"

"He was black."

Victoria remembered the older black man on the train and put a mark by that juror's name. Khloe approached juror number one, a white female who looked to be in her mid-forties.

"How long have you lived in Philadelphia?" Khloe asked, smiling.

"All my life," juror number one answered.

"Have you ever had any experiences with black people that might cause you to be biased?"

"I don't think so," she replied.

Khloe carefully asked probing questions of the panel. After about a half hour she sat down and Victoria took her turn digging for prejudices. She asked each of them about their political party affiliations.

"How many of you own a gun?"

Two people raised their hands. Juror five was one of them, a white guy under forty. Victoria walked over to him.

"What made you decide to purchase a gun?"

"It was a gift from my dad, he likes to hunt."

"Do any of you have family in law enforcement?"

No one raised a hand.

"Have any of you witnessed a crime being committed?"

No one raised a hand.

"Is there anyone who believes that law enforcement is not doing a good job controlling the amount of crime in the city?"

Still, no show of hands.

"How many of you feel you can apply the law to the facts of this case?"

All hands were raised.

Victoria asked several more questions, some of them directed to specific members of the panel. She walked the thin line between enquiring and offending.

"I have nothing further, your Honor," she declared after a little less than an hour.

Judge Kelly pulled back his sleeve and checked the time on his big gold watch, flashing a beam of light all the way to the back wall. It was near the noon hour. Ben Madison could begin his questioning after lunch.

"The court will adjourn until 1:30 this afternoon," he announced.

***

Ben approached the jury and introduced himself and his co-counsel. His presence was bewitching. He pointed out and introduced his client, Edward Landauer and his family. His job of interrogation was easier; the prosecution had already asked all the hard questions.

"How many people think that if you're accused of something that you are most-likely guilty?"

No hands went up.

"Has anyone here heard any negative things about the defendant?"

Juror number nineteen, a black woman, the ideal candidate for the prosecution, raised her hand. Victoria cringed in frustration; she knew immediately that juror would be challenged. Ben was shrewd. He never asked her what she'd heard. He spoke casually with the panel as if he knew them personally. Victoria could already see some were already smiling back at him.

Ben had stood and talked effortlessly before the jury panel for two hours before he concluded.

Neither Victoria nor Ben wasted time with the individual

interviews of jurors. The challenges for cause were lengthy, each side wanted to give themselves an advantage, but Judge Kelly didn't always agree there were clear biases shown. Periodically he checked his watch. He was a stickler for time.

Promptly at 5:00, Judge Kelly checked his watch, ended the striking session, and adjourned for the day.

"Counselors, we have made excellent progress and should be able to finish this in the morning. Be in my chambers at 9:00 sharp."

***

"How do you feel the selection process is going so far?" Khloe asked Victoria as they drove up 11th Street.

"We lost some jurors that would have made it easy but we also eliminated some that would have definitely let him walk. The rest will be wild cards. We should have a jury before Judge Kelly breaks for lunch."

"That means your opening statement will be tomorrow. Are you starting to feel the pressure?"

"Are you for real? I've been feeling it from the day I got the case."

"You can stay at my house tonight if you like."

"No need, Dupree will be home by midnight, I'll be fine."

There was silence in the car for a minute until Khloe coughed and swallowed hard.

"Do you think you should buy a gun?" she said, asking the question that had been stuck in her throat. "It would only be for protection until this thing is over."

"Come on, Khloe, I'm out here preaching the evils of hotheads buying and carrying guns and you want me to join the club."

"What about fighting fire with fire?"

"That's the thinking that gets almost 100 people shot in this country every day."

"You don't have to be Wonder Woman," Khloe said, stopping in front of the house. "Make sure you keep your cell phone close to you."

Victoria got out of the car but before she shut the door she said, "I always do."

Surprisingly, Miss Judy wasn't outside in her spot. Victoria thought about knocking on the door but she wanted to focus on her opening statement. She went straight up the stairs after she bolted the front door lock to shower off the anxieties of the day. For dinner, she finished up some lemon pepper chicken and vegetables warmed up in the microwave, and then she poured herself a rum and coke to relax. She was savoring the moment and coolness of the drink when there was a knock on the door. She peeped through the small glass and was shocked to see who it was. It was Leonard with his hands full of bags. She opened the door.

"Can I come in?" he asked humbly, looking her in the eyes.

Victoria stepped back.

"You should have called first."

"That would have given you the opportunity to say no," he said, walking in.

He put down his bags and sat down on the sofa.

"So what brings you here," she asked, still standing.

"I saw you in court today."

"Is that why you're here?"

"Partially, I want to talk to you about your strategy."

"So this is constructive criticism for the second-best?"

"You know the world loves an underdog, Vee, get them rooting for you. Be good but not too perfect. Have one thing out of place. Let them see you adjust your belt, tuck in your blouse, drop your file. You can't beat Ben Madison playing his own game."

"Is this supposed to boost my confidence?"

"I know you perform your best in red pumps."

"Not everybody can deal with me in my red stilettos."

"I never wanted you in anything but red stilettos."

"Versus barefoot and pregnant."

He laughed. "Maybe, but people have different reactions to a woman wearing red shoes. So I got you some red bottoms to boost your mojo, Christian Louboutin's, five pair, one for every day you're in court," Leonard said, pointing to the bags in front of her.

Victoria was speechless. She sat down, reached into one of the bags and pulled out one of the boxes. The first pair were dark navy pumps, gorgeous, reeking class and good taste.

"Oh hell yeah, I need these in my life," she exclaimed, slipping one of the shoes on her foot and admiring it. "This is by far one of the sexiest moves you have ever made. I just want to take all of your clothes off right now."

Leonard smiled and held his arms out in surrender.

"You know you're no good," she said, putting the shoe back in its box.

"I wouldn't say that's a true statement," he said, giving her a knowing look.

"Stop, I'm not going to let you throw me off. I've got to stay focused."

"That's not my intention, really. I just wanted you to know that I'm proud of you and I'm on your team."

"Thanks, Len. I really need all the support I can get."

"What's the problem with 'little boy blue,' he's not handling his business."

"Don't go there, we're having a moment here as friends and I'm enjoying it. Besides, I saw your picture in the Philadelphia Tribune with Simone Moore at the Homeless Veterans Benefit."

Leonard dropped his head in silence for a few seconds. Then he stood up to leave.

"Call me when you get your head on straight, because you won't find a better man than me."

Victoria walked behind him to the door unable to find

the words to express what she felt, probably because she was completely out of touch with her feelings. She hadn't had time to reflect on her life or what she wanted since she had committed herself to prosecuting Edward Landauer. Leonard had always stayed real with her and she appreciated that. He had always been a concerned friend and she appreciated that too. He had been sexually exciting and she definitely appreciated that, but they had both moved on. The man she once thought was her future walked out of her door without looking back.

***

She went over her notes and re-organized her thoughts for the umpteenth time. Lying in bed she prayed that words wouldn't fail her in the courtroom like they had in her own living room. When she heard Dupree come in the door she turned over and pretended to be asleep.

Chapter Fourteen

Victoria had to force herself out of the bed at 6:00 the next morning. The balance between dread and anticipation had tilted in favor of dread. She opened the closet and searched for the color and outfit that would set the tone for her inner spirit. She decided on navy blue, it expresses importance, power, and authority while being elegant and sophisticated. She reached for the V-neck navy dress that accented the shape of her body without hugging it. Her white Nanette Lepore blazer would complete the look with her mama's pearls.

"What do you want for breakfast?" Dupree shouted on his way down the stairs.

"Everything, I might have to work through lunch," she answered. "I'm coming down in a minute. I want to eat before I get dressed."

Victoria brewed a pot of Jamaican Blue Mountain coffee for the occasion. Dupree made her a three-egg omelet with what seemed like every ingredient in the refrigerator. He had his Beats by Dr. Dre headphones on listening to music which she was grateful for because she wasn't in the mood to talk. She cleaned her plate and finished with a large mug of coffee.

Now it was time for her to pull it together and put on her armor for battle. She showered with an orange ginger aromatherapy body wash hoping that its claims to provide energy held some truth. She moisturized her skin with shea butter and sprayed her body with

"Guilty" perfume by Gucci to add to her aura because Edward Landauer was no doubt guilty.

"I need to own that room, be powerful, unbeatable," she whispered, rummaging through her drawer of underwear. "Nothing makes me feel that more than wearing animal prints," she thought. She chose the zebra print because they confuse their enemy with their stripes. She finished dressing, slipped her feet into the navy red-bottoms, and checked her reflection in the mirror. "I am queen of the damn jungle, baby. It's my world down to my panties," she said, "Stand back, everybody." For a finishing touch to her make-up she applied bright red lipstick. "Red means blood is in the water. Somebody is going down."

***

The morning passed slowly in Judge Kelly's courtroom. There were additional individual interviews with jurors, more excused for cause, and the piles of notes grew higher. At 12:00 Judge Kelly told them to take an hour and come back with their lists of jurors.

Ben and Thomas had the advantage, all they needed to do was keep the jury as white and male as possible and they were set. Their list was made quickly. The hardest thing for them was the wait. Ben made a phone call and ordered lunch to be sent in. He smiled to himself and ordered two more lunches for Victoria and Khloe.

Khloe and Victoria didn't have time to eat. They spent the hour struggling over their notes to come up with one combined list. Out of the 47 jurors in the panel, only 14 were black, adding to Victoria's frustration. Only registered voters are selected for jury duty and young blacks were lackadaisical about the process. Ben had been successful in striking four of them for cause along with two Hispanics, and he still had eight peremptory challenges. They focused on the numbers of the white candidates. They needed to carefully evaluate the white jurors. Still they weren't mind readers and there was no way to know whether the potential jurors were truthful in their answers. There was no barometer to gauge the degree of racism and intolerance.

Back in Judge Kelly's court at 1:00, Victoria gave copies of her list to the judge and to Ben. She had previously struck seven of the 22 white jurors for cause, and she used four of her peremptory challenges to remove four more from the list. There were six white males and four white females left in the pool. The Hispanics were all question marks, they could go either way.

Ben gave his list to Judge Kelly. He had used all of his peremptory challenges to strike seven more blacks from the panel and one young Hispanic man. Judge Kelly made the adjustments to his list and saw they were now only 20 left in the panel of jurors. Judge Kelly gave his list to Victoria and she used the last of her peremptory challenges, leaving 12 in the panel.

Judge Kelly checked his watch, pleased with the time of 1:25.

"Well, counselors, it looks like we have ourselves a jury. Each of you will have one challenge from the list as alternates."

Ben chose juror number 28 a white male, Victoria chose juror number 17, a black female. The jury was made of one black male, five Hispanics, three male and two female, and six whites, three male and three female. They included a bus driver, a college professor, an auto mechanic, two stay-at-home mothers, a hotel manager, and a short-order cook. Ben was pleased with the make-up of the jury. Victoria was disappointed with only one black on the jury.

Judge Kelly thanked and excused the other jurors from the courtroom. Once the prosecution and the defense were back at their respective tables and the selected jurors were in the jury box, court clerk, Mary Brigman, called them to order and swore in the jury. The chosen jurors were given the oath to render a verdict according to the evidence presented to them and by the instructions of the court.

Ed Landauer's family was instructed to leave the courtroom as they would eventually be called as witnesses for the defense. Victoria had successfully objected to the relaxation of court rules that would have let them stay. They begrudgingly left the gallery with Alta blowing a kiss to her son.

***

Pre-trial business had come to an end. The trial was about to begin. Race was the monstrous dragon that hovered over the room threatening to release its rage and consume them all. Benjamin didn't want the case to be about race, that wouldn't be to his advantage, he wanted it to be about fear, the intimidation that a community overrun with crime feels. Victoria didn't want it to simply be about race either, even though she understood that it was racial profiling that got Deshaun killed. She wanted it to be about all the crazies with guns running around looking for opportunities to blow somebody away.

Victoria knew her blood pressure was rising from the increased sound of her heart pounding in her chest and the thumping on her left temple. She sat back and closed her eyes and tried to imagine Dupree's hands massaging away the tension. She was thankful she hadn't eaten lunch, throwing up in court would not have been pretty. She took a swig from her bottle of water to settle down but what she really wanted was a rum and coke to calm her nerves and put those out-of-control butterflies in her belly to sleep.

A text from Len flashed on her silent phone, "You look hot."

She pursed her lips to hold her smile to a minimum.

Judge Kelly began his explanations to the jury.

"Welcome back, ladies and gentlemen of the jury. You will be sequestered for the duration of these proceedings. By those rules you are not to discuss the trial with family, friends, or each other. Now, have any of you read newspapers, gone on the internet, listened to the TV or radio, or had any conversations or created any emails on any electronic device about this case?"

No hands were raised. Judge Kelly continued talking to the jury.

"This is a criminal case, the Commonwealth of Pennsylvania versus Edward Landauer. The defendant, Edward Landauer, has been charged with second-degree murder. The complete definition of this charge will be given at a later time. You have the solemn responsibility to determine whether the Commonwealth of Pennsylvania has proven its accusations beyond a shadow of doubt against Edward Landauer. You as the jury are to listen to all of the evidence conscientiously and refrain from drawing premature conclusions. You cannot consider any other evidence or instructions other than those given by the court in the case before you. You cannot discuss the case with outsiders or each other until deliberation. Is that understood?"

They all nodded in agreement.

"We can now proceed with opening statements. Are you ready Ms. Perry?" Judge Kelly asked, eager to get the trial going and over with.

Victoria rose to her feet.

"Yes I am, thank you, Your Honor."

She stood at the podium and took a deep breath to compose herself while the jury focused on her. She thought about the photo of Deshaun Gardner lying dead in the street. She turned and looked at Mona Gardner sitting on the second row. She had promised her justice for her son. She looked down at her feet and remembered how fierce she was and began to speak.

"Good afternoon, ladies and gentlemen of the jury," and with a nod towards Ben, "Good afternoon, defense counsel. My name is Victoria Perry and I'm an assistant district attorney for the city of Philadelphia. I have lived in the city all my life. All of us that live and work here are weary of the almost daily criminal gun homicides that plague our neighborhoods, yet we as individuals

cannot arm ourselves with guns and become judge and jury.
As an assistant district attorney in the Homicide Unit it is my responsibility to see that the persons who commit these homicides are punished for taking another's life. Today I stand before you with one more sad case of an unsuspecting, innocent, unarmed victim shot without provocation. It is a fear that many of us share that became a reality for Deshaun Gardner when on the evening of March 29th he was murdered, shot through the heart."

She took a moment and spoke to each juror individually as her eyes scanned over the jury.

"This case is about two individuals with two stories, one of a bright and promising teenager and the other of a sullen and unfulfilled man. Deshaun Gardner was a good student planning to attend college this fall. He was well-liked by his teachers as well as his peers. He liked earning his own money and worked three days a week to pay for his high school fees. Edward Landauer was an angry, frustrated, and violent man. He's a man who wanted a position of authority but was rejected at every opportunity, a man who was a disappointment to his parents and to himself."

Ben watched and listened, impressed. She was much more confident and polished than when they were in law school. Her time as an assistant district attorney had served her well. Edward looked at her too barely able to keep from frowning. He couldn't believe this bitch had the nerve to talk about him like that.

"Deshaun Gardner was on his way home from working his part-time job like he had done many times before. He got off the subway to walk the four blocks to his house. It was raining so Mona Gardner called her son to see if he wanted her to pick him up. A very independent teenager, he told her he had his hoodie on and was fine. While they talked a car started following him. Mrs. Gardner was fearful and sent her husband out to meet Deshaun. She was on the phone when her son was aggressively confronted by this stranger. She rushed out to save him but by the time they got to him, only two blocks away, he was dead.

Edward Landauer wanted to be a policeman but he failed the psychological test. He searched for every chance to pretend to be in law enforcement. He worked part-time for Welch Security Company as a security guard for large sport events and started a Town Watch group in his neighborhood. The Commonwealth will prove that on that evening he was bored and alone when a sadistic urge compelled him to come out and look for some action. He strapped on his gun holster and 9mm and went out searching to find something or someone to take aim at and shoot off his pent-up hostilities."

Benjamin fought the urge to object. "Be patient," he said to himself. He would have his chance at bat, and he intended to swing for the fence.

Victoria changed her tone becoming more dramatic. Almost like an old-fashioned radio announcer she created an air of suspense as she described what happened that night.

"He drove down and around the block on his hunt. Then he saw Deshaun, a black teenage boy walking in the rain. He called the police. Surely this person was up to no-good, black and wearing a hoodie. He stalked the boy in his car, terrorizing him and his mother on the other line of a cell phone, even after he was advised by the dispatcher not to follow this so-called suspicious person. Deshaun attempted to run away, but Edward Landauer chased him down and confronted him.

Edward Landauer would like us to believe that he was mild-mannered in his approach to Deshaun Gardner. That he was unexpectedly attacked by this teenage boy and beat to the point of which he feared for his life in just over two minutes, although there was no blood or DNA on the victim's hands. He claims that he had no other choice but to pull his gun and shoot Deshaun Gardner in self-defense. Even if that far-fetched story were based on any truth, Pennsylvania's 'Stand Your Ground Law' modeled after Florida's law was wisely amended by law enforcement officials to state that an individual cannot use deadly force unless the aggressor produces or shows a deadly weapon.

The elements of this case have garnered a nation-wide audience. Many in the media have tried to blame Deshaun Gardner for his own death. The Commonwealth is going to do something different in this trial. We're going to come from a different angle. We're not going to try the victim we're going to actually try the defendant. The evidence will show that on that night, March 29th of this year, Edward Landauer was determined that another asshole wasn't going to get away. Except this wasn't a burglar or a thug, it was a seventeen years old kid, smart, college bound, going home from his part-time job at McDonalds. He was unarmed. His hands didn't stand a chance against a 9mm. The Commonwealth will prove beyond a shadow of a doubt that Edward Landauer with malice aforethought, with reckless disregard for human life, murdered Deshaun Gardner in cold blood."

Judge Kelly threw his arm up to check his watch. He estimated there would be enough time for Ben Madison to do his opening statement and still dismiss the court by 5:00.

"Mr. Madison you may proceed with you opening statement."

Ben rose from his seat self-assured. Victoria had done a good opening but nothing she had said was unexpected.

"Thank you, Your Honor," Benjamin replied as he approached the podium.

He planned to follow Victoria's lead and not bore the jury with tiresome details at this point in the day. There would be ample opportunities to make his case during the course of the trial. Victoria skimmed over the faces of each member of the jury as they focused on Benjamin. She was looking for smiles or any other hint that they were taken in by him.

"Good afternoon, members of the jury. We all are thankful for your indulgence in this matter. There is no doubt that this was an awful event. Anytime a life is loss it is very sad for all of those who are involved in the situation. What we don't want to do is magnify the tragedy of what happened by ruining another life, the life of the defendant," he said, pointing at Ed. "All of us in this room sympathize with the grief that is felt by Darren and Mona Gardner over the death of their son. However, there is another family that has been reeling from the circumstances that have brought us here today. They are Laramie and Alta Landauer and his older brother Emerson. Their anguish began with the arrest of Edward Landauer for the killing of Deshaun Gardner.

Edward Landauer is not an unhappy man or a bad person. He's a kind individual who cares about others in his neighborhood. He is a loyal friend, a loving son and brother, and a gentle human being. He wishes that none of this would have happened, but there was no way for him to foresee the escalation of the situation that took place that night.

First I'd like to remind the jury that buying a weapon and carrying it is legal in Pennsylvania. This is a "shall-issue" state. No one is denied based on political or prejudicial biases. My client purchased the type of weapon that was recommended to him and went through all of the proper procedures to acquire his weapon. He was trained by a licensed instructor at a gun range. He had the necessary license to carry it on his person. On the night in question he was within his legal rights to carry his weapon. He always carried it everywhere he went for his protection, not for use to antagonize anyone else.

The evidence of this case will show that Edward Landauer was lawfully behaving within the rules as a neighborhood watch captain on March 29th. He has not ever considered himself a neighborhood policeman or patrolled the area in that capacity. The streets around him had gone through a rash of robberies and he as well as other members of his community had been told to look out for suspicious persons and not hesitate to call either 911 or the non-emergency number for police. That's exactly what he did on the night in question. He did follow Deshaun Gardner at a distance to keep him in sight until the police arrived. There was no way he could turn his car around and he was sure he would have lost sight of Deshaun if he had tried to circle the block.

He only got out of his car when Deshaun Gardner started to run.

His only impulse was to determine if Deshaun Gardner was there to commit a crime. He tried to have a conversation with Deshaun but as witnesses will later testify the exchange turned confrontational and then violent. One of the witnesses was so alarmed that she called the police. Edward Landauer approached Deshaun Gardner as a preventative measure for those who lived in the neighborhood. Without provocation he was viciously attacked and received a broken jaw in the assault. Edward Landauer has said that during the scuffle, Deshaun Gardner saw his gun and reached for it. It was at that point he drew his weapon. In unbearable pain from his injuries he couldn't fight back."

Benjamin took out an exhibit for the jury to see.

"This is the picture of Edward Landauer when the police arrived. There was no question that my client believed that he would have been killed. In desperation he fired one shot. All three of the witnesses heard a single shot and ballistics have determined that only one shot was fired from the gun. My client was traumatized and dazed when Officer Daly arrived on the scene. Upon seeing the body of Deshaun Gardner on the ground, Officer Daly immediately took the gun out of his holster. He handcuffed Edward Landauer without any resistance. My client was calm and cooperative. Officer Daly saw that he was hurt and called for an ambulance to come to the scene. At the Roundhouse my client did not request a lawyer, knowing that the shooting had been justified. Why would he have called the police if he planned to hurt someone or had bad intentions toward the young man he saw walking.

The prosecution has the burden of proof to show that Edward

Landauer went out looking to kill a stranger. They must prove that he acted out of anger, malice, or hate. That is an impossible task because none of that could be further from the truth. The defense will show that Edward Landauer acted to save his own life and is not guilty of the charge of second-degree murder."

Edward nodded in thanks to the jury and took his seat.

Judge Kelly looked at his watch again. "In light of the hour, we will delay the prosecution calling its first witness."

He explained to the jury that they would be served dinner then he repeated the instructions for their conduct throughout the trial.

He raised his gavel for one strike and announced, "Court will be adjourned until 9:00 tomorrow morning."

Judge Kelly left the courtroom and the jury exited from the side. The lights from the camera went out. Victoria remained seated reviewing her briefs and notes allowing the courtroom to empty before she prepared to leave.

"I think that went well what do you think?" Khloe asked, standing up.

"It was just the beginning. We've got a long way to go."

"I'll go get the car and bring it around if you want a ride home."

"That would be great if you don't mind."

Khloe walked out the rear door as Benjamin walked back in. He moved toward Victoria as she closed her briefcase.

"I was impressed with your open," he said, smiling.

Victoria smiled back. "You, as always, were mesmerizing."

"I followed your lead."

"Until tomorrow," she said, walking out of the courtroom.

She was determined to say as little as possible to Ben while the trial was going on. He always had a trick up his sleeve and she wasn't about to let him get into her head. She took the stairs down to the first floor. The car was waiting on the street outside the entrance. She took a deep breath and stepped quickly, forcing a path through the throng of reporters. Inside the car she exhaled.

"What did he say?" Khloe asked curiously.

"Not much, he was trying to feel me out. Test my fear quotient after his open. I think he still wants to make a deal, the only thing holding him back is his client."

Arthur called Victoria on her cell phone.

"Why don't you stop in my office for a few minutes?" he asked, sounding concerned.

"I've already made my exit. I really don't want to hang around here. I'm spent. You're welcome to conference call me or come by the house."

"No need, I'll see you in court tomorrow."

Ten minutes later Khloe pulled up to the curb in front of Victoria's house.

"Get a good night's sleep if you can," she said. "Call me if you need anything."

"I'm cool, get some sleep yourself, you're looking worried or worn out," Victoria told her.

"Thanks."

***

Victoria felt the weight of the heat on her shoulders when she got out of the air-conditioned car. The direct rays were probably why her neighbor wasn't sitting outside in her usual spot. The first day of the trial had her nerve-wracked and she needed to wind down. She hadn't talked to Miss Judy or Lanetta in over a week. She went to their storm door and knocked.

"It's open," Miss Judy yelled from inside.

Victoria walked in and saw them watching the evening news. The anchor was talking about the first day of the trial.

"Baby, I'm so proud of you," Miss Judy said, reaching her arms up for a hug.

"Damn, Vicki, you're a superstar now," Lanetta exclaimed with excitement. "They showed some of your opening statement and you were hot, girl."

"It's intimidating with cameras rolling all the time," Victoria responded humbly.

"You're in a whole different league now, baby. You have gone national. This is on the news all over the country. If you win, you can go anywhere you want."

"Or I can make a fool out of myself nationally."

"You're definitely gonna have to bring it, sister," Lanetta chuckled, "The other guy is on point and frigging gorgeous."

"I'm not tripping. All I want to be is a big fish in the Philly pond. I don't want to go anywhere else, this is home."

"You mean you don't plan to go on the road with Dupree?" Lanetta joked.

"Who said he's going anywhere," Victoria said, holding her hand up for a high-five.

"That's a rolling stone you're dealing with, Vick. This ain't his home," Miss Judy added.

"What difference does that make? I like him a lot, and he has been very good for me and very good to me. I don't have time to even think about anything else in my life right now."

"Right now your career is your baby," Miss Judy said, "It may not always be like that. Babies grow up and then you need something else in your life."

"He's all that I want right now. Our schedules click. I work late and he works later giving me some time and space to myself. When he goes away on a gig it's not a problem. I don't need a man up under me all the time."

"Well if you like it, I love it," Miss Judy laughed. Then in a poor English accent she asked, "Are you having dinner with us or has Dupree already prepared something for you?"

"If he hasn't cooked, I'll make a sandwich or microwave something light. I've got to be ready to hit the stage in the morning."

"All right, baby," Miss Judy said, "I can't tell you how proud we are of you and what you're doing. Right is right."

Victoria felt her eyes burn from the tears forming.

"Thanks for saying that, it means a lot to me."

"We got your back," Lanetta said, walking her outside to her front door.

As soon as Victoria opened the door she could smell the familiar scent of chicken mixed with vegetables. It was Wednesday and Dupree didn't usually have to play at the club. "Thank goodness," she thought. That was one less thing she had to do. He met her in the living room with a wet kiss and went into the garage to smoke and work on some music. He gave her some quiet time to unwind over dinner so she could concentrate on the case for the rest of the evening. Dupree had gotten used to her habits and moods and didn't seem to mind; he had his own set of idiosyncrasies. Usually he got home or came upstairs about the time she wrapped up for the night. That's when he brought her a rum and coke to help her relax and let the stress go with a massage or some intense sexual activity, whichever she needed the most.

Chapter Fifteen

Victoria hopped out of bed the next morning eager to make her case. She had gotten rid of nearly all of her jitters yesterday during her open but the day still had her a little on edge. She had decided to reverse her strategy with the order of her witnesses. Her first witness would be Mona Gardner. As much as she wanted to spare her any additional pain she needed the emotional impact at the start for the jury that only she could bring. She chose a peach and black color-block dress by Victoria Beckham and put on her beige pair of red-bottoms.

Dupree was still asleep when she finished dressing. She had done her best not to wake him. For some reason which she couldn't explain she didn't like much conversation in the mornings, especially if she was going to be in court. She put a Jimmy Dean biscuit in the microwave and made a pot of coffee. She finished her breakfast, put a peach and some grapes in her briefcase and waited for Khloe to text when she arrived.

Khloe greeted her in the car with a big smile.

"Good morning, Vicki."

"You're quite cheerful this morning, what's up?"

"Nothing, I'm just feeling good today. I guess most of the tension from preparing for this trial over the last three months is over."

"The trial just started, don't exhale yet."

"For me it is, plus I've got a front row seat to watch all the action."

Arthur was outside of the courtroom waiting when they got there. Victoria saw him pacing across the floor before he noticed them. She could tell something was wrong. His tight facial expression loosened and he seemed relieved when he saw them. He scooted Victoria away from the reporters who crowded the courtroom door.

"I don't want to freak you out before court but you got another death threat yesterday."

"Oh my God," Khloe gasped, covering her mouth.

"When, how?" Victoria asked, totally confused.

"It was in a letter that was stopped by security with a suspicious powder residue."

"This is straight-up madness. I'm just doing my job."

"The crazies come out with these high-profile cases. Dt. Rosario is going to be shadowing you from now on as a precaution while they investigate."

"I don't have the time or the energy for this, I've got a case to try," Victoria said, shaking her head, infuriated.

She pushed her way through the throng of reporters hoping for a comment, sat down at the prosecution table, and pulled out her iPad and files for the case. Khloe moved closer to speak in her ear.

"You can make all of this end. I bet Ben Madison would still jump at a deal on this one."

"This isn't about me. It's about getting justice for Deshaun Gardner. Don't forget that."

The courtroom was filled and the cameras were rolling. Ben Madison and Thomas Clancy were already seated at the table with the defendant. The members of the jury took their places in the jury box.

The bailiff called them to order. "All rise. Court is in session."

Judge Kelly walked in and took his seat on the bench and lowered his gavel.

"We're on docket 7631481. This is the case of Edward

Landauer vs. The Commonwealth of Pennsylvania. Good morning, ladies and gentlemen of the jury. Good morning, counselors."

He took a minute to question the jury as to whether they had obeyed the rules of the court while they were out overnight. They responded affirmatively.

"Time is of the essence. Call your first witness, Ms. Perry."

"The Commonwealth calls Mona Gardner," she replied.

Mona Gardner walked slowly but deliberately to take the stand. All the eyes of the jury converged on her with the exception of one, juror six, an older white male. Victoria made a note of it while Mary Brigman swore her in. She figured he was probably leaning towards the defense and didn't want to face her.

"Good morning, Mrs. Gardner. Would you state your full name for the record?"

"My name is Mona Louise Garner."

"How long have you been a resident in Philadelphia?"

"For almost 25 years."

"What is your current address and how long have you lived there?"

"It's 7111 Harbor Street, we lived there for eighteen months."

"Are you currently employed, Mrs. Gardner?"

"Yes, I've been a clerk at PECO, Philadelphia Electric Company for 22 years."

"Are you married?"

"Yes I am."

"What about children?"

"We had one child. His name was Deshaun Nathaniel Gardner."

"How old was he on his last birthday?

"He was born on July 4, 1994, he was seventeen years old."

"Were there any difficulties in raising your son?"

"No, he never gave me a moment's trouble. He was a good son, smart, and respectful."

"Mrs. Gardner, when did you last speak to your son?"

"It was on the day he was killed. He was on his way home from his part-time job. I saw it was raining so I called him to see if he wanted me to pick him up from the sub."

"Tell us what was said on the phone call."

Ben resisted the urge to object on the grounds that it was prejudicial. He knew Judge Kelly would allow it and he didn't want to seem unsympathetic to Mrs. Gardner.

"He told me not to worry about it, he was wearing his hoodie. While we were talking he said that some man was following him. I told him to run away from the car but then he said that the car went past him. It kind of worried me so I told him I was sending his daddy to meet him."

"Did you keep talking to Deshaun?"

"Yes I did. Then he said the car had circled back around and the man was getting out of the car. I fussed at him for not running, I was scared. Then I heard Deshaun ask the man, "Why are you following me?" The man yelled back at him but I couldn't understand what he said. Then Deshaun said, "Back up off me." Then I heard a grunt and the line disconnected."

"What did you do then?"

"I dropped my phone and ran out of the door to help my son."

Mona began to lose the grip on the composure she was fighting so hard to hold on to. Victoria needed her emotion to impact the jury but she needed her to tell the story even more.

"I know this is difficult, Mrs. Gardner. Would you like a glass of water?"

She nodded yes and Khloe quickly poured a glass and handed it to her.

"Were you able to catch up to your husband?"

"Yes, he had gone about a half block."

"How far away from the scene were you at this time?"

"Almost three blocks."

"Did you or your husband hear a gunshot?"

"I don't know. I can't remember. It was raining and we were running and I was so upset. The blocks seemed so long and when we turned the corner I saw police car lights flashing. We ran faster and when we got closer they wouldn't let us through."

"Were you able to see your son?"

Mona paused to gather herself. The courtroom was eerily quiet. Her testimony was gripping.

"I saw him lying still on the cold ground. I screamed and started to cry. I could feel the rain pouring down my face blending with my tears and then I saw the rain drops mixing with the pool of blood from my son. I thought I was going to pass out."

"Did the police tell you what happened?"

"My husband spoke with them, I couldn't."

"Judge Kelly, I have no further questions for this witness at this time," Victoria said, taking her seat.

"Mr. Madison you can begin your cross-examination," Judge Kelly said.

Ben Madison stood up and approached the podium as if he dreaded it. He gave the impression to the jury that it was something that he had to do, something he would have preferred not to do. He paused and spoke in a low tone into the microphone.

"Mrs. Gardner, I am sincerely sorry for your loss."

Judge Kelly admonished him. "You're to ask questions, Mr. Madison."

"Yes, Your Honor. I have only a few questions. Mrs. Gardner, why did you move to South Philly a year ago?"

"We thought it would be a safer environment for our family."

"Were you worried about your son running with a gang in Germantown?"

"My son never belonged to a gang."

"Mrs. Gardner, you mentioned that you heard a grunt before the phone call ended. Were you able to tell the voice of the grunt?"

"I heard it through my son's phone so I don't have any reason to believe that it wasn't him."

"Isn't there a 50-50 chance that it wasn't Deshaun?"

"In my opinion, no."

"So you want the jury to think that it couldn't have been the defendant being hit by Deshaun."

"What I want is to be able to turn back time to that night, to be there standing at the steps when Deshaun came out of the subway, and to bring my son home."

Ben wanted to put the notion out there for the jury that it was possibly Edward Landauer who grunted from being hit by Deshaun Gardner. Going further and antagonizing Mona Gardner was not his intention. He had done enough.

"No further questions, Your Honor," he said, taking his seat.

Judge Kelly motioned to Mona. "You may step down."

Mona walked to her seat without looking in the direction of the defendant.

"The Commonwealth may call your next witness," Judge Kelly said.

"The Commonwealth calls Michelle Banks," Victoria said, standing.

A teenage girl hurried in to take the stand. She exuded energy, bouncing with every step. She was deep brown with big eyes and her long box-braids were pulled back in a pony-tail. She was wearing jeans and a t-shirt.

Mary Brigman swore her in.

"Do you swear to tell the whole truth and nothing but the truth so help you God?"

Sounding sassy with her hand on the Bible she said, "Yes, ma'am."

"Hello, Miss Banks," Victoria said, "May I call you Michelle."

"Go ahead," Michelle answered boldly.

"Michelle, what was your relationship with Deshaun Gardner?"

"We worked together at the McDonald's down in the Gallery."

"How long did you know him?"

"I knew him from the old neighborhood, and he got a job where I work about a year ago."

"Did you like him?"

"All the ladies liked Deshaun. He was fye. He could have been my baby-daddy. He looked good, kept some change in his pocket, and he never called you out of your name."

"Did he belong to a gang?"

"Hell no."

Judge Kelly interrupted. "Watch your language, young lady."

"Sorry, Deshaun wasn't on the streets. He had book smarts, he was going to college."

Victoria continued her questioning. "The media has tried to characterize him as a thug because he wore a hoodie and hung with gang members. Was he a thug?"

"He wasn't no thug," Michelle snapped. "He was loyal to dudes he grew up with, that's it. He didn't try to play extra like he didn't know nobody even when he moved to South Philly."

"Did you ever know him to sell drugs?"

"Hell no. Sorry, Judge. Deshaun didn't do no dirt, he's straight."

"Did he smoke marijuana?"

"He smoked weed every now and then at a party or something."

"Was he hot-tempered?"

"No, he was easy-going."

"Were you working with him at McDonald's on March 29th?"

"Yeah, I was there."

"Did you talk or notice if he was in a different mood?"

"He was like he always was, joking around to make the hours go faster. Nothing special, it was a regular day."

"What did you think when you heard what had happened after work, that he had attacked Edward Landauer?"

Benjamin stood up in his chair. "Objection, Your Honor, it calls for a conclusion."

"Sustained," Judge Kelly said.

Michelle shouted over him. "That man is lying his ass off. He shot Deshaun for nothing."

Judge Kelly spoke to the jury. "Please disregard the last question by Ms. Perry and the response of the witness."

Victoria felt satisfied.

"No more questions for this witness, Your Honor."

Benjamin intentionally brushed against Victoria very slightly as he passed on the way to the podium. It was like telling a fellow fighter that they made a good hit but it didn't hurt.

"Hello, Ms. Banks. You testified that the crowd Deshaun hung around were gang members, is that right?"

"Some were, so what?"

Benjamin had made his point so he moved on.

"Were there occasions that Deshaun smoked some weed when he got off work?"

"How would I know, we went in opposite directions. I went north and he went south."

"You said that Deshaun was popular with the ladies. Did he ever get in any fights with other guys over a girl?"

"No, that never happened. Why would he, plenty wanted to get with him."

"Nothing further, Your Honor."

Edward leaned over to whisper in Benjamin's ear when he sat down. "Is that all you got? When are you gonna earn your fucking fee?"

Ben smiled with no response.

Judge Kelly paused and looked down at his watch, the noon hour was very near.

"The court will recess for lunch until 1:00," he said, bringing down his gavel.

***

Benjamin sat across from Thomas at the 10 Arts Bistro inside of the Ritz-Carlton Hotel. They had gone there to escape the crowds of reporters and spectators during lunch. Benjamin was calmly enjoying his salmon with asparagus but Thomas seemed agitated as he stared down at his plate of mussels.

"No appetite?" Ben asked.

"You're letting her get the upper hand," Thomas complained.

"Who?" Ben asked, amused.

"You know who."

"You sound like Ed. Why are you bothered, your ass isn't on the line?"

"I know you have a thing for her. I'm just making sure you haven't gone soft."

"The war just started, Thomas. You have to pick your battles."

"I prefer to win them all."

"Relax, I have every intention on winning this case. Remember it's all about a shadow of doubt. Besides, it's a win-win situation."

"How so?" Thomas asked irritably.

"Simply put, it won't hurt my career to lose this case. The man murdered a kid."

Thomas bristled at his words.

"Unfortunately I don't have that same luxury. I'm sticking my neck out publicly. If we lose, the glass ceiling for me becomes ironclad and my chances of joining another firm go up in smoke."

"You worry too much. Everybody loves a team player."

Thomas' regrets had grown exponentially. He had always felt like the house-nigger at Rosen and Sullivan and without this win he wouldn't have any dignity. There was no turning back. He had already gone down a path of no return. He pushed his plate away and downed the glass of vodka like it was spring water.

"Good deal," Ben said, raising his glass in a salute.

*****

Arthur had lunch delivered to his office for Victoria and Khloe.

"I like the pace of the trial so far," Arthur said, between a bite of chicken salad. "The sooner this one is over the better. The mayor is blowing my phone up on a daily basis. He wants things to settle down before something else pops off."

"There will be some drama before it's over," Victoria said, "Ben Madison is not an amateur. He's got several surprises for me, I'm sure."

Khloe shifted nervously in her chair and asked, "What about that letter, what was on it?"

"It was ricin," Arthur said, "It wasn't enough to kill you, but it would have put you in the hospital."

"That's some scary shit," Khloe said.

Victoria smirked. "That's the cost of getting in the public eye. You become a target for nut-cases."

"I can put you in protective custody if you want?" Arthur said.

Victoria chewed the last bite of her Cobb salad.

"I'll take my chances at my house. Dt. Rosario has my back and at least I know the people in my neighborhood and they're looking out for me."

"All right, it's your call," Arthur said, gulping down a bottle of Pepsi.

*****

Court convened after lunch with Victoria calling Ronald Flores, the 911 operator who dispatched the call from Edward Landauer, to the stand. Ronald Flores testified that he had worked in the communication center for the Philadelphia Police Department for five years. He described his training and history on the job before the recorded call was played for the jury.

Victoria replayed the part of the call that said Deshaun was suspicious.

"Mr. Flores, did the defendant give you a specific reason as to why he thought the person was suspicious, like something he was doing?"

"Not specifically, he said there had been some burglaries in his neighborhood."

"On the phone call he says "he's looks like he's up to no-good or on drugs." Did he give any specific reason as to why he would think that?"

"Nothing more than he was walking in the rain and looking around at houses."

"I've done that same thing on many occasions as I am sure we all have," she said, glancing over at the jury. "Did someone walking down the street sound like something that was worrisome to you as a dispatcher?"

"Not at that moment, but I did have police dispatched to the area."

"The defendant said, "He's got his hand in his waistband and he's a black male" as if that was significant. Did you think that because he was a black male with his hand in his waistband that he was armed?"

"No, I just told him to tell me if anything else happened."

"On the recording of the call he kept talking about this person's hands and he seems to be trying to make something out of nothing going on. Did you think it was odd that on a cold rainy evening someone would put their hands in their waistband or pocket?"

"I didn't think about it, my job is to keep the situation contained until the officers get there."

"Listening to this call about a perfect stranger from the defendant, did you find all the judgments he was making about someone he doesn't know disturbing, for instance when he said, "These assholes always get away and "fucking coons?""

"I hear people say a lot of things on calls."

"When you hear those characterizations on other calls what do they tell you about the caller?"

"It usually means they are hostile or upset."

"Later in the call he said, "Shit, he's running," and there's movement like he was getting out of the car. Did you think he had gotten out of the car?"

"I wasn't sure so I asked him if he was following him, then I told him that wasn't necessary."

"What does your training say about these kinds of situations?"

"We want to prevent confrontations and encourage persons to get away from situations that might escalate."

"Was that the end of the call?"

"After I told him units were on the way he hung up."

"No further questions."

Victoria returned to her seat.

"Mr. Madison, proceed with your cross-examination," Judge Kelly said.

"Just a few questions, Mr. Flores," Ben said casually. "While you were speaking to Edward Landauer during this call, did you feel there was anything unusual or different about the call?"

"No, it was pretty typical."

"Is it usual practice to ask the race of someone during a call?"

"Yes, we are trained to try to get a description of suspects."

"At any time during the call did my client sound like he was in a rage?"

"No, he seemed calm, maybe aggravated before he hung up."

"Was there anything that he said that gave you a reason for concern?"

"Not really."

"When you suggested that he not follow the person, why was that?"

"We don't want callers to jeopardize their safety by provoking a confrontation."

"Speaking with him, did you think that his behavior was dangerous or threatening?"

"No, sir, not from what I heard on my end of the phone."

"Nothing further, Your Honor." Ben said, ending his cross.

"Would you like to re-direct, Ms. Perry, or will you proceed with your next witness?"

"No redirect, Your Honor."

The next witness for the prosecution was a representative from the Town Watch Integrated Services. Victoria wanted him to clarify what their duties were and what training they received to become certified.

He obliged when he testified, "The overall responsibility of a Town Watch group is to observe, document, and report it to the police. Carrying weapons is highly discouraged."

She also had him verify the records submitted into evidence that were kept by their Town Watch Group. The records showed that Edward Landauer had made a total of 42 non-emergency and 911 phone calls to the police in the last 10 months. Of those calls, 22 were made about suspicious persons, and in all but two of the calls the suspicious persons were young black males.

In Benjamin's cross-examination he asked the representative to confirm that Edward Landauer was acting within the scope of his duty when he was reporting what he thought was suspicious or criminal activity. The records also indicated that there were no other incidents where Edward Landauer had intervened in a dangerous situation. He and Victoria went back and forth with objections and re-directs for over an hour. Judge Kelly checked the time intermittently and when the Town Watch representative left the stand at 4:35 he gave the usual instructions to the jury and adjourned the court.

***

Victoria collapsed on the sofa as soon as she stepped inside her house. Her body ached like she had just competed in an Ironman Triathlon. Fatigued down to her bones her muscles held on tight and tense. She needed Dupree to give her a thorough rub-down but it was Thursday and he would be playing a late set at the club. Her phone chirped signaling another message. When she finally checked her phone there were seven texts and fourteen missed calls. She decided to take a hot bath to loosen up.

The sound of the running water in her bath was soothing. She added some lavender and Dead Sea salts to help her de-stress. She eased her tired body down into the warm soft bubbles and relaxed. While she rested her thoughts drifted back to the late dinner she had with Khloe after they had reviewed the report from the Medical Examiner's Office. Khloe was noticeably distracted. She kept checking her phone and seemed on edge. Victoria had sensed that there was something going on with her for a week or two but she hadn't asked her about it yet. It wasn't that she didn't care, it was that her plate was filled and piled high until the trial was over.

The hot bath helped a lot. She crawled into bed with her phone and answered the texts from Tamika, Angeline, and Joshua. She hadn't talked to any of them since the First Chance gala. She checked the list of missed calls and promised to take time on the weekend to catch up with everybody. She set her phone alarm and rolled over to go to sleep.

It was late in the night when Dupree slid in the bed beside her.

"Are you awake," he whispered.

"I am now. I haven't slept soundly in weeks."

"Can I get you something, do you want a drink?"

Victoria chuckled. "My body won't have time to metabolize it. I can't show up to court with alcohol in my blood."

He reached his hand under the thin satin gown she was wearing.

"How about a quickie?"

"Oh yeah," she moaned, "Give me some of that but don't make it too quick."

Whatever kinks were left after the hot bath they were smoothed out by Dupree. Victoria thought she knew all of his talents but multi-tasking was one he hadn't previously shared. After a short session of kissing, rubbing, stroking, and kneading, she was in a deep sleep.

Chapter Sixteen

It was only 9:00 am and the temperature had already reached 93 degrees. Tempers had flared overnight in the city after court testimony regarding the recording of the 911 call had been broadcast on every news channel in the country. The faithful line of demonstrators outside the Criminal Justice Center which had thinned as the months passed was more robust with renewed vigor. Dupree dropped her off in front of the Widener Building after Khloe called saying she was running late. That raised a red flag in Victoria's head. Khloe had never been late before and she was on schedule to question the morning witnesses. It wasn't like her not to be prepared.

Every seat in the courtroom was filled and the buzz of voices speaking in low tones blended in with the drone of the air conditioning that was puffing on blast. Sitting with her back to the courtroom, Victoria could feel the pressure of Mona Gardner's eyes on her. If she were in her shoes she might not have come today. Reliving the moments after her son's death and having to see the pictures of his body was too cruel for her to imagine. She considered turning around to speak to her when Judge Kelly walked in and took his seat on the bench. The jury entered and then court was called to order.

Victoria's first witness of the day was Sgt. Robert Kline, the first police officer on the scene. She stood and did her best to smooth the wrinkles from her linen dress before she reached the podium. She went through the usual questions of how long he had been employed by the Philadelphia Police Department, his education and training, and then to the night of the shooting.

"How far away from Shiloh Street were you when you received the radio transmission of a suspicious person?"

"I was about five minutes away."

"Did the nature of the call change?"

"While I was in route it became a disturbance and then later a shot was fired."

"What did you see when your arrived."

"I saw a man standing over a body in the street."

"Do you see that man who was standing over the body in the courtroom?"

"Yes, that's him sitting over there."

He pointed to Edward Landauer.

"Let the record show that Sgt. Kline identified the defendant," Victoria stated. "How was the body positioned?"

"He was lying on his back."

Victoria handed Sgt. Kline a photograph.

"This is Commonwealth exhibit 11, do you recognize this?"

"Yes, this is a photo of Deshaun Gardner's body."

Victoria went through several Commonwealth exhibits that were identified by Sgt. Kline.

"Did you check to see if the victim was alive?"

"Yes, I checked for a pulse, but there was none."

"Did you call for an ambulance?"

"Yeah, but back-up and an EMT arrived just after I called."

"Once the investigators and crime technicians arrived on the scene did you have any more contact with the defendant?"

"No, I did not."

"Thank you, Sgt. Kline," Victoria said, taking her seat.

"Your cross, Mr. Madison," Judge Kelly said.

"Thank you, Your Honor," Benjamin said, rising. "Sgt.

Kline, you seem to have an exemplary record with the police department."

"Thank you, sir."

"When you arrived on the scene was it still raining?"

"Yes, but not as heavy."

"What was the defendant doing when you saw him?"

"He was just standing there."

"Did he have a gun in his hand?"

"No, it was in his holster."

"Did you have your gun drawn?"

"Yes, I did?"

"Why was that?"

"The radio transmission said there had been a shot fired. I wasn't sure by who or why."

"Was the defendant agitated or combative when you approached him?"

"No, he was calm."

"Did you notice any injuries to the defendant?"

"His face was swollen."

"What did you do first?"

"I took the defendants gun, removed the magazine and ejected the round from the chamber. Then I checked the victim to see if he was breathing. I called for help but like I said they arrived while I was on the phone."

Ben studied his notes on his laptop then said, "Nothing further."

"You're excused, Sergeant," Judge Kelly said.

During the time Sgt. Kline left the stand, Khloe strode quickly through the galley and eased into her seat at the table.

"Everything okay," Victoria asked in a low voice.

"Yeah, I'm ready."

Khloe took her laptop from her briefcase.

"Ms. Perry you may call your next witnesses," Judge Kelly said.

Victoria stood at the table.

"Ms. Luskin will be examining the next witness, Your Honor."

"All right, proceed, Ms. Luskin."

Khloe stood at the lectern and called Jason Liu, the crime scene technician, to the stand.

The dismal testimony of the crime scene technician went on for almost an hour with him explaining the photographs that had become the evidence exhibits thirteen through thirty three. His testimony covered the physical evidence that had been cordoned off with the yellow crime scene tape attached to orange cones, the gun, the cell phones, finger prints, and the contents of Deshaun Gardner's pockets.

Victoria looked over at Edward, he was sitting there making notes on a legal pad, detached, as if he were watching a movie unrelated to himself. Khloe hurried through the results of the DNA residue on Deshaun's hands and the exhibits that were photographs of Edward Landauer's face and then ended her examination.

Victoria sensed a strange vibe as Khloe returned to the table and Benjamin went towards the lectern. He smiled at her but Khloe looked down and avoided making eye contact with him. It made her wonder if he had spoken to her about the case without her knowledge.

Ben's cross-examination started with photos of Deshaun's body and the lack of bruising or swelling on his face or body. He focused heavily on the photos of Edward Landauer's swollen face and his complete cooperation with the investigators. He went over the procedures by the technicians. After Benjamin finished his cross, Judge Kelly shifted in his seat as the time clicked past twelve o' clock. It was like an even boxing match each taking their turns on the ropes.

Victoria did a re-direct with one question.

"What was in the victim's pockets?"

"A wallet with fourteen dollars in it and a school ID."

When the crime scene technician finally finished testifying at 12:40 Judge Kelly called a recess for lunch until 2:00.

"Good job, Khloe," Victoria said. "I'm eating lunch in my office. Do you want to join me?"

"No, I think I have a stomach virus. I'm going to take something for it and rest in my office."

"All right, but if you don't feel any better go on home. I've got it under control."

"Thanks, Vicki."

Victoria dodged the usual reporters and their questions on the way back to her office.

***

"You may take your seats," Judge Kelly instructed when court was back in session. "Call your next witness, counselor."

Victoria went to the lectern.

"Thank you, Your Honor. The prosecution calls Janet Falco."

There was quiet while Janet Falco was sworn in.

"Good afternoon, Ms. Falco. Would you please state your name for the record and where you're employed?"

"My name is Janet Falco and I'm employed with the Philadelphia Police Department."

"For how long and what is your present position?"

"I've worked there as a Program Coordinator for Crime Prevention for eight years."

"Would you tell us what a Town Watch Program is?"

"It's a group run by members of a community who have an interest in deterring crime in their neighborhood. They act as the eyes and ears for the police department."

"Do some of your duties include the organizing of Town Watch Programs?"

"Yes they do. I act as a facilitator when a community makes a request for a Town Watch Program in their neighborhood."

"What does that entail?"

"A meeting is scheduled and volunteers are invited to attend. We explain the history and objectives of Town Watch Integrated Services. We talk about crime prevention and making their homes more secure. They're given materials stating the rules and procedures. Then they are introduced to the officers patrolling their community and we do a power-point as part of the training."

"Are there designated positions in the group?"

"There is the Town Watch coordinator, the block captains, and the participants in the neighborhood."

"Your Honor, with your permission, I would like to show exhibit 42, which was the power-point shown to the defendant at the organizing of the Town Watch program for his community."

"Proceed," Judge Kelly replied.

Victoria directed the jury to look at the screen.

"Ms. Falco, can you take us through the power-point and show us the specifics of training?"

"First, they are not to act as vigilante police, not to take matters in their own hands, or to put themselves at risk. We explain the difference between emergency and non-emergency phone calls and which numbers to call for them."

"What about following or engaging someone they feel is suspicious?"

"They are instructed not to follow or confront anyone, they are told to call 911. They are to be the eyes and ears of the police."

"No further questions, Your Honor."

"Cross, Mr. Madison," Judge Kelly said.

Benjamin moved to the lectern.

"Have you ever met the defendant, Ms. Falco?" he asked.

"Yes, he was a coordinator at one of the Town Watch organizing meetings."

"Did he tell you what his motivation was for starting a watch program?"

"He said there had been several robberies in the neighborhood."

"So his concern was for the safety in his community?"

"From what I could tell, that's the way it seemed."

"Nothing more, thank you."

Judge Kelly nodded to the witness. "You're excused."

Victoria decided to call only one of the two credible witnesses who lived on Shiloh Street who called the police that night. Benjamin had both of them on his list of witnesses.

"Your Honor, the Commonwealth calls Ariana Angulate."

She was sworn in, and spelled her name for the record.

"Mrs. Angulate, are you married?"

"I'm divorced."

"Do you have children?"

"I have a 26 year old son."

"What do you do for a living?"

"I'm a teacher, tenth grade English."

"What is your current address?"

"I live at 5301 Shiloh Street."

"How long have you lived there?"

"I've live there for 19 years."

"During those years, have you met or come in contact with the defendant?"

"Not really, I've seen him a few times but I knew his mother. His parents owned a grocery store in the neighborhood for years until they moved away."

"So you weren't a participant in the Town Watch group in your neighborhood."

"No, I keep to myself."

"What were you doing on the night of March 29th?"

"I was at home grading papers in my living room."

"Does your living room face the street?"

"Yes it does."

"Did you hear any commotion that evening?"

"I heard cars driving past from time to time and then I heard a car door open and close. I heard running and then male voices."

"Were you alarmed at that time?"

"I stopped to listen. I couldn't understand what they were saying but it sounded like they were arguing. There was a heavy aggressive voice and another voice in a lighter tone. Then it sounded like there was scuffling, I could hear grunts."

"What did you do?

"I picked up my phone to call 911, then I heard a gunshot."

"How much time do you think passed from the time you hear the voices until you heard the gunshot, Mrs. Angulate?"

She paused and answered, "Less than two minutes."

"At that point did you look out of the window?"

"Yes, I saw the defendant standing over a body in the street and then a police car with flashing lights pulled up."

"Thank you, Mrs. Angulate."

"Your cross, Mr. Madison," Judge Kelly directed.

"Thank you, Your Honor."

"Good afternoon, Mrs. Angulate. I won't hold you long. I just have a few questions. I was wondering, why you didn't go to the window when you first heard the noises?"

"So much has been happening in the neighborhood lately and I live alone."

"Were you afraid to go to the window?"

"I wasn't scared. I was just being cautious. I didn't know what was going on. It happened so fast. Then it was over."

Benjamin nodded graciously. "No more questions."

Judge Kelly checked his watch and said, "Call your next witness."

Victoria called the representative from T-Mobile USA who testified about the time of the phone call between Deshaun and his mother. It was established that they were on the phone at the same time that Edward Landauer was on the phone with 911. Their conversation continued up until sixteen seconds before the second 911 call was received by dispatchers and less than fifty-three seconds before the shot was heard. The defense declined cross-examination.

Two more witnesses testified, one of Edward Landauer's former instructors from Philadelphia Community College who testified that Edward had aspirations to be a policeman and had applied to the police academy, and his instructor at the gun range where he took a firearm safety class.

It had been a long day and Victoria had no complaints when Judge Kelly checked his watch again and adjourned until tomorrow morning. Out the side of her eye she watched Benjamin converse with his client before they left the courtroom. She didn't feel like answering any questions so she lingered at the table putting her papers in order. Once the courtroom was about empty she hurried out and took the stairs down to the vestibule.

Victoria didn't want to go home. She needed to breathe some different air, see some different faces, eat some Soul food, and have a stiff drink. She picked up her cell phone and called her friends, Marvin, Angeline, and Joshua to see if they could hang out with her at Warm Daddy's. She knew it was short notice but they had been blowing up her phone with messages wanting to get together. Besides, it was Thursday and Dupree was playing there tonight. It would give her a chance to show him some support after all he was doing to make things easier for her.

She changed into faded skinny jeans, a white flowing blouse, and red sandals. She pulled her hair up in a ponytail added some big earrings. Her brief case fit nicely in her large straw tote, she put it on her shoulder under her arm, and wearing her big white framed sunglasses she barely recognized herself. She walked about two blocks down Market Street to clear her head before she hailed a taxi. It felt good to feel free, no cameras, no judge, and no jury.

***

Tamika and Angeline were waiting outside when Victoria got to the restaurant.

"Thank you guys for coming out," Victoria said, giving them both quick hugs before they went inside. "Where are Marvin and Gerald?"

Angeline answered first. "Gerald is being an old man today. He didn't feel like going out."

"Girl, Gerald is an old man every day," Tamika laughed.

"He was an old man when you married him," Victoria added.

"At least I know where he is every night," Angeline snapped.

"For your information, Marvin is out of town on negotiations. He's a free agent," Tamika added, exasperated.

"As long as you know it," Angeline said, insinuating something else.

Tamika rolled her eyes but held her tongue as the hostess asked, "How many in your party?"

"It will only be five of us," Victoria responded cordially.

"I don't know why you wanted to come here. You know I'm on a gluten-free diet," Tamika complained, glaring down at the food on the plates of other patrons.

"You can eat a salad," Victoria said, unaffected.

"You've been looking good on the news, Vick," Angeline said after the waitress sat them at one of the side tables. "Those shoes are banging, you've been shopping without me."

"I haven't had time. Leonard gave them to me for good luck."

"Are you two back together?" Angeline asked nosily.

"No, we're just friends."

Tamika pursed her lips and shook her head. "I don't know what's on your mind, Vicki. I wouldn't let Leonard get away."

"I told you at the Gala that I'm with somebody else now, his name is Dupree."

"That's right, I forgot. Mr. Music Man," Angeline teased.

"Neither of you are going to work my nerves, he's good for me. I would be struggling through this trial without him," Victoria said, concentrating on the menu.

The waitress came back and was taking their order when Joshua and Hannah joined them at the table.

"How rude, you all weren't even going to wait," Hannah said, sitting down.

The waitress paused for a second. "Would you all like a few more minutes?"

"No need," Joshua said after giving Victoria a hug, "We'll have the blackened tilapia and beef ribs with two tequilas."

"Now that we're all here, there's somebody that I'd like you all to meet," Victoria said happily.

"I get it," Angeline announced, "Dupree is playing here this evening."

"Yes he is," Victoria replied proudly.

Tamika rolled her eyes again.

Joshua changed the subject. "Anyway, Victoria, I just want to tell you that you are doing an impressive job as a prosecutor. I've never seen you at work before."

"I hope you'll say that when it's over."

"The defense attorney is all that," Hannah said, smiling slyly. "I bet he works on the case day and night."

"Why are you saying that?" Joshua asked, irritated.

"The Commonwealth's second chair is sleeping with the enemy."

Victoria was stunned. "What are you talking about?"

"Miss Khloe, she stayed at the hotel after the Gala to hook up with Benjamin Madison."

"How do you know that?" Victoria demanded.

Hannah grabbed her chest. "Oooh, now I'm being questioned by the famous Victoria Perry."

"Be quiet, Hannah," Joshua said, "I told you it's not your business."

"Excuse me, I thought she knew."

The waitress brought their food to the table. No one said a word until she was done serving.

Joshua spoke first. "Look, Victoria, don't get sidetracked on some irrelevant bullshit. I wouldn't even deal with it. The only thing you need to think about is how to put that asshole where he belongs, locked up in the pen."

The background music volume lowered and the band started to play.

Victoria turned her attention to the stage. "You're right, Josh. I'm done with that foolishness."

"Which one is he?" Angeline asked nonchalantly.

"He's playing the sax," she answered.

Angeline appraised Dupree from his dreads to his purple polo shirt, down to his bleach-washed jeans, then the huaraches on his feet, and raised her hand for a high-five.

"I'm not mad at you, girl."

"Oh shit, now I get it," Tamika said, putting down her fork. "The brother is all that. I've got to hand it to you Vicki, you don't play. I'm not going to say another word."

Tamika and Angeline had stopped eating and were both engrossed in the show. Victoria smiled to herself as she crunched on her Southern fried chicken plate and sipped on a Margarita while the Voyagers played their set. She was determined to take Joshua's advice and let the music lighten her up. She ignored the annoyed whispers between Joshua and Hannah.

The waitress cleared the table and they ordered another round of drinks just as the set ended. Dupree walked by giving Victoria a wink as the band gathered at the back to refresh themselves before their next set.

"He's got skills," Joshua said, nodding.

"I'm so sure," Tamika added.

"Well, do we get to meet him or what?" Angeline asked, feeling snubbed.

Victoria slid out from the long cushion bench and walked over to where the band was sitting. Every eye from the table followed. Victoria leaned over and spoke in his ear.

"There are some friends of mine here that I would like you to meet."

"I'm kind of working right now, baby."

"It will only take a minute."

Slightly perturbed he relented and came over to the table.

"Dupree, this is Angeline, my roommate from college, this is Tamika, and this is Joshua, and his wife, Hannah. We all went to school together."

"It's very nice to meet all of you," Dupree said, extending his hand to each of the women.

"Please join us," Tamika said, smiling.

"I wish I could but we only get a short break before the next set."

"Another time," Joshua said, standing up for a good brother handshake.

"No doubt," Dupree said, putting his arm around Victoria.

She walked towards the back with him stopping before they got to the band's table.

"That wasn't hard. They're good people."

"I'm sure they are," he said, giving her a quick kiss. "I'll see you at the house."

Joshua and Hannah were both standing when she got back to the table.

"We enjoyed it, but I've got an early morning," Joshua said, giving her a hug. "I'll call you this weekend."

"Thanks for coming, it was good to see you guys," Victoria said before they left. "I probably need to call it a night myself."

Angeline reached for her purse. "I'll drop you off, Vick."

"What about you, Tamika?" Victoria asked since she was still seated.

"I'm going to stay for the second set. There's no reason for me to rush home early."

"All right, girl," Angeline chuckled, "Don't get in any trouble."

"There's no ring on my fingers," she answered, taking another sip of her drink.

Angeline was almost to Victoria's house before she turned down the radio to talk.

"How long do you think the trial will last?"

"Probably another week, I should get through my witnesses tomorrow."

"Then we need to have some real girl-time after it's over. I need to catch up with you."

Victoria stepped out of the car.

"Hopefully we can get to Atlantic City for a weekend."

"Take it easy, Vick. You have a lot going on."

That was an understatement. Now that Victoria felt she couldn't trust Khloe, the full weight of the trial would be on her shoulders. She would have to prepare her own briefs and do all examinations of the witnesses. There was no need to confront Khloe. She had a right to privacy in her personal life. She wasn't the only woman to fall for a pretty face and a smooth tongue.

Chapter Seventeen

Victoria walked in the courtroom more focused than ever. The air of a conspiracy gave her another reason to fight harder to win. She nodded at Mona Gardner when they made eye contact as they did each day. She crossed her legs and looked at her feet. Her black pumps were so fierce, she felt like a panther ready to attack.

"Are you feeling better?" Victoria asked when Khloe slipped into the seat beside her.

"Oh yeah, I must have caught a stomach virus like you said."

"Hmmm, I hate when that happens."

 "What's the game plan for today?"

"Take it easy, I've got it."

Benjamin sauntered in as usual with his client sandwiched between him and Thomas Clancy. Victoria gave him a polite smile as he sat down at the table. The bailiff announced court was in session and Judge Kelly walked in, then the jury, and the session was called to order. Judge Kelly greeted the jury as usual and followed with the barrage of questions as to whether they had discussed the case with anyone outside the jury.

He took a gulp of water and said, "The Commonwealth may call the next witness."

"Good morning, Your Honor, ladies and gentlemen of the jury, we call Detective Maria Rosario to the stand."

Dt. Rosario was sworn in and took the stand. They went

through the usual questions of name, length of employment, training, and experience.

"Detective, how many were there when you arrived on the scene?"

"There was Sgt. Robert Kline and the defendant standing by Deshaun Gardner's body, and two other police officers. The EMT got there just as I did."

"What happened after you got out of your vehicle?"

"I asked them what happened. Sgt. Kline explained that the defendant told him that he shot the person lying on the ground. At that point I handcuffed his hands behind his back. Took the gun from Sgt. Kline and put it in a gun box."

"What was he wearing?"

"He was wearing a beige jacket and blue jeans."

"Were his clothes torn, ripped, or disheveled in any way?"

"No they were not."

"Was there any blood noticeable on him or his clothes?"

"His mouth was swollen and there was some blood around his lip."

"What happened after that?"

"The EMTs were checking the vitals of the victim lying on the ground. One of them asked the defendant if he was hurt."

"What did he say?"

"He said his jaw was hurt. I asked him if he wanted to go to the hospital but he said no."

"What happened next?"

"I walked him to my car and transported him to the Roundhouse."

"Did the defendant have any trouble walking or need assistance getting to the car?"

"Not at all."

"Thank you, Sgt. Rosario."

Benjamin only asked three questions in his cross-examination.

"Did my client resist or was he uncooperative at any time?"

"No he didn't."

"Was he angry or agitated in any way?"

"No sir, he didn't seem to be."

"Did he make any comments about Deshaun Gardner?"

"Not to me."

"Nothing further, Your Honor."

Victoria called the doctor who attended Edward Landauer at the hospital. His testimony was short. He said that Edward Landauer had a hairline fracture of lower jaw bone that did not require surgery or wiring. Benjamin declined from cross-examining the doctor. Judge Kelly called for a fifteen minute recess. The two cups of water he drank while the witnesses testified had made their way through his system and urged to be released.

After the break, Victoria called Dt. William Carlton the Chief Investigator on the case to the witness stand. She made the decision not to play the recording of the interview since she would not be able to cross-examine the defendant's account of what happened. She moved quickly through the preliminary questions to the details of the statement and interrogation of Edward Landauer.

"Dt. Carlton, how did your investigation begin?"

"I told the defendant his rights and I let him know the interview would be recorded. He signed the form that stated he understood and agreed to talk without an attorney. Then I asked him to tell me his story."

"What did he say?"

"He explained that he started a Town Watch group in his neighborhood. He mentioned that he had seen several suspicious people around the area and that they always got away."

"Did the defendant say why he thought Deshaun Gardner looked suspicious?"

"He said the suspect was taking his time casually walking in the rain looking at houses and he hadn't seen him before. I asked him what the person looked like and he said he was African-American, wearing a dark hoodie and jeans, tall, late teens or early twenties."

"Was that when he claimed he called the police?"

"That's right. We used a google map of the scene and asked him where he was when the person known as Deshaun Gardner passed him."

"How did the defendant claim he made contact with the person?"

"He said the person came up to his car and then ran across the street. Then he got out of his car to pursue Deshaun, although he said the dispatcher told him he didn't need to follow him. He said the victim jumped at him and said, "What's your problem, muthafucka?" He said he asked him what he was doing around here and he said, "Shut your fucking mouth," and starting punching him in the face. He said the victim told him he was a dead man. He said he called for help but no one came out to help. He said he thought the victim was going for his gun, that's when he pulled it out of his holster and shot him."

"What did the defendant claim happened after that?"

"He said that Deshaun said, "You shot me," and tried to get up but he told him to stay down. Then a police car pulled up."

"I've read the defendant's written statement and he referred to Deshaun Gardner as the suspect over and over throughout the statement. Isn't that a law enforcement term to describe a person thought to be guilty of a crime?"

"Yes it is."

"Deshaun Gardner was walking casually in the rain. In your knowledge and training, Dt. Carlton, is that a crime?"

"No it's not."

"Is it a crime to wear a hoodie?"

"No, ma'am."

"Do you think that people who wear hoodies are suspicious?"

"No I don't."

"Have you found any evidence that Deshaun Gardner was committing a crime or was armed with a weapon of any type?"

"No we haven't found anything that indicated he was committing a crime and he did not have a weapon on him."

Victoria hesitated a moment before she said, "So, the only thing that we can say Deshaun did that night was defend himself against an attack?"

Ben leaned forward into his microphone. "Objection, You Honor, speculative and argumentative."

"Sustained," Judge Kelly said.

"Did the defendant show any outward emotion to demonstrate that he was upset with having just shot and killed someone?"

"He didn't and that concerned me at the time but I didn't know him or his personality enough to judge."

"No further questions, Your Honor."

"Your cross, counselor," Judge Kelly directed.

"Dt. Carlton when you mirandized my client did he waive his rights?"

"Yes he did."

"Was he cooperative in your interview and during the reenactment of what happened?"

"Yes he was."

"Were you concerned at all when he said he followed the suspicious person?"

"I didn't think about it."

"Did he seem to have any animosity or contempt toward Deshaun Gardner?"

"No, he didn't seem to."

"Was he evasive in any way to deem he was hiding anything?"

"Not from what I could tell, he answered all of my questions."

"So, you didn't have any reason not to believe what he was saying, wherein the prosecution referred to his statement as claims?"

"At that point, I was collecting evidence. I made no judgement."

"Were you concerned when he referred to Deshaun as the suspect?"

"I wasn't bothered by it."

"In your experience as a police officer have you seen circumstances where individuals were numb after undergoing mental or physical trauma?"

Dt. Carlton folded his hands. "I have seen that."

"Was there anything that my client did or said that led you to believe he took the situation lightly?"

"He was anxious to get it all over with so he could go home, so he could get some sleep for work the next day."

"So you were charged with looking at the evidence to determine if this case fell within the statute of self-defense?"

"In general, yes, but I don't make the decision to indict."

Benjamin spent fifteen minutes trying to minimize the language Edward used as harmless slang and showing pictures of Edward's face and close-ups of his bloody mouth in an effort to convince the jury that he had been viciously attacked. Victoria resisted the urge to re-direct, her next witness would show who the real victim was.

Judge Kelly checked his watch again and it was 12:20. He sat up like an alarm had gone off. "The court will be in recess until 1:30."

Victoria felt her cell phone vibrate in her briefcase as she walked out with Khloe trailing her. She waited until she was out of the courtroom before she looked to see who was calling. It was Arthur, saying he had lunch in his office.

"The boss is feeding us today," Victoria said.

What Victoria really wanted was a quiet peaceful lunch alone in her office. Holding her tongue had been tough enough sitting beside Khloe in the courtroom all day.

"Is that a good or bad sign?" Khloe asked apprehensively.

"You never know with Arthur Mitchell, we'll find out shortly."

When they got to his office, Arthur was stretched out with his feet up on his desk wearing a big grin on his face.

"Come on in, ladies. Sit down. We're having Chinese today. Victoria, I would offer you a drink but I don't want to take your edge off."

"May I ask what are we celebrating?" Victoria asked guardedly.

"It looks like you'll rest your case this afternoon. Mayor Turner called and he's very pleased. So am I. Win or lose, you have put on a good case. It was enough to put all of this civil unrest behind us and have a profitable summer in the city."

"So it doesn't make any difference to you whether the killer of a young black boy walks?" Victoria asked indignantly. "Where's the justice in that?"

"The system is doing its job."

"I thought the days when a white man could kill a black man on the streets without any provocation and walk away a free man were behind us but evidently they are not."

"Victoria, I'm surprised at you," he said, amused. "I thought you wanted my job. You'll never be D.A. with all those idealistic notions clogging your brain. This is real life."

"I think I just lost my appetite," she said, turning to leave.

Khloe moved to follow her out.

Arthur laughed. "Sit down, Khloe. I don't want this good food to go to waste. We can talk. Maybe you'll be my successor."

That was a reality check. Victoria took deep breaths on the way to her office. She knew she had to make some changes in her life. She refused to work in the D.A.'s office until she became cold and hard like the marble under her feet. She was absolutely certain she didn't want Arthur's job, her goal in law school hadn't been to work in the D.A.'s office. It just happened to be the office that sought her out. She would have gladly accepted an offer from a firm like Rosen and Sullivan with a pent office suite and a view.

The words of her mother repeated in her head, "The devil is truly busy." She refused to give in to the negative energy around her. She was determined to recycle it and let it serve as the fuel to propel her through the trial and hopefully to another position. She wasn't an idealist harboring delusions of saving the world. She had watched her daddy try to do that his whole life.

***

The courtroom gallery had refilled after the lunch break. The cameras, the reporters, Benjamin, Thomas and the defendant, Edward Landauer were all back in place. Khloe was seated at Victoria's right side. The jury was present as Judge Kelly raised his gavel. The only person absent from the room from the morning session was Mona Gardner. The sense of dread Victoria felt evaporated. She hadn't wanted to inflict any more suffering on her with the details of her only son's murder.

"The Commonwealth may call its next witness," Judge Kelly said firmly.

"Thank you, Your Honor, the Commonwealth calls Dr. Godfrey Diallo."

Victoria adjusted her notes as the doctor approached the stand and was sworn in.

"Good afternoon, Dr. Diallo. Would you please begin by stating your name, then give us your occupation, where you are employed, and for how long."

After stating his name and spelling it for the record, Dr. Diallo stated that he was the Chief Medical Examiner and had held the position for 26 years. He went on for an additional four minutes detailing his education, degrees, training, and residencies. He listed his credentials and certifications as a licensed surgeon and forensic pathologist.

"What evidence was given to you to determine your findings in this case?"

"I examined the re-enactment and records from the clinic where the defendant was treated, videos related to the case, autopsy photographs, and the toxicology report."

Dr. Diallo testified that the facial injuries of the defendant were insignificant, not life-threatening, no stitches were required. He never lost consciousness, and in his opinion they were from one blow. He further testified on his report of the autopsy performed on Deshaun Gardner.

"What were your initial findings from the autopsy report?" she asked.

"We found he had been shot in the aorta above the left ventricle of his heart. This was the cause of death. Three bullet fragments were removed, two in the heart area and third in the lung. There was no other disease present in the body."

"Were there any other injuries on the body?"

"Only a small abrasion on the middle finger of his right hand."

"Was there any blood on his hands?"

"Not from the abrasion, but there was some on his left hand."

"What did the DNA tests reveal about that blood?"

"It was the blood of the deceased, Deshaun Gardner."

"Was DNA from the defendant found on the victim's hands?"

"No ma'am, none was detected."

Victoria continued with the long examination of the gory details of the Deshaun's death. Khloe accompanied her on the computer as she moved methodically through the presentation of exhibits that were the pictures of the entrance wound and the exit wound in Deshaun's chest and back. The doctor testified that the gunshot came from an intermediate range, less than four feet. He described the straight path of the bullet once it entered Deshaun's body, each part of the heart that was pierced and where the fragments tore his flesh and where one fragment lodge in his lung. He talked about the amount of blood that collected in his chest and estimated that he lived for possible two minutes from the time he was shot and that he had a zero chance of survival."

Benjamin's cross-examination reviewed Dr. Diallo's testimony about the injuries sustained by his client.

"Isn't it possible that my client was hit many more times without there being marks left from those blows?"

"Objection, Your Honor, he's asking the witness to speculate," Victoria called out.

"Sustained," Judge Kelly answered.

Benjamin moved his questions to the toxicology report. "There was THC from marijuana found in the body of Deshaun Gardner wasn't there, Dr. Diallo?"

"Yes, there was about 1.7 milliliters per milligram detected."

"Isn't it possible that was a sufficient amount to have a mental or physical effect on him?"

"It's possible but that would depend on a number of factors and variables."

"Nothing further, Your Honor."

Victoria thought about re-direct but decided against it. She didn't want to make a big issue about the small amount of THC.

"The witness may be excused," Judge Kelly said, checking his watch. "Call your next witness, Ms. Perry."

"The Commonwealth calls Darren Gardner."

When Darren Gardner walked up to take the stand, Mona came inside the rear door and took a seat in the back.

"State your name for the record, Mr. Gardner."

Mr. Gardner stated his name and spelled it. He answered questions about where he lived, his education, place of employment, and marital status. He wore his pain all over his face as he talked about Deshaun and the plans they had for him to attend his alma mater in Tennessee.

"Was it your decision for your family to move out of Germantown?" Victoria asked.

"Yes it was. I thought it would be safer for Deshaun but I was wrong."

"Was Deshaun in a gang?"

"No, he had big plans for his life. He was never in any trouble."

"Did you know that he smoke marijuana?"

"No, but I'm not surprised, I smoked some myself when I was his age. It would not have worried me."

"Your witness, Mr. Madison," Judge Kelly said.

"No questions for the witness, Your Honor."

"You may be excused," Judge Kelly said, looking at the time.

"The prosecution rests, Your Honor."

Judge Kelly nodded sedately, containing his pleasure that they would get done before 6:00. He was more than ready for a tender piece of meat and a stiff drink. He gave the jury his usual admonishments for their behavior during the weekend, raised his gavel and announced, "The court is adjourned until Monday morning at 9:00."

Victoria exited quickly before Khloe could even shut down her laptop. She wanted to get out without making any statement to the press about the case. It had been the most challenging and significant week in her career. Khloe struggled to catch up to her as she ducked into the stairwell.

"I'll pull the car up to the front," she said, giving up the chase at the top of the staircase.

"All right," Victoria shouted up to her.

The red light showing voicemails was flashing when Victoria got to her office. She ignored it. Whoever it was would have to wait until Monday. She gathered her laptop and files for the case and headed back out the door. She was grateful for the police barriers that held the demonstrators and most of the reporter away from the entrance. She easily made her way to the curb where Khloe was waiting.

"Thanks," Victoria said as the car pulled away. "So, what are you plans for the weekend?"

Khloe hesitated before she spoke. "Not much, I was thinking about driving to Richmond for the weekend. I haven't been home in a while. Do you need me to work?"

"No, go on and enjoy yourself. I would love to get a break out of the city for a few days."

"I don't want to feel like I'm leaving you in the lurch."

"Don't worry about it. All the research has been done. The rest is in the presentation."

"Just call me if you need anything."

"Take this weekend to recharge, unless you don't need those batteries anymore," Victoria said facetiously.

Khloe blushed. "I haven't needed them lately."

"Who's the lucky guy?"

"I don't want to talk about him yet. I might jinx it."

"Okay, I hear you."

Victoria's feelings of anger and betrayal waned and she felt sorry for Khloe. She was being used. Knowing Ben, this wasn't a budding relationship. She didn't think he was even capable of truly caring for someone. He was a warrior. Divide and conquer was his modus operandi. Khloe was just the latest conquest. She got out of the car in front of her house and waved.

She rushed in the front door not wanting to talk to anybody. She was spent and needed some time to herself. She warmed up some leftovers Dupree had in the refrigerator and then laid down in the living room in front of the muted TV looking at the posts on her Facebook page. A text from Leonard flashed up, "I was wrong. You did your thing in court this week."

She texted back. "Thanks, but Benjamin gets to put on his show next week."

"You'll be ready for him."

"I don't have a choice."

When Victoria woke up it was after midnight. She climbed the stairs to her bedroom and went back to sleep. She didn't wake up when Dupree got home, and she barely opened her eyes when he said he was going to the Northeast to check on his friend's house.

***

Victoria spent most of the morning in bed. She hadn't realized how tired she was. She showered, dressed, ate a bowl of cold cereal, and then went next door to visit before she ran a few errands.

Victoria knocked hard on the screen door before she went in.

"Hey in here, it's the law."

"It's about time," Miss Judy joked, "I called you over an hour ago."

"I must have been in the shower. What do you need, ma'am?"

"Lanetta had to fill in for somebody at the half-way house and I need to get some things from the store."

"I'm here, where do you want to go?"

"I want to go to Pathmark if you don't mind."

"Not a problem, I've got to pick some clothes up out of the cleaners on the way."

Miss Judy put her handbag over her shoulder and opened the refrigerator.

"I'm going to grab a bottle of water, it's so hot today. You want one?" she asked.

"Sure, why not," Victoria answered, holding out her hand.

Victoria unlocked the passenger side door for Miss Judy to get in before she double-checked the bolt on the front door. In the car, she put on the shades she kept in the glove compartment, backed out of the driveway, and zoomed out of the block. They turned right off of Girard Ave onto Broad Street.

"I've been watching the trial every day, Vicki," Miss Judy said. "I feel like my mama back in the day when she was watching her stories, I stop everything I'm doing."

"Well, unlike those soap operas, this will soon come to an end."

"I hope it comes out in your favor, baby."

"Not for me, for Deshaun and his family."

"That's right, I can't stand seeing that man sitting up there like he didn't do anything wrong, it makes me sick."

"It's worse in person. What kind of crazy sonofabitch does something like that and expects to walk away."

"I don't know. There are some sick people out here."

"Tell me about it."

"I've got a taste for some fried pies," Miss Judy said, gazing thoughtfully out of the passenger side window.

"Ooo, that sounds so good, I haven't had those since my momma cooked some for me when I was a little girl. I loved them."

Remind me to get some dried peaches and apricots when we get in the store. I'm going to make some this evening."

The two of them were leisurely cruising through green lights up Broad Street talking about the delicious desserts that they hadn't had in a long time, rice pudding, lemon meringue pie, and Good Humor popsicles, when Victoria sped through a yellow light just as it changed.

"I better lighten up on the gas pedal, Old Faithful didn't have time to slow down on that one."

Miss Judy chuckled. "I know that's right."

Victoria could see the traffic light ahead of her at Broad and Huntingdon was red. She pressed the brakes firmly but the car didn't slow, she pressed it down as far as it would go, and it still kept speeding forward.

Alarmed she said, "Miss Judy, the brakes aren't working."

"Oh my God, Vicki, can you pull the keys out to stop it?"

"No, they won't come out with the car in drive."

Victoria beeped the horn loudly and dodged traffic as the car sped through the red light.

Miss Judy grabbed her heart. "Lord, Jesus."

"I put it in neutral but it's driving out of control."

Victoria held the wheel tightly in one hand while beeping the horn with the other as they roared through another red light at Lehigh Avenue. Car horns blared at them as they left the sounds of skidding tires behind them. Old Faithful plowed forward with Victoria weaving between lanes and other cars as they sailed through a green light at Somerset and W. Indiana. As they approached a red light at Clearfield a burgundy sedan with tinted windows started speeding on the left side of them.

"What the hell is going on?" Miss Judy shouted.

"I don't know. Call 911."

Miss Judy grabbed her phone out of her purse as the car sped forward. She lost her grip, the phone dropped, and slid under the seat when the sedan veered into their front fender hitting it on the driver's side. Driving on instinct Victoria moved to the far right lane bearing down on the horn to clear the street. The burgundy car edged in front of them forcing them closer and closer to the curb until they bounced up on the sidewalk and then down again. Victoria held the wheel as the car began to swerve. The burgundy sedan hit them again pushing the right tires back onto the sidewalk. Victoria braced herself as Old Faithful rammed into a fire hydrant just in front of the crowded intersection of Allegheny Avenue. Jerked forward into exploding airbags, Victoria and Miss Judy were thrown back against the seats and then flung to the front. Water jutted out the hydrant and rushed into the street.

"Are you okay?" Victoria asked frantically, reaching for Miss Judy despite the throbbing pain growing in her shoulder.

"I hope so, I can't tell yet," Miss Judy said, lifting her head up.

All of sudden somebody snatched the driver's car door open.

Victoria turned and looked. "Dt. Rosario, how did you get here?"

"Are either of you hurt? The fire department is on its way."

"Mostly we're shaken up. My brakes failed and this car just ran into me."

"That was me driving the burgundy car. Did you forget you're under protection because of the death threats?"

"I hadn't notice you."

"You're not supposed to, neither is the person threatening you. I saw your brakes went out so I did what I had to do to stop the car."

"Well thank you, Jesus, and thank you, detective," Miss Judy said, "The situation was getting real ugly and we could have been killed."

"That's why I'm here. Let me help you both out. I'll run you up to Einstein Hospital where you can get checked out.

Victoria winced as Dt. Rosario grabbed her left elbow.

"I'm good, help Miss Judy."

They heard the sirens of the fire trucks and EMTs.

"Give me a minute, I'll be right back," Dt. Rosario said after they were settled in the back seat of the burgundy car.

In a delayed reaction Victoria felt like crying.

"Look at Old Faithful, my daddy would be heartbroken," she said with tears in her eyes.

"No he wouldn't. He'd be praising God that we made it out alive. That car can be fixed."

"I'm so sorry about all of this. I wouldn't put you in danger for anything."

"No harm done, baby, except we won't be getting those fried pies this evening."

Chapter Eighteen

Benjamin had been too busy to see her for most of the week. It bothered her but she respected his obligation to prepare to put on his defense next week. She was looking forward to the end of the trial just as much or more than everyone else in Philly.

"I love you," she said barely above a whisper, inaudible below the sound of his Bose stereo.

She loved every part of his body and the scent of his skin. She loved breathing the same air he breathed. To her he was like a drug and she was turning into a junky.

Khloe crawled up from under the sheets to look him in the face.

"Benny, I think I should tell Victoria about us seeing each other."

He hated to be called, Benny, he wasn't a child. He refrained from telling her because she wouldn't be around long enough for it to matter.

Khloe rolled over and laid beside him. "I don't feel comfortable keeping it from her. I think she can sense something is going on."

Ben hesitated and thought about the repercussions. Would Vicki be jealous or angry? It wouldn't send her running into his arms that's for sure. The deception with her second chair gave him an adrenalin rush. It was just the push he needed to make this trial interesting.

"What purpose would it serve right now? She would only misconstrue it as a ploy to sabotage her prosecution."

"Whatever you think," Khloe said, snuggling happily under his arm.

For once in her life she had the captain of the football team, homecoming king, the rock star, the one who always picked the cheerleader, the homecoming queen, or the fashion model. It felt good to be the chosen one for a change. She only wished she could parade him up the steps of City Hall arm-in-arm.

Benjamin lay beside her full of regrets, the first being that last shot of Scotch at the Gala. Getting involved with Khloe had been a mistake. He had broken the eighth Cardinal Rule, combining orgasms with professionalisms. It was nothing more than a game at the time, something to amuse himself, and now she was acting like a lovesick teenager.

***

On Monday morning at 8:45 the courtroom was packed as usual. The press and spectators waited in anticipation before the jury and Judge Kelly took their assigned seats. Victoria had been drinking coffee like it was water after a four mile run but she didn't feel like it was having much of a reviving effect. She had lain awake the last two nights in pain, sore from her neck down, and the shock that Miss Judy could have been seriously hurt in the accident. Against doctors' orders she had decided not to wear the neck brace they provided her with in the emergency room. She didn't want to distract the jury. The other big thing disturbing her was the revelation from Dt. Rosario that the brakes going out on the car wasn't an accident.

Victoria ambled in through the gallery of the courtroom biting the inside of her lip to steel herself from the aches she felt in her shoulders, neck, and back. It also helped to contain the frown that creeped to her mouth when Laramie Landauer gave her the stink eye as she walked passed him in the back. She thanked heaven for the respite when she finally set her briefcase down on the prosecution's table. She got some additional comfort when Khloe entered the courtroom, if things got too rough she might have to stand in for some of the cross-examinations.

Khloe sat down and scooted her chair close to Victoria.

"I just heard you were in a car accident on Saturday. How are you, were you hurt?" she asked, genuinely concerned.

"The upper half of my body is killing me but I'm okay."

"What happened?"

"I was driving up Broad with my next-door neighbor and the brakes went out. Thank God Dt. Rosario had my back. She had to run me off the street to stop the car. Now she's saying that the car had been tampered with."

"That's incredibly scary. Do they know who did it?"

"They're investigating, that's all I know."

A hush came in the room when Ben Madison walked in with his client, Edward Landauer, and co-counsel, Thomas Clancy. Ben dropped his briefcase in his chair and crossed the aisle. He put his hand on the back of Victoria's chair and leaned over to speak privately.

"Good morning, counselors. It's good to see you, Victoria. I'm sorry to hear that you were in an accident. How are you feeling?"

"I'm well, thanks for asking."

"If you want a continuance I wouldn't object."

"I appreciate the consideration but it's not necessary."

"All right, but I'll leave the offer on the table," he said, patting her on her sore shoulder.

He returned to the defense table just as the court clerk and bailiff entered and declared court was in session. The jury came in and took their seats while Judge Kelly took his place on the bench. Benjamin went right into his defense with four witnesses who were neighbors of Edward Landauer, one whose house had been broken into and the others who were familiar with the break-ins in the area and had worked with him on the Town Watch group. He kept them on the stand for the whole morning attempting to drive home that his client was acting as a necessary hero on behalf of the community. Victoria took a time out and Khloe did the cross-examinations. When Judge Kelly called for a recess for lunch, Victoria could have kissed him.

"What do you want to do for lunch?" Khloe asked as they left the courtroom.

"I need to lie down. Can you get me a hotdog with mustard and sauerkraut from the corner?"

"Sure, no problem."

Victoria hurried to the restroom, the cups of coffee had run through her system. Back in her office she wanted to pop one of the serious pain pills that had been prescribed but they would probably knock her out and she had a long afternoon in front of her. When Khloe got back, she ate the hotdog in three bites and washed it down with a bottle of fruit juice. She took two Aleve tablets set the alarm on her cell phone and stretched on the couch.

***

In the afternoon session Benjamin called Alta Landauer to the stand. She seemed nervous but she calmed down after he asked her the preliminary questions of who she was and her relationship to his client.

"Was your son raised in the house where he now resides?"

"Yes he was."

"Would you say he had a stable childhood?"

"For the most part, yes. When he was very young my husband was in the military and we moved around a lot until he retired, that's when we bought a grocery store in the neighborhood."

"Did he give you any problems at home?"

"Definitely not, he didn't give us any trouble at all. Eddie was always trying to do things to please his father."

"Were there any complaints or reports from his teachers about his behavior at school?"

"No, just the opposite. Eddie was the one who was bullied at school all the time. The kids picked on him all the time because of his weight."

Ed grimaced as he listened to his mother testify. He couldn't stand her bringing up the past and calling him, Eddie, he was a man goddamit. When Alta glanced over at him and saw his displeasure she realized her error.

Ben asked one more question. "Were you aware of the increase in criminal activity in the area where you used to live?"

"Yes I was, and I was proud that Edward was doing something to help. He always wanted to help people. He even applied to the Philadelphia Police Academy."

"Your witness, counselor," he said, moving back to his table.

"Good afternoon, Mrs. Landauer," Victoria said politely. "I just have a few questions. You mentioned your husband was in the military. Did your sons serve as well?"

"No, Edward wanted to go in the service but he wasn't able to."

"Was that because of physical or mental reasons?

Benjamin interrupted. "Objection, Your Honor, leading the witness."

"Sustained."

The implication was put out there so Victoria moved on to her next question.

"You also said that the he applied to the Police Academy. Was he denied admission?"

"I'm not sure what happened with that," Alta said thoughtfully.

"Would you say that your son was trying to please his father with his attempts to enter into the military or law enforcement?"

"He may have been."

"Since he couldn't pass the tests, didn't he start the Town Watch to try and fulfill his desire to police the neighborhood?"

Ben stood up. "Objection, Your Honor, it's inflammatory."

"I withdraw the question, Your Honor," Victoria interjected.

"Edward only wanted to be a hero," Alta exclaimed, her eyes filled with tears.

"No more questions, Your Honor," Victoria said, taking her seat.

"The witness is excused," Judge Kelly said, "Defense, call your next witness."

"We call, Emerson Landauer," Benjamin responded as he stood at the lectern."

Emerson was sworn in and gave his name and where he lived.

"As an older brother, were you always protective of Edward?" Ben asked.

"Of course I was, that's only natural."

"And are you trained in martial arts?"

"Yes I am, I have a Black Belt in Taekwondo."

"Did Edward take up the discipline or any other form of self-defense?"

Emerson shook his head. "It wasn't his thing, he's not very coordinated."

"If he were attacked by a strong guy, could he effectively defend himself?"

"Objection, Your Honor," Victoria interjected, "He's assuming facts and calling for a conclusion from the witness."

"I'll allow it," Judge Kelly said indifferently.

"He's never been a fighter, he's a little clumsy," Emerson said, looking at the jury.

Edward winced at his brother's words. He hated that he always made him look like he was weak. Emerson was always better, no matter what he did. He couldn't believe it, people were saying he killed that boy in cold blood but beside his older brother he still looked like a wimp.

"I know you've heard all the comments made about your brother in the media about him being a bigot. Is your brother a racist?"

"No way, he doesn't have anything against blacks or people of any color. He was friends with several blacks on the street where we grew up."

"Do you think he was racial profiling when he saw Deshaun wearing a hoodie?"

"Not at all, Ed said he thought the person was trying to hide his identity."

"No more questions, Your Honor."

Victoria left her laptop on the table, her shoulder felt too weak to carry it to the lectern. She only had a few questions so she could make it without her notes.

"Hello, Mr. Landauer. I'm curious, what made you take up Taekwondo?"

"It's a form of mental and physical discipline, and it's a great workout."

"Did you encourage the defendant to take the classes also?"

"Sure, and he did for a while, but like I said it wasn't his thing."

"Do you think that maybe he got tired of you showing him up and fighting his battles for him? So tired in fact that he bought a gun?"

"No way, the gun was to defend his home. He wouldn't use it unless it was life or death."

"Except he carried it concealed on his person when he was out in public, did he not?"

"I don't know. We don't hang out a lot."

"Have you ever referred to a black man as a fucking coon?"

"No, I haven't," Emerson said, outraged.

Benjamin rose to his feet. "Argumentative, Your Honor."

"Sustained, tread lightly, Ms. Perry," Judge Kelly said, peering at her over his glasses.

"No more questions, Your Honor."

Victoria grit her teeth to stave off the pain as she returned to her table.

"Why don't we take a fifteen minute break," Judge Kelly said, his second glass of water was stressing his full bladder.

Victoria kept her seat, not wanting to expend any unnecessary energy. Benjamin walked out leaving his client with Thomas.

"I'm going out for a cigarette," Khloe said, standing up.

"I didn't know you smoked," Victoria said skeptically.

"It's one of my secret vices."

Victoria shook her head in disbelief. "And I thought I was complicated."

After the recess Benjamin called another medical examiner as an expert witness. His testimony for the first hour focused on the injuries of Edward Landauer and the power with which he had to be hit to break his jaw. Then in the second hour he moved to the autopsy and the gunshot wound, and how long Deshaun may have lived after he was shot. Victoria was bored and she suspected the jury was too. They had all been through it with the Commonwealth Medical Examiner. The facts were that the defendant pulled the trigger and shot the victim. Who cared about the wound size? It killed him. The only relevant thing he offered to the trial for his $1400 fee was that the nozzle of the gun was 3-4 inches away from the victim.

Victoria yielded to Khloe for the cross-examination. By the time the witness was excused it was after 6:00 and Judge Kelly looked like he was about to explode. He gave the jury their usual instructions without taking a breath, adjourned the court, and stormed out of the courtroom.

"We need a new strategy," Victoria said when they got back to her office.

"What's on your mind?" Khloe asked, plopping down in a chair.

"We've been in court for six days and the scales haven't tipped one way or the other. Ben is going to put Jamaal Taylor on the stand tomorrow and it might be the pivotal point in the trial."

"Can you block it as prejudicial?"

"I'll try, but I need a contingency plan. I need Edward Landauer's crazy ass to testify."

"There's no way Mr. Madison is going to put him on the stand."

"I know he doesn't have any intentions of doing that but he can't stop his client from testifying if he insists."

"How are you going to manage that?"

"He's easily provoked. I just need to push his buttons."

"How?"

"Starting tomorrow morning, I'm going to be more accommodating to the press."

***

The next morning Victoria dressed in a fuchsia sheath dress with matching duster and her gray pair of Christian Louboutins. She was leaving early so Dupree made her a breakfast smoothie to drink on the way. On her request Dt. Rosario dropped her outside of the police barrier; she had been escorting her back and forth to the Justice Center since the accident.

A rogue reporter stuck his microphone in her face.

"It doesn't look like Edward Landauer is going to take the stand. Are you disappointed?"

"I'm not surprised, it's expected. He's not used to fighting his own battles," Victoria answered smugly.

"Why should he? All he has to do is sit there quietly and wait it out," the reporter said with a smirk.

With an air of self-righteousness, Victoria replied, "My daddy always preached that the truth will set you free."

The reporter wouldn't let it go. "That's a chance they probably won't take."

"The innocent don't have to be scared of telling their story."

"Maybe they're being smart."

"Most cowards are, but don't quote me."

Victoria smiled and walked through the barrier and into the Justice Center. She couldn't have scripted it better.

Today when she passed Mona Gardner in the Gallery she wasn't apprehensive about making eye contact. Victoria was confident that she was doing all she could to bring their son's murderer to justice. Both Mona and Darren had been stoic maintaining their dignity under the horror of the trial as the Prosecution and the Defense launched attacks at each other in their public war. Nevertheless, she knew Benjamin well enough to know that he planned on firing a torpedo at them today that could possibly sink her case.

Khloe paused from organizing their briefs when Victoria sat down.

"You look like you're feeling better today."
"I got a good night's sleep."

As soon as Judge Kelly sat down Victoria asked to approach the bench. It was a longshot but if at all possible she needed to block Jamaal from being called as a witness. She knew his testimony could definitely hurt the prosecution's case. Her argument was that Jamaal Taylor would be a prejudicial witness not bringing any evidence to the actual event. Benjamin argued that it was relevant to the defense's case, that Deshaun Gardner may have previously been involved in gang activity and was prone to violence.

Judge Kelly asked the jury to leave the courtroom when he realized that both Victoria and Benjamin had dug their teeth in this rag and neither wanted to let go. While the sidebar conference between the prosecution and defense went back and forth for an hour and a half citing cases to substantiate their position, sidebar conversations among the audience in the gallery were becoming just as contentious. In the end, Judge Kelly ruled in favor of the defense, bringing all the arguments to a close.

Judge Kelly brought the jury back in, apologized to them for the delay. He went through the usual formality and asked the group the same questions he asked every day and they answered them in the same way they did every day, with silence.

"Call your witness, counselor," he said, checking his impressive watch.

Benjamin called Jack McCullough to the witness stand. Edward sat up tall in his chair. He knew Jack wouldn't let him down.

"How long have you been friends with Edward Landauer?"

"We met at Welch Security Services six years ago. We both worked there part-time on the weekends. Then we started hanging out after work. We've been friends ever since."

"So, you both hung out together socially pretty often?"

"Yeah, we did," Jack answered, glancing over at Ed.

"On any of those occasions did the defendant get into an altercation?"

"On a couple of nights, people were always trying him."

"Was my client, your friend, ever beat up?"

"At least once, he wasn't a fighter. He got hurt pretty bad."

"Is that the reason he bought a gun?"

"Not really, he told me one of his ladies was scared to stay over after a robbery in the neighborhood so he bought the gun to make her feel safer."

"Nothing further, Your Honor."

Victoria moved to the podium for cross-examination.

"Good morning, Mr. McCullough," she said courteously. "You mentioned that the defendant got into a number of fights. Was there something about him that turned people off, something that made them react angrily to him?"

"Ed didn't take any B.S. from anybody."

"Was it like he had something to prove?"

"Maybe he did. People can't disrespect you all the time."

"Isn't it possible that he provoked these fights?"

Benjamin stood up. "Objection, argumentative, Your Honor."

"Overruled," Judge Kelly responded, "The witness may answer."

"It might have looked that way," Jack answered, "People will always push you around if they think they can get away with it."

Edward shrank down in his seat discontented. He couldn't understand how this bitch was putting words in Jack's mouth and twisting everything he said.

"You testified that the defendant bought the gun for his house but then he applied for a license to carry it concealed. Did he ever carry it on him when you two went out?"

"Sometimes, I don't know. He kept it inside his waistband."

"Did you worry about somebody getting shot with his hot-temper?"

"Objection, its inflammatory, Your Honor."

"Sustained."

"No further questions."

"The witness is excused," Judge Kelly said, sipping from his glass and checking the time, "The court will break for lunch until 1:00."

***

The seed Victoria planted in the morning had borne fruit by the afternoon. Her comments had been broadcast all over the news media. Arthur was waiting to meet with her and Khloe outside when court was adjourned for lunch. A pack of reporters that had gathered outside the door intercepted them and pushed forward to get an interview with the Assistant D.A.

Victoria made an uncharacterized statement to the press.

"Although the Defense Counsel is well within his rights, their entire defense is relying on other witnesses who have no knowledge of the event to testify while the defendant who has full knowledge of what took place on the evening of March 29, 2012 sits silent. I'm sure it's in the best interest of his client not to give us the truth."

Arthur moved in to stop the interview, taking Victoria by the elbow.

"Victoria, you're on the line, careful or you may cross it."

"I'm done, Arthur, don't worry."

Thirty minutes later she was back in her office picking over a plate of barbecue when she got the expected visit from Benjamin. He sat down in the chair opposite her.

"I know what you're trying to do," he said haughtily.

"I've been completely transparent," she said, wiping her hands.

"I'm seeing another side of you, Momi," he said grinning at her. "I'm intrigued."

"Suddenly I realized I was in Rome," she said, grinning back.

"Touché."

"Why are you here, Ben?" she asked him.

"I was just wondering if your newfound relationship with the press might be a hint of desperation. I'm here to make a deal if there's one on the table."

"As you can see there's nothing here except chicken and potato salad."

He jumped to his feet energized. "I love it. A worthy opponent brings out the best in me."

"Glad I could help," she said nonchalantly.

"You are so sexy, Momi, have dinner with me."

"Why, you're already sleeping with my assistant."

Ben paused for a moment while he recovered.

"Where did you hear these rumors?"

She gave him a look that told him not to waste his breath lying.

"You weren't very discreet."

"My mistake, I usually have better judgment."

"You're both consenting adults."

Benjamin was speechless, something that rarely happened. Victoria continued to eat. When she was done, she stood up and tossed the plate in the trash.

"As I said before, there's nothing on the table."

"Fair enough," he said on his way out.

Chapter Nineteen

Victoria watched the jury's reactions as Jamaal meandered into the courtroom wearing baggy jeans that hung low despite his belt and a long Boondocks t-shirt. Their facial expressions of disapproval confirmed that it wasn't a good look. He was sworn in and took his seat in the witness box. He made no attempt to tone down his cockiness for the benefit of the court as he stated his name, age, and address. Benjamin couldn't have been more pleased.

"Do you mind if I call you Jamaal?"

"Why would I mind, that's my name."

"Would you say that you were a good friend of Deshaun Gardner?"

"No doubt, he was my boy."

"How long were you two friends?"

"Since we was in elementary school."

"You hung out together after school?"

"Oh yeah, we kicked it all the time."

"Did you ever skip school together?"

"Yeah we did, what's the big deal?"

"What kind of things did you and Deshaun like to do to past the time?"

"Nothing in particular, hoops or just chill in the hood."

"There are a number of gangs in Germantown. Have you ever belonged to a gang?"

"I don't know what you're talking about, unless you calling my family and friends a gang."

"Jamaal, doesn't your juvenile record have a couple of robberies and a drug charge on it over the past three years?"

"I don't know, man," he sneered, "I haven't memorized it."

"Were any of your family and friends involved in those activities?"

"People are always accusing me of things I didn't do. The cops got me on a "stop-and-frisk." They couldn't prove any of those charges; they didn't have a reasonable suspicion to stop me."

"Weren't you picked up in the Badlands, the area in North Philly known for drug dealing?"

"It's real hot up there right now, man," Jamaal answered, "I stay away from the Badlands. I don't go nowhere near there. I'm not hustling drugs. Another friend of mine just got killed out there last week."

"Weren't you sent to the Youth Study Center for robbery?"

"I know you ain't ever been hungry, so you don't know nothing about being on the grind. I did what I had to do to make that dough. I'm trying to survive out here."

"In the mugshot taken when you were arrested you were wearing a grey hoodie just like the one Deshaun Garner was wearing. Aren't hoodies worm by gang members in Germantown?"

"Come on, man, are you for real? Hoodies are worn by everybody all over town."

"For you and Deshaun Gardner to stay friends all of these years, the two of you must have had a lot things in common?"

"He was a good dude, he was loyal."

"Your witness," Benjamin said, returning to his seat.

Victoria rose for the cross.

"Jamaal, as a friend, what did you like most about Deshaun?"

"He kept me laughing all the time. He was always joking about something."

"Deshaun didn't have a juvenile record. Is that just because he didn't get caught?"

"No way. He didn't get in any dirt. I wouldn't have even let him. He had too much going for hisself. He was real smart. He always said he was going to make it and then help me out."

"Did he act like a thug or try to be hard?"

"No, man, he was comfortable in the streets but he wasn't made from the streets. He didn't have to pretend, he was down with everybody."

"Would Deshaun use language like, "You're gonna fucking die?""

"Uh-uh, he didn't cuss like that, he was cool, but me, I might have said that and more if somebody ran up on me."

"Nothing further, Your Honor."

Benjamin considered re-direct but it might do more harm than good.

Edward started coughing uncontrollably like he was having a fit or choking on something.

"Does your client need a recess?" Judge Kelly asked Ben, concerned.

"Just a moment, Your Honor."

Ben spoke to Edward while Gayle handed him a glass of water. The fit seem to subside so Ben called his next witness, Anita Donati, a supervisor at the insurance company where he worked. She wobbled up to the stand nearly as wide as she was tall with bright red curly hair and heavy make-up. The jury was more fascinated by her appearance than by anything she would offer as a witness.

She testified that Edward was congenial with his co-workers and extremely dependable. In the winter months when it was dark at the end of the day he often walked her to her car. He was always concerned about crime and being safe. He wasn't the type to hurt anybody. He even notified her personally about what happened that night.

When Victoria cross-examined her, it turned out that aside

from work she didn't know much about her employee. She didn't know he had family that lived in the city. She wasn't aware that he had taken classes at Community College while he worked there. Victoria was about to end her cross when she decided to ask one last question.

"When Edward told you what happened, how did he say he felt about it?"

"He said if he could do it over he wouldn't have done anything differently."

"Thank you, Ms. Donati," Victoria said sincerely.

Judge Kelly checked his watch while the witness waddled down from the stand and back out of the courtroom. He was torn. It was only 4:15 but if he allowed for one more witness they would most certainly go past 5:00. His carafe of water was empty and the fact that he was sweating under his robe helped him come to his decision.

Judge Kelly turned towards the jury.

"Ladies and gentlemen, in light of the hour, we'll recess at his point. Court will adjourn until tomorrow morning at 9:00."

Victoria tapped her foot in a moment of private praise. Benjamin hadn't rested his case. She needed more time for her seed to come to full fruition. She sucked in the sides of her jaw to contain the smile that strained to spread across her face.

***

They barely got down the steps into the Lincoln MKT that waited for them daily outside of the Criminal Justice Center before Edward exploded in a rage.

"You're letting them kill me in there, man."

Benjamin rolled his eyes up in his head.

"What's your problem, Edward?"

"You're bullshitting. I'm tired of sitting in there next to you with your mouth shut while they're making me look bad. I want you to put me on the stand. I got something to say."

"It's not necessary, Edward. It's not our job to prove anything."

"I don't care about that," he bellowed. "I hear what they're saying about me."

Thomas couldn't hold his tongue another second.

"Mr. Landauer, you've got the best representation that money can buy. Let us do our job."

"What the hell do you know about it?" Ed said, looking at him with contempt, "You're the fake nigger paid to sit beside me and make it look good for the jury."

"Calm down, Ed, we're on the same team," Ben said. "The situation is under control."

"Don't try to play me. That bitch has been punking me all day."

"Nobody can play you unless you step in the trap," Ben said, getting impatient with his tirade.

"I got a right to speak for myself. I said I want to testify."

"As your attorney I have to advise you against it."

"It's not your ass they want to throw under the jail."

Benjamin leaned back in the seat. He refused to waste rational words on someone who was completely irrational. Hopefully this was a temper tantrum and his client was merely venting his frustration. Edward breathed heavily through his nose with his chest rising high every time he inhaled until they reached the condominium in West Philly, one of several the firm maintained for expert witnesses.

"Think about it, and then sleep on it," Ben said when the car stopped.

Edward got out and slammed the door.

Thomas looked out the window disgusted.

"I can't believe he's so ungrateful after all we've done on this case."

Benjamin shook his head, reached for his cellphone and called Laramie Landauer.

"Good evening, sir," Benjamin said after Laramie was on the line. "There's been a new development in the trial."

"I know, chronic indigestion and high blood pressure for myself."

"Edward is insisting on testifying."

Laramie groaned. "What can I possibly do to assist you?"

"I need you to speak with him, change his mind."

"If you couldn't, what makes you think I can? That kid doesn't care what I think."

"I don't agree, sir. He's been trying to earn your approval for most of his life."

"Try as he may, he's been a disappointment to me most of his life. He's a grown man now. He can make his own decisions."

"All right, sir, have a pleasant evening."

"I'll try," Laramie said and hung up the phone.

Benjamin opened his briefcase, pulled out a silver flask with an emblem of a horse head on it and poured a big swallow down his throat.

***

Victoria went straight to Miss Judy and Lanetta's door as soon as she got out of Dt. Rosario's car that evening. She still felt guilty about what happened.

"Knock-knock," she said, walking inside the unlocked screen door.

"What's up, girl," Lanetta said cheerily.

"I came to check on Mom. How's she feeling?"

"She's good. She went to bed about a half hour ago. Go on up, she might not be asleep."

Victoria looked at her watch and saw it was after eight o' clock.

"No, I don't want to bother her," she said, sitting down at the kitchen table.

"Have you eaten yet? Mama made some shrimp fried rice

today."

"No, I haven't, that sounds right on time."

Lanetta fixed her a plate and put it in the microwave.

"So, how are you doing?"

"I'm still sore and tripping over it but I can't call in sick this week."

"I know that's right. I watch as much of it as I can while I'm working and I loved the close-up you had this morning. Get your fame, sister."

She handed Victoria the plate with a fork and poured her a glass of iced tea. Victoria said a quick blessing and started to eat.

"It's not about that," she said with her mouth full, "I'm trying to win this thing."

"You might have some sense in that head after all," Lanetta joked. "You called that psycho out today. Let's see if he steps up to the mic."

She took a big gulp of tea.

"Tomorrow is 'do or die.'"

Dupree was playing at the Blue Note tonight so Victoria stayed there with Lanetta and watched two episodes of *Girlfriends* before she went home. She made sure the front door was securely locked and headed straight upstairs to take a shower. The warm water felt so good to her aching muscles she hated to turn the water off. Standing there under the gentle streams cascading over her back it reminded her of when she was a teenager. She could almost hear her momma shouting through the door, "Turn off that water."

She smiled to herself as she stepped out of the shower, put on a big t-shirt, and went into her daddy's office. She curled up in his lazy-boy chair where she did her late night reading and studied the briefs Khloe had prepared until her eyes started to itch from fatigue. Once her files were organized Victoria couldn't make up her mind what she wanted most, a cool drink of rum and coke or a pain pill. She settled for the pain pill and crawled into bed.

***

Victoria stepped out of Dt. Rosario's car at the entrance of the Criminal Justice Center dressed in a khaki colored safari jacket with matching skirt wearing her chocolate colored red-bottom heels. She was charged and ready to go in the jungle and capture her prey, right down to her leopard print bra and panties. She thought about what Leonard had said about being understated but she couldn't resist carrying the Louis Vuitton briefcase with her outfit.

She strutted in the courtroom like she owned it. She wanted to make eye contact with Benjamin but he was engrossed in a conversation with his client. Victoria couldn't help but notice the navy suit and blue and white striped shirt the defendant was sporting. She had to admit the gold tie with dark blue polka dots set it off nicely. Victoria had anticipated Benjamin being a rival for 'most-fashionable' but the defendant had been showing up in a different suit and tie every day. They had been in court for eight days and he hadn't worn the same color suit or tie twice.

Benjamin leaned in close to whisper to Edward.

"Let it go, Ed. We haven't had time to prepare you."

"I don't give a shit, I'm ready," he insisted

"I'm not sure the jury will react positively to you."

"I'm not changing my mind," Edward said stubbornly.

When Judge Kelly came in promptly at 8:59, Benjamin jumped to the lectern and requested to meet with him in his chambers. Victoria stood up and resisted the urge to do a hallelujah dance as they all went out the side entrance to the judge's office.

"What's this all about, counselor, you know I like to run a tight ship?" Judge Kelly asked, pouring himself a glass of water.

"Your Honor, my client insists on testifying."

Victoria mouthed the word, "Yes."

"You just have to roll with it, counselor. If you came in here with a motion for withdrawal, it's denied. It's too late to withdraw without causing an adverse effect to your client."

"Your Honor, we request a recess until tomorrow morning to prepare."

Judge Kelly stood up to leave.

"Request denied, counselor. Now, if there's nothing else, let's get on with it."

Benjamin had planned to call Laramie Landauer as his first and last witness of the day before Edward insisted on testifying. His father was the only one who could make Edward seem like a sympathetic character. With that in mind he called his client to the stand.

"State your name for the court, please," Benjamin said.

"Edward Landauer, E-d-w-a-r-d L-a-n-d-a-u-e-r.

The jury stared at Edward while he gave his address and place of employment.

"Mr. Landauer, explain to the jury what motivated you to start the Town Watch group in your neighborhood."

Edward leaned forward towards the microphone to speak.

"When I was growing up in the neighborhood it was a nice place, you didn't have to worry about anything. Over the past three years the crime was getting worse and worse. There were burglaries all the time and then a friend of mine down the street had this guy come into her house while she was at home. She's lucky to be alive. It was so scary that my girlfriend at the time encouraged me to buy a gun for protection. That's when I decided to start a Town Watch group."

Benjamin flinched and tried to disguise his reaction with stretching his shoulders. Victoria whispered to Khloe while she typed feverishly on her laptop.

"You were properly licensed and your gun was registered was it not?"

"Definitely, it was all above board."

"Had you ever canvassed the streets around your house before the night of March 29, 2012?"

"Many many times, especially if the dogs down the street were barking a lot, just to check things out."

"What happened on the night of March 29th?"

Ben held his breath while Edward answered.

"It was a regular day. I was sitting in my house watching the TV when I heard the dogs barking again. I came out and looked around but I couldn't see anything. It was raining so I went back in to get my car keys to drive around. I got my gun and holster too. I thought that since I was going out I might pick up my friend, Jack, and go get a beer or something. I turned onto Oak Street where the dogs were barking but I didn't see anything at first. Then I turned onto Shiloh Street and that's when I saw this guy wearing a hoodie walking on the street."

"Could you tell if the person was black or white at that time?"

"Not then, I couldn't see his face and his hands were in his pants or either in his pockets. He was moving slow at first, like he was trying to look at houses that didn't have their lights on. That's when I called the police. When he saw me he darted across the street and started walking fast."

"Did you try to approach him at this time?"

"No, I circled the block. When I came back he saw me and he started running. I pulled my car past him to keep an eye on where he was going until the police got there. I walked over to him to ask what he was doing around here and that's when he pushed me and said, "Get the fuck out my face." I told him not to put his hands on me and then he started punching me in the stomach. He punched me in the jaw so hard I felt it crack. When I grabbed my face he tried to snatch my gun out of the holster. I reached it first. Then he started punching me again and I felt like I was going to pass out. I knew if I did he would shoot me. I raised my gun and fired one time. Then I heard the sirens coming. An officer pulled up, he got out of his car and took my gun. I wasn't trying to kill anybody. I was trying to save myself."

"Did you feel like your life was in imminent danger, that you had no other choice?"

"Absolutely, I wouldn't have used my gun if it wasn't."

"Are you a racist?"

"No, I'm not."

"No more questions, Your Honor."

Benjamin returned to the defense table, Victoria paused for a few seconds before she went to the lectern. She had the defendant right where she wanted him.

"Good morning, Mr. Landauer. You testified that a girlfriend convinced you to purchase a Kel-Tec PF-9 9mm semi-automatic pistol."

"Yes, she felt safer staying over after I bought it."

"Tell me about the day you bought the gun. How did it make you feel?"

"I didn't feel any particular way about it."

"Did you have any reservations about shooting someone?"

"It was for my protection, I never wanted to kill anybody."

"If you have no intent to kill, why buy a gun?"

Benjamin jumped up. "Objection, Your Honor, argumentative."

"I withdraw the question, Your Honor," Victoria said.

The question was more directed to the jury.

"So, Mr. Landauer, you said you weren't excited about finally having the gun you wanted? Whenever I make a major purchase it gives me a thrill."

"Not really, it was just for protection."

"So you planned to use it only for protection at your home?"

"At first yes, that's right."

"I know how I feel when I get a new pair of shoes I can't wait to take them out on the town. Did you feel like that when you bought the holster and applied for the license to carry a concealed weapon?"

"That wasn't the way I felt."

"Are you saying that you paid $400 to $1500 for something that you hoped and prayed that you would never have to use?"

"I thought I might need to carry it when I go clubbing, sometimes things get out of hand."

"That's understandable. I don't buy anything I don't intend to use."

"Objection, Your Honor," Ben shouted.

"Careful, Ms. Perry," Judge Kelly said.

Victoria moved on.

"You said that March 29th started off as a regular day. My morning thoughts always set the course of my day. What were you thinking about that morning? Were you edgy or upset?"

Edward shrugged his shoulders.

"No, it was a regular day."

"All right, so what were you doing that evening before you heard the dogs barking?"

"I was relaxing in my house."

"Do you drink a beer to help you relax?"

"Sometimes I do but I didn't that evening."

"So you couldn't relax, you strapped on your gun, and went out in your car to hunt for a black thug to shoot that night?"

Edward eyed Victoria with revulsion. He despised everything about her. She was a woman who didn't know her place. He wandered who she thought she was talking to him like that. He was about to give her an earful when Benjamin shot up out of his seat.

"Motion to strike, it's prejudicial, Your Honor, Ms. Perry is badgering the witness."

"Sustained, Miss Perry, you have been warned," Judge Kelly said harshly.

"I apologize, Your Honor," Victoria said.

She paused for a moment to check the notes on her laptop before she resumed her cross.

"Excuse me, Mr. Landauer. Did you say you were in your car investigating the noise from the dogs and then you saw Deshaun Gardner?"

"That's right."

"Was the hoodie an immediate red flag for you?"

"No, he seemed to be lurking around like he was casing the neighborhood."

"Were you against him because he was black?"

Ben interrupted. "Objection, Your Honor."

"Overruled," Judge Kelly replied.

"I told you already, I don't have anything against black people," Ed said irately.

"You told the police dispatcher that he looked like he was suspicious or on drugs. I'm curious about what that looks like? What does that look like to you?"

"Like I said before, he was walking real slow in the rain, lurking around. I've seen some young guys around like that before when we had a burglary around the corner from me."

"You said that when you circled back, Deshaun started running. Was he running towards your car or away from it?"

"He was running away."

"How could he run away and attack you at the same time?"

"I pulled my car in front of him."

"When you got out of the car did you have your gun drawn?"

"No, I just wanted to talk to him, see what he was doing."

"When you approached him did he strike you right away?"

Edward shifted uncomfortably. He was tired of answering questions.

"No."

"Who spoke first?"

"I did."

"What did you say?"

"I asked him what he was doing around here and he told me to

"Shut the fuck up." Then he pushed me. He kept coming at me. I cried out for help but nobody came to help me."

"You had the gun, he was unarmed. You had the upper hand. He was a teenager, you're a grown man. Why were you calling for help?"

"He was a strong kid. He was attacking me."

"When did you reach for your gun?"

"He broke my jaw and I thought he was going for my gun so I pulled it out and shot him."

"Did you mean to intimidate him or did you feel you needed to shoot him?"

"I panicked. I didn't have time to think."

"You had to be feeling something because you grabbed your gun."

"I felt like my life was in danger."

"How can we be led to believe that within the time span of less than five minutes, the time between when you ended the call with the dispatcher to the time shots were heard that you found yourself in the equivalent of a championship beat down where you feared your imminent death?"

He looked over towards the jury.

"It's the truth."

"Are you telling us that if you hadn't shot Deshaun Gardner that you would be dead today?"

"I'm sure about that."

"Hadn't you called the police minutes before and been assured that they were on their way."

"Yes, but I feared for my life, I wasn't even thinking about that."

"I find it hard to believe that packing a loaded 9mm gun against who you described as a teenager would cause you to fear for your life."

Ben stood up again, exasperated. "The prosecution is making

statements again."

Victoria yielded. She had made her point.

"Nothing further, Your Honor."

Benjamin sighed as his client left the stand. No chance for a mistrial.

"The witness may be excused," Judge Kelly said. "The time is approaching 12:00 so we'll take an hour recess for lunch. Let's return at 1:00."

Victoria got a quick look over at Benjamin on her way out. He was fuming. She almost felt a tinge of empathy. As long as she had known him she had never seen him in a situation where he wasn't in control. He would have never put Edward Landauer on the stand in a million years. She had pushed his client's buttons until he didn't have a choice.

"What are you plans for lunch?" Khloe asked on the way out.

"I'm going out with Dt. Rosario. I got a text that she has something important to discuss with me about my secret nemesis."

"Okay, I'll see you back here at 1:00. By the way, good job this morning."

"Thanks. Unfortunately, he held his temper but at least the jury got to know him better."

The reporters outside the courtroom were in more of a frenzy than usual. No one had expected Edward Landauer to testify. Victoria was back in her mode of offering no comment. Outside she hopped into Dt. Rosario's car thankful for the tinted windows.

Chapter Twenty

"What's on the menu?" Victoria asked, looking out the window.

"Mexican, there's an El Azteca restaurant not far from the Roundhouse," Dt. Rosario said, zooming down Market Street.

"Chili's is right on the corner."

"I don't eat Mexican unless there are Mexicans cooking in the kitchen."

"I'm not particular," Victoria laughed, "As long as it tastes good.

Dt. Rosario made a right turn on to Eighth Street, another right on Chestnut Street and parked the car in a space marked 'no standing or waiting.'

"So tell me, what's the big news report about my psycho-stalker?" Victoria asked, getting out of the car.

"It can wait until after the appetizer," Rosario said, getting out of the car.

Prolonging the mystery sparked Victoria's curiosity. It peaked when she saw Dt. Carlton and Arthur sitting at a table.

"Come join us," Arthur said, sounding like he was on his second shot of Tequila. "I hope you don't mind me ordering for you, they had this neat entrée of 'five things for $10, it should have something you like in it."

"Thank you, Arthur, but you shouldn't have spent so much," Victoria said humorously.

Arthur smirked. "Very funny, don't quit your day job."

"Being that our esteemed D.A. did not order appetizers, can we get to the meat of the matter?" Victoria asked impatiently.

Dt. Carlton inhaled deeply before he spoke.

"This investigation went in a totally different direction than we thought it would. We're all here to discuss when and how you want to go forward on this.

Victoria frowned up, confused. "Okay, now I'm lost."

"Initially we thought that the culprit making the threatening phone calls was just some crazed redneck venting out his frustrations. We had to take it more seriously when the ricin showed up in the mail. We went over every inch of your car and one of the fingerprints came up as a match to that of a small-time hood who thinks he's a big-time hit man."

Victoria backed up her chair from the table.

"This is too much for me to deal with right now."

Dt. Carlton continued. "Look I don't want you to get upset, we have the suspect in custody and we know who hired him. We got his cell phone and there was only one number that we couldn't connect to anyone. It was traced to a pre-paid phone. We found out where the phone was purchased from the serial number. It was sold in a Target on Monument Rd. We looked on the camera footage from the date and time of the sale and we saw a familiar face."

"Who was it?" Victoria asked, barely audible.

Dt. Rosario put her hand on Victoria's shoulder to brace her.

"It was the Defense Attorney's second chair, Thomas Clancy," she said.

"You have got to be kidding, that's ridiculous. Benjamin wouldn't risk his career doing some insane shit like that," Victoria said, shaking her head in disbelief.

"I can't say who did what or who knew what. I just know what we saw," Rosario said.

"The phone number is the same as the calls that made the death threats," Carlton added.

"This doesn't make any sense," Victoria said.

Arthur put both his elbows on the table and folded his hands.

"The question is what are we going to do about it and when?"

A waiter brought their food and drinks to the table.

"What are the options?" Victoria asked, looking at all the food on her plate.

"We can go back to the Justice Center and arrest Thomas Clancy right now," Arthur said, "I can guarantee that it will mean a mistrial. Another option is to sit on this until the trial is over."

Victoria threw up her hands in disbelief.

"How do we know if they've given up on killing my ass?"

"You know I have your back, Vicki," Rosario assured her. "Besides, the attacks were probably meant to affect the trial and it's coming to a close."

"It's your call," Arthur said before he took a big bite out of his burrito.

Victoria thought about the consequences. She couldn't go through the drama of the trial all over again. The city needed a reprieve from the tension and conflict that had gripped them all since that night in March. What if the defense plan was to derail the trial all along? She had worked too hard to give them that satisfaction.

"Let's hold off until the case goes to the jury," Victoria said.

"Good deal," Arthur said, taking another huge bite.

***

Victoria sat at the prosecution's table as if she knew nothing about the conspiracy across the aisle with defense counsel. "Don't look over there," she repeated to herself but it was almost impossible not to stare. She had sat within arm's length of the man who had threatened and then attempted to take her life. "If I don't get a guilty verdict they should give me an Oscar or an Emmy for my acting performance," she thought. Then she chuckled to herself, "Thomas Clancy probably deserves an award too."

"How was lunch?" Khloe asked, sliding in her seat.

"It was delicious. I'll have to take you there sometime."

"Come on, Victoria, do they know who tried to kill you?"

"They have suspects and they're close to making an arrest."

"So what do they know about him?"

"Not much, but I can't deal with that right now. I've got to keep my mind on this case."

The bailiff called for order in the court and Judge Kelly came in just before the jury. He asked the same questions he always did every time they came back in the courtroom. If any of them ever talked about the case, they never admitted it. Then he instructed Benjamin to call his next witness. He called Laramie Landauer to the stand.

"You were a military man weren't you, Mr. Landauer?"

"Yes, I was, twenty years in the Marine Corp."

"With the level of discipline you were accustomed to in the military, did you raise your sons in a strict environment?"

"Not necessarily, I raised both my sons to be law-abiding citizens?"

"With your military background, did you teach your sons the art of self-defense?"

"Emerson was athletic and held his own, but Edward, his mother raised him soft. He never did learn how to fight."

"Were they raised with any racial biases in the home?"

"Absolutely not, Edward is not any more prejudiced than anybody in this room."

Ben changed the subject after that response from Laramie.

"Mr. Landauer, were you aware of the increase in crime in your old neighborhood?"

"Edward talked about it a lot and we knew he started the Town Watch program? I was proud of him for taking a stand."

"When you heard about what took place on the evening of March 29th what did you feel?"

"I was sorry about what happened. I hurt for the Gardner parents, and for Edward. He didn't have anything against that kid. He was just tired of these young thugs ruining the neighborhood."

Alta covered her mouth as if it would stop her husband from speaking but he kept on.

"You can't live in peace around them, that's why I moved away from there."

Benjamin's plan for gaining empathy backfired on him. Instead of making the jury feel sorry for Edward, his testimony had only shown the apple didn't fall far from the tree. He closed his laptop.

"No more questions."

"Your witness, Ms. Perry," Judge Kelly said, nodding his head.

Victoria took her position at the podium.

"Good afternoon, Mr. Landauer. From your record you had a stellar career in the military. Wasn't it hard for your sons to live up to that legacy?"

"I never asked my boys to follow in my footsteps."

"No, but isn't it natural that they would want to? Edward tried to enlist in the military after high school didn't he?"

"Yes, he did."

"He also applied to the police academy didn't he?"

"Yes, he did, and if my son had the badge he wanted we wouldn't be here today."

"Are you saying that the Police have a license to murder in the street?"

"You watch the news don't you, madam prosecutor, what do you think?"

Ben felt like kicking himself in the head. He was the one who put Laramie on the stand. He would have a lot of persuading to do to minimize the damage in his closing statement.

"Nothing further from this witness, Your Honor.

"Do you have another witness, Mr. Madison," Judge Kelly asked.

"No, Your Honor, the defense rests."

"Ms. Perry, do you have any rebuttal witnesses."

"No, Your Honor, the prosecution rests."

"Ladies and gentlemen of the jury, no more witnesses will be testifying, that portion of the trial has concluded. The counselors will meet with me in my chambers. Due to the hour, you will be excused for the remainder of the day. Court will be adjourned until 9:00 tomorrow where final arguments will be presented."

Judge Kelly then marched out of the court room while the jury filed out. Victoria loaded her laptop and files into her briefcase while Khloe did the same. A feeling of dread and paranoia was coming over her. The last place she wanted to be was closed up in a room with Ben Madison, Thomas Clancy, and Khloe Luskin. She couldn't trust any of them. It reminded her of Julius Caesar walking outside of the Pompeii theatre where he was taken to a small room by his conspirators and knifed to death.

***

Surprisingly the meeting in Judge Kelly's chambers went smoothly. Possibly the opposing sides were saving their energy for the closing remarks. Benjamin went through the motion of declaring that the evidence supported his client's declaration of self-defense and requested that the charges be dropped. Judge Kelly denied the request and in about an hour they agreed to the instructions that would be given to the jury. Victoria lingered in her chair a few moments to be the last one out of the door. She wasn't going to give them free aim to stab her in the back.

***

"I don't want to hear any objections, Victoria," Arthur said strongly. "We can't take a chance on any drama at this juncture in the trial. We've booked you a room at the Ritz Carlton. Dt. Rosario is going to escort you home to pick up whatever you need."

"I want to argue with you but that offer is hard to refuse."

"It's a matter of safety and convenience, after tomorrow you're on your own. Do you need Khloe to come and help you prepare your power-point?"

"No need, I don't want the distraction of a power-point tomorrow. I won't be teaching. I want them to hear my argument not read it, this is real life."

Dt. Rosario waited outside Victoria's house while she packed an overnight bag and her garment bag. Tomorrow was the big finale and she wasn't sure what to wear. The attack mode of the trial was over so she didn't need to be fierce, animal prints were no longer required. It was time to be precise, direct, sincere, serious, and impressive. It was time to lead Edward Landauer to the gallows; it was time to wear black. She chose a sleeveless black linen dress with asymmetric buttons down the front, bulky gold jewelry would soften the look. She packed her sleek black red-bottom pumps and lace underwear in the bag with her toiletries and hurried back out to the waiting car.

She wanted to take a few minutes and visit with her family next door but she had kept Rosario waiting long enough. She would call them as soon as she got settled in the hotel. Rosario opened the trunk and put her bags beside a red rolling suitcase.

"I get the adjoining room next to yours," Rosario said, smiling. "It's going to be rough duty, but somebody's got to do it."

Victoria looked back at her house as the car pulled away. It looked so empty without Old Faithful sitting in the driveway. She made a promise to her daddy that she would have it repaired as soon as possible, right now it was being held as evidence. Victoria leaned back against the headrest wondering how long it would take for her life to return to normal.

***

The opulent and formal exterior of the Ritz-Carlton with its huge columns reminded Victoria of the architecture of City Hall across the street. The valet rushed to Rosario's car door as soon as they pulled in and a bellhop stood at the entrance waiting to assist with their luggage.

"I already have the room keys, Victoria," Dt. Rosario said, going towards the elevator.

They rode to the nineteenth floor. "We're in 1914 and 1916."

The room was completely luxurious. Victoria looked around the large suite taking it all in, along with the view of William Penn above City Hall.

"Now this is where I'd like to recuperate after the trial," Victoria said, falling back on the plush sofa. "Then I could really enjoy this place."

"I'm sure the hotel won't mind extending your stay for however long you want," Rosario chuckled, unlocking the adjoining door.

"Not at these prices, they don't pay me like that."

"You don't have to tell me, I work for the city too. I intend to enjoy these few hours starting with a hot bath and then plenty of room service. Knock or call if you need me," she said closing the door between the rooms.

Victoria pulled out her phone to make some calls before she ordered up some food and polished up her closing argument.

Miss Judy answered. "I was just about to call you. I saw you drive off with that detective. Is everything okay?"

"It's all good. My boss wants me to stay in a hotel near the Justice Center as a precaution. The case will probably go to the jury tomorrow."

"I'll be glad when all this mess is over."

"You are not alone on that. Is Lanetta around?"

"No, baby, she's out with this guy she met at that club you took her to."

"Wow, we really need to catch up. I'll stop by tomorrow after court."

"All right, baby. Take care of yourself."

Victoria pushed the button to end the call feeling like she had lost touch with her life. She had been consumed with the case since the morning after the shooting. She felt isolated and alone. She checked the time, Dupree shouldn't have started his set at the Blue Note yet.

"What's up?" he answered.

"I'm at the Ritz Carlton for the night, it's beautiful, come by here when you get done."

"It'll probably be real late. I'll be off tomorrow and we can hook then."

"I need you tonight, Dupree, the full treatment. I have to be on in the morning."

"If it's like that, wait for me at the house."

"Why can't you come here?"

"I don't need to be in a high priced hotel to enjoy my lady."

"It's not about this hotel, it's about me wanting to be with you."

"I'll be at the house when I get off."

"You're more of a snob than anyone I know."

"What's that supposed to mean?"

"It means you refuse to be in the company of people you perceive to be different from you."

"Vick, I'm basically a minimalist and you surround yourself with people and things of excess. I've told you before, it's not my scene."

Victoria didn't respond. She couldn't understand what that had to do with him coming to be there with her.

"I've got to go, I'll call you later," he said, hanging up.

Victoria ordered a ribeye steak, baked potato, asparagus tips, a bottle of red wine, and strawberry shortcake for dessert from room service and took a hot shower. She sat and ate at the dining table where she could see the city lights and worked for a couple of hours before she stretched out along the pillow topped mattress and fell asleep.

Chapter Twenty-One

This was the day, the closing round of the fight, and Victoria Perry's last opportunity to convince the jury that the death of Deshaun Gardner was indeed murder in the second-degree. She had to be better than she had ever been. That meant she had to forget the disappointment she felt from Dupree not coming to the hotel, even though she could have used a massage and some good loving to relax her. Benjamin would no doubt be charming as usual, and with five women on the jury he stood a good chance of getting a hung jury. She took one last look at her dress in the mirror and wondered if the black was too subdued. Then again, it was too late to second-guess. They were due in court in a half hour.

Dt. Rosario tapped lightly on the adjoining door.

"Good morning, Vicki," she said, obviously in a good mood.

Victoria opened her side.

"Buenos dias, come on in. You must have slept well."

"I ate well, slept well, and ate well again this morning. I don't have any complaints."

"I ate like a pig last night myself. I just had toast and coffee this morning. I need to stay light on my feet for this last round. Then it's up to the jury to render a decision."

"I'm ready to close this one myself, not that this detail has been among the worst, but I like to tie up loose ends without delay. As soon as the jury goes in to deliberate we'll make the arrest."

Victoria grabbed her briefcase.

"Vamonos, partner, we've got business to handle."

"Okay then, you are speaking my language," Rosario chuckled. "I figure it will save time if we walk across the street. I'll come back and get the car."

"Si, that'll work," Victoria said, smiling.

Inside the Justice Center, Dt. Rosario said, "I believe you'll be fine from here."

Victoria nodded. "Hasta la vista, baby."

"They're not ready for you today," Rosario laughed.

"They better be," Victoria said as the elevator door closed.

Reporters with microphones and cameramen in tow were positioned around the door to the courtroom. Khloe was standing to the side of the entrance speaking with Arthur.

"You look well-rested," he said as she approached them.

"I am, thank you."

"It's too late to consult on your statement. I don't think you need it. I just want to let you know you have my moral support," Arthur said, leading them into the gallery.

He took a seat beside his executive assistant in the second row of the packed gallery. Alta and Laramie Landauer and their son Emerson were seated on the same row across the aisle. Victoria and Khloe took their seats at the prosecution table. Mona and Darren Gardner were there seated behind them in the first row. Benjamin swaggered in like he had every day of the trial with his client, Edward Landauer, behind him and Thomas Clancy in the rear. Judge Kelly came in at his usual prompt time, one minute before 9:00. The jury took their seats and the bailiff called the court to order.

Judge Kelly spent a few minutes on his usual questions to the jury. Then he told them that they would hear final arguments on the case, first from the Commonwealth and then the defense. When he finished he turned to the prosecution.

"You may proceed, Ms. Perry."

Victoria rose and stood at the lectern.

"May it please the court. Good morning ladies and gentlemen. This case, the Commonwealth of Pennsylvania versus Edward Landauer, is a result of the homicide of Deshaun Nathaniel Gardner, a young promising teenager, on the evening of March 29, 2012. May I approach the jury, Your Honor?"

"Yes, you may," he responded.

Victoria moved towards the jury.

"The unfortunate events of that night were caused by the reckless behavior of the defendant, Edward Landauer, when he placed himself in the role of police officer, judge, and jury. From his own call to the police we can hear him assume that Deshaun Gardner was a criminal, one of those assholes who never get caught. However, the truth was Deshaun was not a suspect as the defendant described him. He was an innocent teenager on his way home to his family.

In his argument, the Defense Attorney brought forth several witnesses who testified that the defendant was not a racist, yet his actions said otherwise. There is no question that he racial-profiled the victim in this case. By definition racial profiling is the use of a person's race by law enforcement as a factor in deciding whether to stop and search someone. He saw Deshaun Gardner was black, wearing a hoodie, and then he decided that he was a thug up to no good. That's a very strong emotional reaction towards someone you don't even know. So how did he come to that assumption? Deshaun wasn't engaged in any illegal activity. It was based on his personal feelings alone, he stalked this child, confronted him, and then he killed him."

Victoria slowly paced across the front of the jury box, pausing and making eye contact with each one of them.

"Mr. Madison has gone through great efforts to convince you that Edward Landauer was the victim in this case. That he was scared, that he was attacked, and acted in self-defense. That he went out of his house that evening with good intentions even though he strapped on a fully loaded 9 mm gloc. He said that on his way to meet some friends he was acting as a captain of the Town Watch when he went to check out the area where dogs were barking. Then he saw Deshaun walking in the rain wearing a hoodie. He wants us to believe that he was fearful of this teenager, yet he said he followed him and approached him, even though the dispatcher told him he didn't need to follow him. Then he said Deshaun reacted aggressively to him, cursing him, pushing him, and then punching him."

Victoria stopped suddenly and gripped the cool brass-covered railing of the jury box.

"Now I want you to take a deep breath and put yourself in Deshaun Gardner's shoes, heading home after a long day at school and then work. You get off the train as you have done many times before and someone starts following you in the darkness. You're wondering who this is, what do they want, are they going to hurt you? For a grown man it might be disturbing. For a woman or a kid it's terrifying. When this stalker approaches you with a 9mm it quickly becomes life or death. Fight or flight kicks in. Deshaun Gardner stood his ground and he was murdered at the hands of Edward Landauer. He was without any doubt the victim in this case."

Edward chest heaved and he shook his head with displeasure at Victoria's words.

"The defendant's mother testified that her son wanted to be a hero. The evidence showed that he was denied admission by the military and the police force but that didn't dissuade him from wanting to be in authority and police people. He bought himself a gun and got a license where he could carry it like he was a cop. We have a full staff of police enforcement; we don't need private citizens on the street taking it upon themselves to be judge and jury. What happened to Deshaun Gardner could happen to any of us. Right place at the wrong time, the time when Edward Landauer was out looking for a so-called criminal to act out his fantasy. Over and over he referred to Deshaun Gardner, an innocent kid walking home, as 'the suspect.'

We all have our demons, there is no law against being angry or frustrated with our lives, our significant others, our jobs, or crime in the streets. It doesn't give us the right to buy a gun and stalk our fellow citizens waiting for the opportunity to release those demons. We are accountable for our actions. It doesn't even matter whether he was a racist or not, you can't go out in public and shoot down anybody you want because you think they're suspicious, or wearing a hoodie, or walking slow with their hands in their pockets. You've heard from many witnesses but the circumstance speaks for itself. I submit to you that the defendant is guilty of murder in the second degree and ask that you come to a just verdict. Thank you."

Victoria took her seat. Mona bowed her head. Darren looked at his hands. Alta closed her eyes. Laramie looked at the ceiling. Edward shook his head defiantly. Judge Kelly checked his watch and called for a fifteen minute recess.

***

"Mr. Madison, you have the floor," Judge Kelly said when they returned to the courtroom.

"May it please the court?" Benjamin asked from the lectern. May I approach the jury?"

"Yes, counselor, go ahead."

Benjamin knew what the task in front of him required to get an acquittal. It was to insure that the jury liked him more than they disliked his client. He rested his hands on the jury box.

"I want you all to know that I understand the gravity of the assignment that we have asked you all to carry out. This is my job, but being here has been a personal sacrifice for all of you. With the seriousness of this duty, I want you to understand that you must weigh all the evidence that you have heard throughout this trial, and follow the law. That means your verdict must be subject to reasonable doubt. It is the responsibility of the Commonwealth to prove their case, they have that burden. The defense does not have that obligation. My client is to be presumed innocent unless they prove otherwise."

Ben moved towards the side of the jury where four of the women were sitting and leaned in close on one arm.

"During the course of this trial you have heard things about my client, Edward Landauer, things that may have given you an impression about him. We are all complicated people, I know that I am. So unless we can get inside another person's head it is virtually impossible to know what makes them tick. So I want to caution you on making assumptions about my client when you deliberate. Among all the criticisms that you have heard about Edward Laudauer, you have also heard that more than anything he wanted to serve his country and his community. Even when he was denied those opportunities he found ways to be a concerned citizen in his neighborhood by coordinating a Town Watch group.

The prosecution has referred to my client as someone who wanted to be in law enforcement, a cop-wanna-be. I don't know about you but I don't see that as a bad thing. We need policemen in our society. It's a noble job. They say he was a vigilante who took the law into his own hands, but then they also showed that he called the police for assistance in his neighborhood on many occasions. They said that my client's story changed each time he told it, but he never tried to deceive the detectives or declined to answer any questions that he was asked. He never even asked to have a lawyer present which was his right. He simply answered them as he remembered it. Nothing that he did was unlawful on the night of March 29, 2012."

Ben moved to the other side of the jury box and casually folded his arms.

"The prosecution has asked you to put yourself in the victim's shoes and now I ask you to put yourself in my client's shoes. The evidence shows that there were quite a few burglaries of homes in his neighborhood, including the home invasion of his neighbor. He was urged to buy a gun by his girlfriend. They were all on edge and frightened. The records also show that the individuals who had been arrested were all young black males. That is what contributes to my client's frame of mind at the time when he was looking into the noise he heard on the street and when he saw Deshaun Gardner. He saw someone he thought was suspicious and he called the police which is exactly what we are all advised to do in that situation. He followed Deshaun Gardner because the dispatcher said to let him know if the person does anything. He didn't have any hostility towards this person. He wasn't feeling anger or hatred. He didn't know him. He didn't come out of his house planning to shoot anybody. He was only acting out of concern for his community.

He approached Deshaun to ask him what he was doing around there. That wasn't an aggressive act. If somebody approached me and asked me that question I would tell them I live down the street and I'm on my way home, but Deshaun reacted with anger telling him to "get the fuck out of my face." Witnesses testified about seeing and hearing an argument and struggle. Deshaun was taller and more muscular in the scuffle with my client. Edward Landauer was beaten up and his jaw was broken. At that moment he feared that he was in danger of great bodily harm. He had a reasonable belief that his life was in danger. Under this circumstance the law says that he can act in self-defense and use deadly force."

Benjamin talked for another half hour. He tried to get the sympathy of jurors who might be intimidated by these young men wearing hoodies. He explained how Deshaun had brutalized his client and the definition of self-defense and how his client was basically defenseless while Judge Kelly shifted anxiously in his seat. The proceedings had gone past the lunch hour. It was approaching 1:00 and the pressure from the last glass of water made him feel like his bladder was about to burst.

"This incident was a tragedy for everyone involved. I feel sympathy for Mr. and Mrs. Gardner as I'm sure you feel for them also, but that doesn't allow us to ignore the law. My client admits that deep down he may have pre-judged Deshaun Gardner because he was black. He had seen more than one black man suspected of burglaries in the neighborhood, but the dynamic changed after he approached Deshaun. He was brutally attacked and he shot the victim in self-defense. If you're not absolutely sure, then you must find him not guilty. Thank you."

Judge Kelly promptly called a recess until 2:30 and rushed from the room. Victoria left out of the rear door just as quickly. She didn't have much time to work on her rebuttal.

"You may be worth a quarter after all," Edward said, watching Ben shut down his laptop.

"It's not me that you need to worry about," Ben said offhandedly.

Laramie moved up the side aisle toward the defense table like a fed-up parent coming to collect an unruly child.

"Let's go," he said in a huff, "Your mother wants to eat lunch with you."

The arrogance faded from Edward's face and he followed his father without comment to where Emerson and his mother waited outside the courtroom.

"Well, Thomas, how about I buy you a drink?" Ben said with his briefcase in hand. "You look like you could use one."

"I could use several but it probably won't make much difference," Thomas said sullenly.

Benjamin poured Thomas a drink from the bar in the limo

before he checked the messages on his IPhone. He thought it was kind of strange when Thomas threw his head back and poured the Scotch down his throat. Why was he looking like he was the man whose life hung in the balance.

"I thought I did a damn good close," Ben said, attempting to lighten his mood. "What's got you so glum?"

Thomas shook his head in dismay. Ben put his phone down and poured him another drink and one for himself.

"You know you can't take these cases personally. It's a job, nothing more, nothing less. Whatever will be, will be."

Benjamin was glad the trial was almost over. He was tired of watching a successful black man cry the blues every day.

"It's easy to be philosophical in your position," Thomas said, frowning.

"My philosophy is simple," Ben said, raising his glass, "Don't make excuses."

***

Relieved with a new pitcher of water and a full stomach, Judge Kelly asked everyone to take their seats.

"You may proceed with your rebuttal, Ms. Perry."

Victoria took a deep breath and got up to speak.

"Thank you, Your Honor. May it please the court? The Defense has attempted to complicate the occurrence of March 29, 2012 by clouding what took place that night with the defendant's motivations. The burglaries in the neighborhood, the lack of ill-will of the defendant, and his inability to defend himself are not pertinent in this case. This tragedy began when the defendant went out looking for trouble, looking for a chance to be a hero.

He saw Deshaun Gardner walking home talking on the phone with his mother. He called the police but he was determined to handle this person who he referred to as a 'fucking coon.' Then the confrontation escalated. Why? The defendant said that Deshaun told him to "get the fuck out my face." He said he was afraid but he didn't walk away and wait for the police. His best friend, Jack McCullough testified that Edward Landauer didn't take 'bullshit' from anybody. So surely he must have responded verbally or physically.

I don't know how many of you are boxing fans, but you probably are familiar with the sport. In a championship fight there are twelve rounds, three minutes per round. The defendant wants us to believe that a 1-2 minute struggle with a seventeen year old boy had him in fear of his life. Yet there was no blood or DNA from the defendant on Deshaun Gardner's hands. The defendant is a liar. In order for him to claim he shot Deshaun in self-defense it had to be because it meant his life or death."

Victoria's voice rose and fell with emotion.

"The fact is that Edward Landauer brought his gun out in a fist fight, a fight that he initiated. The law is clear, it says he had to retreat before using deadly force, but he didn't. Deshaun was the one who tried to run away. It was his life that lay in the balance and his life that was taken. I submit to you today that there was no justification for shooting Deshaun Gardner. The defendant knew the police would be there at any minute, but he was itching to use his new toy, so he got out his gun and pulled the trigger. Sadly, this man who is supposed to have no anger or hatred in his heart had no compassion after this child was killed, no regret or remorse for the life he took. He didn't try to assist this boy in any way. He only sought to justify his actions once the police arrived on the scene.

All that took place before the moment Edward Landauer got out of his car and confronted Deshaun Gardner doesn't matter. The previous burglaries are irrelevant and the Town Watch program is irrelevant. We are here because a child was murdered. Mr. Madison wants you to think that this was a justifiable homicide but it wasn't. Pennsylvania's Castle Doctrine expansion says that an individual has the right to stand their ground in a confrontation in a public place. It also says that deadly force cannot be used unless the aggressor produces or shows a deadly weapon. The defendant had no legal right to use deadly force. He committed homicide based on an unreasonable belief. In this instance Deshaun Gardner had the right to use deadly force against Edward Landauer when he brandished a gun. Unfortunately, he was unarmed. We can't turn back time or make this wrong right. What we can do is give Deshaun Gardner the justice that he deserves in this case by finding the defendant guilty. Thank you for your patience."

She took a breath and ran her hand across the brass on the jury box until it felt warm. Then she took her seat.

Judge Kelly sat tall in his chair after a quick glance at his watch.

"Ladies and gentlemen of the jury, thank you for your attention during this trial. Now I will read your instructions for deliberation."

In his charge to the jury, Judge Kelly read that the defendant was accused of second-degree murder and their duty to decide the circumstances of the killing. They were told they could decide on second-degree murder or manslaughter. He defined self-defense and when deadly force is justified. He explained when killing is excusable, what a dangerous weapon was, and what a firearm was. They were told to use their common sense in considering the evidence and the witnesses. He reiterated that it was the Commonwealth's obligation to prove the defendant's guilt to overcome the presumption of his innocence. His tone was steady, even monotonous, most certainly repetitious, and from the faces of the jury and the spectators in the gallery, many had already zoned out by the time he read the portion on deciding on the verdict.

The jurors were escorted to the jury room by the court deputy and Judge Kelly announced that court was in recess. Edward rose to his feet anxious to get out of the room with so many anticipating eyes focused on him.

"Where are you headed?" Benjamin asked, standing and resting his hand on his shoulder.

Edward shrugged his shoulders from under Benjamin's hand.

"I'm going to wait for the verdict with my folks. I hope they got their money's worth?"

Benjamin held his tongue and nodded. He watched Edward as he joined his family and supporters who were waiting near the rear door.

"He has no idea," Thomas said, lifting his briefcase from the defense table.

"It's just a day's work," Benjamin said as he walked out.

***

"Good job, Vick. How do you feel?" Khloe asked as they gathered up their laptops, files, and notes spread across the table.

"I feel sick to my stomach."

"Why, I thought you would be relieved."

"Not in the least, it's out of my hands now," Victoria said, hurrying to the elevator, "I've got to get out of here."

Victoria led Khloe out of the building looking neither to the left or the right. She refused to make eye contact with anyone. She refused to make a statement to the throng of reporters clamoring outside the Justice Center door.

"Let's go to Capitol Grille, I'll buy you a drink," Khloe offered, pulling her eyes away from Benjamin and Thomas as they moved toward his waiting limo.

Just then Victoria caught sight of Dt. Rosario and Dt. Carlton as they jumped out of their parked car in front of the long black Lincoln.

"In a minute," Victoria replied, "I want to see something first."

"What is it?" Khloe asked, following the direction of her eyes.

Dt. Rosario cut off Thomas while Dt. Carlton moved behind and handcuffed him. She could see Rosario's lips move as she informed him of his arrest and rights that he obviously knew.

Victoria waited to see his shock and outrage but there was none. Without a word he dropped his head and got into the back seat of their unmarked car. Benjamin stood there stunned for a moment as the car pulled off. A swarm of reporters converged on the scene but Ben made off in his car before the reporters could get to him.

Khloe raised her hands.

"What was that about?"

"That was my secret admirer."

"You're kidding, Thomas Clancy."

"Indeed."

"Is anybody else involved?" Khloe asked cautiously, thinking about Benjamin.

"I have no idea. I guess we'll know soon. Anyway, time for that drink you promised me."

It was less than a block to the restaurant. Victoria read text messages and listened to voice mails until they got to Capital Grille. They found two seats at the end of the bar. Khloe ordered vodka and Victoria ordered cognac. The bartender recognized her from the newscasts and poured her double shot of Pierre Ferrand.

"Thank God these seats have backs," Victoria said, taking a sip and leaning back.

"How long do you think the jury will be out?" Khloe asked.

"There's no telling, but I doubt they want to be sequestered over the weekend. Unless there is a stubborn holdout, there should be a verdict anytime between the next minute and tomorrow evening."

"Where are you going to wait?"

"I've got a quick stop to make and then I'm going home. I can be back in court in fifteen minutes from my house."

Khloe drank her drink quickly but the worried look on her face had not softened. Victoria felt for her.

"Girl, aren't you ready to confess yet?" she asked, acting impatient.

"What are you talking about?"

"I know you've been seeing Benjamin."

Chapter Twenty -One

"How did you find out?"

"You can't keep a secret in this city."

"I'm sorry, I should have told you."

"You're free to do what you want with who you want, my only problem is the timing. There was a conflict of interests. I probably should have replaced you but I thought it would bring more attention and raise more questions."

"Thanks for not judging me."

"I understand the attraction, Ben is hard to resist."

"He's also hard to pin down."

"I don't like to give relationship advice, but I wouldn't pin any hopes on Ben. Have some fun and let him go."

"Too late, I'm in love with him."

Victoria chuckled. "In that case, let me buy you a drink before I go. We can either toast to your future or you can cry in it."

***

Victoria changed clothes in her office to go down to the Roundhouse. It was rush hour and traffic was heavy. She could probably walk in the same time that it would take a cab to get there. Besides, she needed to get some air, some sun, and some exercise. Preparing the case and the trial had kept her from getting all three. She walked down Market Street listening to the symphony of voices, sirens, and engines along the way. On 12th Street she went inside the Reading Terminal. She had a taste for something sweet, ice cream or water ice, except she didn't have enough time to sit and enjoy it. She bought some candy instead and took the back exit out to Race Street.

Dt. Carlton and Rosario had finished questioning Thomas and were standing outside the interrogation room when Victoria walked in.

"What did he say?" Victoria asked, looking through the glass of the one-way mirror.

Dt. Carlton shook his head in amazement.

"He copped to the phone threats, the broken window, the ricin in the mail, and hiring somebody to take out the brakes on your car."

"Why, was anyone else involved?"

"He says no, he acted alone, apart from that he won't say any more," Rosario answered.

"Can I talk to him?" Victoria asked.

"It's up to him," Dt. Carlton said, opening the door for her.

Victoria walked in. Thomas looked up and motioned for her to sit down.

"What was this all about, Thomas?"

"What it's always about, winning."

"It wasn't that serious, it was only one case, not your entire career."

"From where you're sitting, maybe, it was more than that for me. It was my chance to make a name for myself in the firm."

"You could have killed me and my family."

"I didn't want to hurt you. I simply needed you off the case. You cared too much."

"Did Ben or your client know what you were doing?"

"Why would you ask that, is it that you don't think I'm capable of orchestrating it by myself? People always underestimate me."

"You risked the most but you had the least to gain by your actions."

"What difference does it make now, I'm fucked."

"The difference is you fucked yourself."

"You don't know what it's like to be the token black, ignored, and ridiculed. I'm as good as Madison but they treated me like the janitor."

"Don't waste that bullshit on me, I grew up in the same world you did."

She sat there for a minute wanting to help Thomas, wishing there was a way out for him, but he had thrown his career away.

"Good luck," she said on her way out.

Chapter Twenty-Two

The sun was setting and a slight breeze blew across the porch. Barefoot, wearing blue jean shorts and a white tank top, Victoria mulled over the last four months while she sipped raspberry iced green tea with Miss Judy and Lanetta.

"It's past happy hour," Victoria said, looking up in the sky, "We might need to spike this tea."

"Don't rush it, sister, the jury is still out." Lanetta said. "We're going to need that drink soon enough, one way or the other."

"I know that's right," Miss Judy said, sighing. "Either way it goes, I'm glad it's over."

"This has been so drama-filled, I don't know if I want to go through this again," Victoria said with her eyes following the path of a firefly.

"You're just battle-weary, you're a fighter to the heart, baby," Miss Judy said, patting Victoria on the arm. "You'll be ready for the next one."

A dark limo pulled into the block and stopped in front of the house. The window rolled down and Victoria could see it was Benjamin. She set her glass down beside her chair and walked to the car. The driver opened the door for her.

Benjamin held his hand out. "Come in, I want to talk to you."

Victoria slid in onto the seat across from him.

"So, to what do I owe this visit to my home?"

"I'm here to offer you my sincerest apologies. I had no idea that it was Thomas behind the threats and attempts on your life. I go low from time to time but I would never resort to anything like that, and I would never do anything to hurt you."

"Thank you for saying that and thanks for coming by. I thought you might be waiting for the verdict with your client."

"He's enjoying the comfort of family and friends."

"What about Khloe? She might like some company."

"It was you I wanted, Momi," he said, looking at her bare legs.

"Then you shouldn't have settled for my second chair," she said, knocking on the window for his driver to open the door.

"I'm relentless," he said, smiling. "I'll see you in court."

"I'm sure."

Victoria went back on the porch and they watched the limo float out of the block like a yacht on smooth water.

"All right, ladies, I'm going to call it a day. I've got some phone calls to make," Victoria said, picking up her glass of tea.

"I guess I will too since you let our ride get away," Lanetta joked.

"Well, I'm going to stay out and enjoy myself by myself," Miss Judy said, lifting her glass.

***

Victoria laid in the bed with the TV volume turned low on the evening news. She had more texts messages and voicemails than she had the energy to answer. She pressed Angeline's name for efficiency. Calling her was like making eight calls, she put any pertinent info she got out on the wires to everybody.

"Hey, Angel, what's going on?"

"Girl, you are going to live a long life," Angeline answered out of breath, "I was about to get in my car and drive to your house. I have been calling you every day all week. I know you've got a lot going on but damn. Call a sister back sometimes. I've been worried about you."

"It's been a crazy week."

"I heard about the accident. If it wasn't for the news I wouldn't have known if you were alive or dead. What's up with that?"

"Come on now, give me a pass. This case has run me ragged. You know we're going to Atlantic City when this is over."

"Then the jury better quit playing, I'm ready to go."

"It probably won't be tonight so relax."

"Anyway, how are things going with Mr. Melody?"

"I don't know, lately between his schedule and mine we haven't spent much time together."

"Bring him on the trip, it'll be fun."

"For some reason he's not comfortable with my friends and colleagues."

"What's his problem?" Angeline asked with an attitude coming on.

"He's a bourgeois-hater."

"Hmm, sounds like your spring fling won't make it to Labor Day."

"Don't say that, he'll make the adjustment."

"Uh-huh, and fat folks hate fried food."

Victoria laughed. "You are so cold."

"I keep it real."

"Too real for me, we'll talk after the verdict comes in."

"Bye, girlfriend."

The phone rang in Victoria's hand before she could put it down. She saw Leonard's name and number on the screen.

"Hello, stranger," she answered.

"Hello, Vee. I can't believe I get to talk to you instead of your voicemail."

"I know, I know. Angeline just wore me out."

"Okay, so I can skip that part. How are you?"

"I'm getting better."

"You're one of the best, I watched the trial."

"Thank you, that means a lot coming from you."

"I truly mean it."

"I appreciate that."

"I miss you, Vee."

"What's got you feeling so sentimental this evening?"

"Not just this evening, every morning, noon, and night."

"You weren't when we were together."

"I was wrong."

"Wow, those are words I never heard you say."

"Don't give me a hard time, baby."

"It's late, where is Simone?"

"She wasn't the right woman for the role."

Victoria leaned back on her pillow.

"This sounds interesting, tell me all about it."

They talked until Victoria heard Dupree come in the door. Then she said a quick goodbye. She smelled the ganja when he walked into the bedroom.

"Is this what you wanted?" he asked, running his hand under her sleepshirt.

"You know it is," she whispered.

They made love for what seemed like all night. Victoria turned over on her side. The numbers on the clock shone 2:35. She wondered if the reason she was so turned on was because of her conversation with Leonard. Then she wondered if it was just the weed that had Dupree fired up.

***

Victoria called in and took a personal day. She was exhausted and didn't feel like waiting for the verdict in the office. Dupree brought her some toast and coffee in bed before he left around 10:30. It was almost 1:00 and she hadn't taken a shower yet. Doubts were flooding in on how she handled the case, what she should have done, what she should have said, and all the things she wished she hadn't said or done.

She found a half-eaten hoagie in the fridge and washed it down with a bottle of ginger ale before she finally took a shower. The quiet in the house was unnerving, she needed some music to drown out the misgivings she was having about her prosecution. She put on a Kem CD to take the edge off. Restlessness set in about 3:00, what was taking so damn long. It wasn't a good sign for the Commonwealth. Dissension is the only thing that causes a delay. She decided to get dressed and wait at the office where she could get moral support. She chose a bright green suit to lift her spirits and called a taxi. It was time to go back out and face her world, the judge and jury.

It was about 4:00 and she was less than three blocks from the Justice Center when the call finally came in. The jury had a verdict. Victoria slipped through the crowd of zealous reporters gathered outside the building and caught an elevator to the eleventh floor. Ben had an attractive blonde woman seated next to his client to replace Thomas. The families were seated in the first row of their respective sides. The Landauers looked relaxed. The Gardners look nervous. Their faces added to her anxiety. What had she missed?

Khloe walked in and Benjamin stepped over to speak.

"Counselors, whatever the verdict, I want to tell you it was a great experience having such formidable opponents."

"You're so full of shit, Ben," Victoria said, "This isn't the time or the place."

Khloe looked over at the attorney who had taken Thomas Clancy's spot.

"Is this the last time we'll see you?" She asked.

"Who knows?" he answered with a shrug and a smile before going back to his client.

Arthur came in and squeezed into a small space on the end of the second row.

"All rise," the bailiff said.

Judge Kelly walked in.

"Please be seated. There is a verdict." He nodded to the bailiff. "Have the jury come in."

The jury came in and not one of them would look toward the gallery. Some focused on the judge, a few looked at the far wall, and the rest were looking down at the floor. The foreman gave the verdict to the bailiff who handed it to Judge Kelly.

"There are not to be any outburst during the reading of the verdict," Judge Kelly said after he read the slip of paper.

He handed it back to the bailiff for the court clerk to read. Benjamin motioned for Edward to stand up beside him.

The clerk read. "In the case of Docket number 7631481 in the Commonwealth of Pennsylvania, we the jury find the defendant, Edward Landauer, guilty of murder in the second degree, so say we all."

Victoria started to shake as all the uncertainties and fears were expelled. She bit the inside of her jaw to stifle a scream. Mona Gardner sprung up and shouted, "Thank you, Jesus," and then collapsed down in her seat against Darren. Alta Landauer covered her mouth and Laramie shook his head in disgust. Edward Landauer stood there like a blowfish inflating as his anger grew. Benjamin whispered in his ear to calm him. Khloe threw her arms around Victoria.

"Mr. Madison, do you want to poll the jury?"

"Yes, Your Honor."

The jurors were polled and the verdict was unanimous.

"Thank you jurors for doing your civic duty," Judge Kelly said. "You are now discharged."

Benjamin made a motion for Judge Kelly to override the jury and acquit his client which was swiftly denied. Sentencing was set for the Wednesday of the following week. A clamor came over the courtroom. Mona leaned over and gave Victoria a kiss on the cheek. Arthur pressed through the gate and extended his hand to Victoria.

"Congratulations, be at my house at 6:30," he said before making a quick exit.

"What's next?" Khloe asked.

"I need to regroup and my phone is blowing up. Do you still have the car?"

"Yeah, it's parked in the lot across the street."

"Can you get a ride over to Arthur's house without it?"

"Sure, no problem."

"Walk with me."

A semi-circle of reporters holding microphones and yelling questions enclosed around them when they stepped outside the Criminal Justice Center asking them about the verdict.

***

Victoria parked the car in her empty driveway. Miss Judy's chair was unoccupied. She banged on their door before she went in.

"Wake up in here," she shouted, marching into the kitchen.

Miss Judy walked in from the living room smiling.

"Go ahead, Vick, you're strutting around like you're Johnny Cochran after he won Michael Jackson's case."

Victoria smiled back. "After this, I'm starting to wonder if my momma was true to my daddy, I believe I'm his outside baby."

"Stop your mess, child. Your momma and daddy would be so proud of you today."

"I wish they were here so bad, Miss Judy."

"Don't get the blues about it, they're here. I know your daddy was probably standing up there right beside you today."

"I know somebody was because my legs were like jelly when they read the verdict."

"So what are you going to do to celebrate?"

"You know we have plans to go to Atlantic City tomorrow. Where's Lanetta?"

"She's at work. I called her when I heard the news."

"I've got a lot of calls to make myself and I need to take a 20 minute power nap before I head back out," Victoria said as she walked towards the door. "My boss is having something at his house this evening."

"Enjoy yourself, baby, you deserve it."

She grabbed Miss Judy and gave her a tight hug.

"Thanks for being there for me."

"Where else am I going to be, child? I love you."

"I love you too," Victoria said on her way out.

In her own living room she kicked her shoes off and dropped down on the sofa. She talked to Joshua, Marvin, and Angeline before she called Dupree.

"It's all over but the shouting," she said when he answered.

"That's dope, babe," he said, "I knew you could make it happen."

"I don't think I could have gotten through without you."

"It was all my pleasure."

"Are you gigging tonight?"

"Not sure, what's on your mind?"

"I want you to go with me to a reception at my boss's house in about an hour."

"You go on, I'll catch up to you later."

"All right," she said, disappointed.

She knew Dupree wouldn't want to come with her before she asked. He didn't want any part of her that existed outside of her house or a club. Still, she refused to let him upset her, not today. She leaned back on the couch and closed her eyes.

***

Victoria changed into a pastel peach cocktail dress and caught a taxi to Arthur's townhouse on South 3rd Street. The door opened after three taps on the doorknocker and a hostess invited her in. Whenever Arthur entertained at his home, he did it big. It was part of his calculated climb to higher offices in the city and possibly a move to Harrisburg. She followed the woman dressed in a black skirt with matching vest and white shirt through the foyer and into his great room.

Arthur clapped when he saw her walk in.

"The lady of the hour has arrived."

Victoria smiled graciously with all the eyes focusing on her as Arthur moved closer to greet her and shake her hand, holding it as he lead her through his many guests over to where Mayor Russell Turner was holding court.

Mayor Turner gave her an unnecessarily tight hug.

"My hat is off to you, Victoria. This could have turned into a real nuisance for the city."

"Well, we have the jury to thank that the real nuisance will be locked up," Victoria said, backing up to find some personal space. "Now he can play policeman, warden, and soldier boy all day and all night long."

Arthur laughed loudly. "I'm sure there are enough suspects and criminals at the Curran-Frumhold facility for him to patrol for as long as he wants."

"This win was a boon for our national reputation, Victoria," Mayor Turner said, patting her on the back. "You are to be rewarded. How do you feel about being the Assistant Chief of the Municipal Court?"

Victoria was bowled over. "That's very generous, Mayor. Give me some time to catch my breath."

"The appointment is yours if you want it. Think about it and come see me in my office. We can discuss your future in the city. You're our brightest rising star right now."

Mayor Turner excused himself and rejoined the cluster of 'movers and shakers' he had been mingling with. It was clear to her that none of the people in the room really cared about justice for Desahun Gardner. He was just another black boy shot down in the streets. The only thing they cared about was maintaining their comfortable positions of authority with no friction.

Arthur steered Victoria to the bar and got her a glass of champagne.

"It's you moment, Vicki. Don't blow it. You don't get many.

Right now you're almost guaranteed my job when I give it up."

Victoria took a sip from the glass.

"Arthur, how many times have I told you I don't want your job?"

"I have no idea, I never believed you. You're ambitious. Why else would you push so hard?"

"That's a good question?" she asked, noticing Khloe across the room near the food. "Anyway, I don't want to keep you from clearing the path."

Victoria made her way to the buffet table. She hadn't eaten anything since breakfast. She gave Khloe a squeeze around her shoulders while she looked at the spread.

"I haven't said thank you for all of your help."

"I guess you're glad to get rid of me," Khloe said, continuing to fill her plate. "I didn't mean to be a pain in the ass."

Victoria chuckled. "Believe me, you weren't. You helped me out more than you realize. Things got a little bit sticky when you succumbed to the charms of our opponent but we made it through. No harm done."

"It was worth it," Khloe sighed, "Even though he dumped me like spoiled milk."

"I'm not surprised but at least it was worth it."

They relaxed and joked while they ate. Between bites Victoria responded to the congratulations from her colleagues, councilpersons, and even Police Commissioner Mancini on winning the case. She had a mouthful of crab dip when she saw Leonard watching her from out on the terrace. She downed her glass of champagne and went out to speak to him.

"I've been waiting to talk with you," Leonard said after she closed the double doors.

"Why didn't you come inside?"

"I wanted to talk to you alone."

"This is probably as alone as we'll get."

"Congratulations again, you did what you were supposed to do."

"Coming from you that's special but I think I owe a lot of it to the shoes," she said, flexing her ankles.

He smiled looking at her feet.

"You wear them well."

"I think you're right for a change."

Leonard gripped her hands in his and moved closer.

"Vee, I want us to get back together."

"Len, don't do this, I'm with somebody else now."

"No you're not, baby, where is he?"

It was the first time in her life that Victoria didn't have a snappy comeback line.

"I think I better go back inside. It was good to see you."

For the rest of the evening Victoria laughed and smiled and pretended to enjoy herself but the cloud she had floated in on had turned dark and it was pissing her off. She deserved to savor this moment. She didn't know how to respond to criticism of Dupree because she didn't fully understand his reasoning. Without question he had supported her in his own way. She accepted that he wasn't comfortable in crowds unless he was on stage but she didn't like making excuse for anybody. She couldn't say he hated the establishment, it sounded so 1970s. She gladly called it a night around 9:00 and went home.

Dupree gave her a greeting at the door that brightened up her mood.

"You're my hero," he said, lifting her off her feet in a bear hug.

"Is that so? Then I'm ready to receive all my accolades."

"Come on upstairs, I want to do this right."

He took off all of her clothes and caressed every inch of her body and kissed her from head to toe. He was an attentive lover. Inside the privacy of the house he denied her nothing. Outside of the house they shared nothing. She was too busy to make all of his gigs and he had no interest in spending time in courtrooms or social gatherings. She lay quietly beside him, her body satisfied, while her thoughts raced and screamed that she needed more.

Chapter Twenty-Three

Victoria made reservations for a luxury suite at the Borgata for the night. Angeline and Gerald had other plans and couldn't make the trip. She got up early before Dupree, packed her bag, and gave him a goodbye kiss. She would eat breakfast with Miss Judy and Lanetta before they got out on their overnight road trip.

The door was open but Miss Judy and Lanetta were still busy pulling their things together.

"We're about ready, Vicki," Miss Judy said, coming down with her bag in hand.

Victoria grabbed a pack of peanut butter crackers and a cup of milk to eat in the car. She put their bags in the back of the minivan she rented to make the trip.

"Don't forget the cooler," Victoria shouted back towards the door.

Lanetta came out with her arms full.

"I got that covered. Did you bring some extra towels?"

"Oh yeah, I'm ready, I've got the lounge chairs too."

"You two can lay out on the beach in all that sun if you want to, I'm going to spend the day inside the air-conditioned casino taking all their money," Miss Judy said from the back seat.

Victoria started up the car.

"Help yourself, I intend to let the waves wash over me and carry all my worries back into the ocean. Then I'm going to the spa for the works before we sit down to a gourmet meal."

"I'm down with that," Lanetta said, "I don't gamble with my own money and you said this was girls only."

"I might play a little, I feel lucky," Victoria said.

"So what was Dupree's excuse this time for not joining us?" Lanetta asked.

Victoria frowned. "I didn't bother to ask him."

"Uh-uh-uh," Miss Judy grunted.

"This is our celebration," Victoria announced, putting on her sunglasses.

They turned off of Girard Ave onto 6th Street, crossed the Ben Franklin Bridge, and landed in New Jersey. They merged onto the New Jersey Turnpike towards Atlantic City.

"That's the way we should be traveling," Lanetta said, checking out the limousine driving beside them.

Victoria chuckled. "Most definitely, we will if Miss Judy hits the jackpot today."

"All right, Mama. Now you know your assignment for the day," Lanetta said cheerily.

They got to Atlantic City before noon. The three of them walked on the boardwalk for a while before Miss Judy got tired and was ready to settle down in front of a slot machine. Victoria and Lanetta found a spot on the beach and waded out into the ocean until the water was chest high. They let the force of the waves push them around for almost an hour before they stretched out under an umbrella and drank apple coolers.

When the sun got too hot they headed to the casino. It wasn't easy but they got Miss Judy to move from her lucky spot long enough to go to the spa and salon where they got hairstyles, manicures, and pedicures. They got dressed up and Victoria treated them all to a great meal in the hotel restaurant. They gambled some more after dinner trying to stay even with the house and later caught one of the lounge acts. Miss Judy turned in early but Victoria and Lanetta partied in the lounge until 3:00. Several people recognized Victoria and bought them drinks.

The women slept late and ordered room service and didn't leave until it was over an hour past check-out time. After Victoria and Lanetta put their bags in the car they did some window shopping at the mall on the Boardwalk. They walked along the edge of the beach while Lanetta told them about her new man. Then they got custard cones and started the drive back home. It was starting to get dark by the time they got back to Philly.

"I'm going straight to bed so don't get in my way," Miss Judy said, marching in the house.

"That's fine with me because I have a hot date," Lanetta replied, walking behind her. "We'll talk later, Vick."

"Definitely, I'll catch up with you when you and your new man slow down."

Lanetta laughed. "That might be a while."

"All right, sister, that's what's up," Victoria said, going inside her front door.

She could smell the sauce from the jerk chicken wafting through the air. She followed the aromas into the kitchen and found Dupree slicing peppers for the salad.

"It smell delicious," she said, kissing him on the cheek. "I'm going to take a quick shower."

"Take your time. I'll make you something to drink."

Victoria could feel a different vibe in the air. When she stood next to Dupree she could feel the distance between them. His hair was tied up, he always wore it down in the house. She wondered if he was feeling angry about her not asking him to go to Atlantic City. She assumed he wouldn't go, besides she needed a girl's day and night out to decompress.

They ate the dinner without much conversation and sat at the table sipping on rum and cokes.

Dupree broke the silence. "The Voyagers are about to go on a tour."

"Wow, that's great. When?"

"Come on in the living room, I wrote a song for you. I want you to hear it."

She trailed him into the living room and sat on the sofa watching as he carefully put his saxophone together. That's when she noticed his duffel bag packed beside the case. Before she could say anything he brought the mouthpiece to his lips and began to blow. As he played the music lifted her up, took her on a ride, and brought her back again. The high notes made her want to holler with joy and then the melody made her want to cry. It was magical. It was like the night she first heard him play at Warm Daddy's except this wasn't a beginning, it was goodbye. When he stopped the easiness between them was gone and she tensed up.

"That was beautiful," she said.

"I'll stay the night if you need me to."

"I always need you."

"No you don't. It was temporary, and to be honest, I prefer not to be needed. I like my freedom."

"Don't you need somebody?" she asked with all seriousness.

"I need my music, it's my only constant."

"So what was this about?" she asked with open hands.

"It was about living life. I gave to you and you gave to me. It was all good."

"It's that simple for you."

"No, but I've got to go wherever the music takes me," Dupree said, standing at the door.

"So just like that you're walking away."

"I'm crazy about you and you're welcome to come with me. This is who I am. It's what I do. It's what I eat and what I breathe. I don't think you can accept that.

"I never asked you to choose."

"You are now."

The stiffness went out of her backbone. He was right. She got up off of the sofa, walked over to the door, and gave him a long kiss.

"Be happy," she said sincerely.

"You too," he said, closing the door behind him.

*****

The Labor Day picnic at Fairmount Park with Angeline and Gerald, Marvin and Tamika, and Joshua and Hannah had Victoria feeling lonely. For better or worse they had somebody to share their lives with. Whenever she thought about her relationship with Dupree she didn't know how to categorize it in her memory. They had never really gotten much time to spend together and it was over as abruptly as it had begun. Her whole life was in transition.

"Vicki, come on over here and help me cook this food," Angeline insisted, walking over to the grill. "I'm not going to let these men ruin perfectly edible meat by burning it. These birds are already dead."

Victoria grabbed the barbecue sauce and joined her friend while she cooked. She could sympathize with the chicken that Angeline turned over on the fire. Just when you adjusted to your circumstances somebody comes and flips the script. She had withstood the heat of the trial, she was a more seasoned attorney, and now everybody wanted a piece of her.

"So how are you hanging?" Angeline asked.

"Professionally, things are great. Personally, I still feel like I'm walking up an escalator that's coming down."

"I know you're not brooding over Dupree. He's wasn't you, Vick."

"He's a good guy. He just didn't want to be a part of my world."

"That's okay because I wasn't feeling him either."

"He was cool. You never got a chance to know him."

"And whose fault was that?"

"I know, but I miss him. He was good company."

"Now you know I'm your roommate. Any time you need me to come and stay with you just let me know and I'm there."

"Victoria laughed. "I don't think that would make Gerald happy, besides there are some skills that Dupree had that aren't on your resume."

***

Victoria woke up from a daydream as she worked late on a case in her office. The black letters had blurred on the computer as she mentally floated back over the last four months. Edward Landauer had been sentenced two weeks ago and the fever pitch around the D.A.'s office and the Criminal Justice Center had died down. The news media was a fickle suitor and had shifted its attention to 2012 Summer Olympics and the oncoming presidential election.

At the center of her contemplation was the lunch meeting that she had attended at the invitation of Frederick Rosen, senior partner of Rosen & Sullivan. They had extended the offer that she had dreamed about when she finished law school. She couldn't deny the entrance looked like a palace and they had unquestionably given her the royal treatment. The offer included a more than generous salary, a corner office suite comparable to Benjamin's, and the promise of a partnership with the firm.

She wouldn't have hesitated for a second to accept their offer six months ago, but the craziness of what happened with Thomas Clancy had given her serious doubts. The opportunity to be their new token black wasn't part of her master plan. Accepting the mayor's promotion to Assistant Chief of the Municipal Court wasn't high on her wish-list either. The only thing she was certain of was that there had to be more out there for her than attacking the poor and defenseless citizens of Philadelphia every day.

She packed up her briefcase and slipped her cross-over bag on her shoulder. The hot temperatures of the afternoon had dropped and the usually stifling air was breathable. She glanced up Broad Street and felt like walking home and even more like running, but her feet wouldn't appreciate the gesture with the heels she was wearing. Old Faithful was in the shop, the government car Arthur had provided had been returned to the city garage, and she wasn't ready to rejoin the hustle and bustle below the street on the subway. She hailed a taxi for the straight shot ride down 13th Street. In the back seat she pulled out her phone and ordered a salad and a small pizza from City View.

She was surfing the channels on the TV in the living room when she heard the knock on the door. She reached in her purse for a twenty dollar bill to pay for the delivery. She opened the door and was shocked to see Leonard standing there holding the pizza and her salad.

He smiled. "It seems I'm just in time for dinner."

"I guess you are," she said, smiling. "Come on in."

He stepped in and set the pizza down on the coffee table.

"I'd like to take you out for a real meal," he said, reaching for her hand.

"I'll take a rain check, the pizza smells good and I'm ready to eat. Sit down, I'll get us some plates and something to drink."

Victoria came back with plates and a bottle of zinfandel that she found in the refrigerator.

They ate and drank, talked about her career options, and teased each other about Simone and Dupree. They kicked off their shoes and watched a re-run of *Love Jones*. It was close to midnight when Leonard stood up to leave.

"Now, if you're done with all that Baby Face bullshit, I'm telling you old-school like Teddy Pendergrass, come on and go with me over to my place."

"What are you talking about, Len?" she asked playfully.

"I want us to get married."

"You say that now. What if I'd lost?"

"I wouldn't have asked you until after the next election?" he laughed. "But seriously, I have to admit you handled your business thoroughly and professionally."

"You didn't believe in me."

"It wasn't that. The media can kill you dead. I wanted to live to fight another day."

"I don't blame you for that. Honestly, for the most part I thought it would help my career. I guess I'm a bigger gambler than you are."

"That's true, and to your credit, you won. Now you don't need anybody. Do your thing. Start your own firm."

"I hate to profit off the misfortunes of other people," Victoria said wistfully.

"Get over it, baby. That's the American way," Leonard said, squeezing her waist.

Epilogue

Victoria sat in the office looking at the certificates on the wall, the books stacked neatly on the bookcases, the Oriental rug on the floor, the cherry desk, and William Penn on top of City Hall from the corner view. It was hard for her to believe that it all belonged to her. The frame on the end of the desk was also something she would have never predicted; it was a photo of her on her honeymoon with Leonard. She had the wedding her mother always dreamed about, the only disappointment was that her momma and daddy weren't there.

The intercom buzzed. "Angeline Irving is here," Sandra said.

"Thanks, I'm expecting her."

Sandra Irving was her administrative assistant. Khloe decided to come with her when she left the D.A.'s office and she had just hired a paralegal, John Guyette, a fresh graduate from her Alma Mater. They were already preparing briefs for their first case.

"What's going on, newlywed?" Angeline asked, strutting in her office.

"It's all new, new husband, new house, and a new office."

Angeline looked around the room nodding her head in approval.

"Now you're the woman who has everything."

"Not quite, I don't know what you're waiting on but I want a family."

Angeline sat down in one of the green leather wingback chairs in front of the desk.

"I think you may have gotten enough new things for a while without having a baby. You'll need to take some time to get your firm established."

"I'm my own boss, I can do it. I have good support."

"Okay, I won't argue with you, you're going to do what you want to do no matter what I say."

"That's a fact."

"So what interesting cases are you working on since you've gotten back?"

"I'm defending a professional tennis player who was accused of raping one of the contestants of the Miss America Pageant."

"Stop, you mean you're going to be representing Foster Griswold."

"The one and only."

"I thought you wanted to stay out of the limelight, the press is having a field day on him."

"I know, the media has already been the judge and jury. I didn't want my face out there again so soon but he was my first client. How could I have said no?"

"What is our esteemed State Senator Leonard Sterling saying about this one?"

Victoria laughed. "He's on the fence for right now, although he did say that I need to be more discriminating in choosing my clients."

"So how do you like living out on the Mainline?"

"It's not as bad as I thought. I miss the neighborhood but I like the peace of it for a change."

"What are you going to do with your parents' house? You know I can sell property in York Town in a heartbeat."

"Lanetta is going to be living in it. It gives her some privacy and she can keep an eye on Miss Judy at the same time."

Just then Khloe burst through the door.

"You will not believe who I just got off the phone with," Khloe said excitedly.

"I'm going to take your word on that. Why don't you tell me." Victoria replied.

"It was Brent Matthews, the CIA guy who accused the National Security Agency of going above and beyond their legal boundaries in surveillance, and then leaked the documents to prove it. He outed them. They were monitoring internet use, google accounts, emails, and cell phone use in their surveillance, over-reaching all levels of confidentiality."

"No way. I saw him all over the news. He said the NSA spied on Brazil, Britain, China, France, Germany, and leaders all over the world. The whole thing is unbelievably deep. He had to leave the country. Why is he calling us?"

"He wants a consult with you. He's being charged with stealing government property and revealing classified details of United States surveillance programs."

"Oh shit! That's way over my head."

Angeline was trying to stay quiet but couldn't hold her tongue another second.

"Victoria, don't even think about it. I know you haven't forgot about those death threats and your car accident."

"Don't remind me. He might be too hot for me to handle, Khloe. Get back with him and tell him that I need to do some research on the charges."

"I'm getting out of here, I don't want to be seen anywhere near you." Angeline said, half-joking but moving out the door. "You better tell him like Whitney Houston, hell-to-the-naw."

"If you want to go high-profile, Vicki, it won't get any bigger than this," Khloe said on her way out.

Victoria picked up the phone to call Leonard. He was up in Harrisburg for a legislative meeting.

"Hey, baby," he answered, "I knew you were about to call me, my ears were burning."

"I bet they were. I just got a phone call from Brent Matthews."

"Do you mean the Brent Matthews aka traitor to his country."

"The very one. He wants me to consult on his case."

"Come on, Vee, cut me a break. I trying to get my foot in Congress. I don't even want to think about the repercussions of touching that one. Not only would my political career be over we would probably have to leave the country."

"I'm not considering the case at the moment but you have to admit it would be an interesting argument for the justice system. The most powerful federal agencies were caught breaking their own laws and they are so gangster that they want to lock up their accuser."

"Sweetheart, we can't even have this conversation on the phone."

"That's the problem."

"Let's talk about how much I miss you."

"All right, I rest my case, you win."

The End